Each
New Morn

L.G.Thomson

ISBN-10:1499377444
ISBN-13: 978-1499377446

For Charlie, Caroline
and Mary Kate Thomson.

Each new morn,
New widows howl, new orphans cry, new sorrows
Strike heaven on the face

Macbeth Act IV, Scene III
William Shakespeare

PART ONE

1

The sound of breaking glass.   And something else.
Voices.   Some distance away yet, but coming closer.
Chrissie Cunningham crouched by the side of the
bedroom window and peered out.

They were at the end of the street.   Some brandished
burning torches, naked flames licking into the night air.
Others carried flashlights.   They didn't look or sound like a
rescue party.

They swarmed over the road, cocky, claiming the streets
for themselves.   Tension sparked the air around the mob
like static electricity.   A bottle smashed against the
windscreen of a car.   The sound excited them, setting
them screaming and yelling even louder than before.

Chrissie pulled back from the window as they drew
near.   The bedroom was on the first floor, but there were
too many eyes out there for her to risk drawing attention
to herself or the house.   She hadn't been conscious for
long.   Was still trying to make sense of the world she'd
woken to.   She sat down, back against the wall, and
listened.

The noise intensified.   A sudden scream scorched the
air, high pitched and intense, piercing and painful to listen
to.   She fought the urge to cover her ears as it went on and

on. She couldn't afford to miss anything - like the sound of the front door being kicked in.

She ground her teeth until her gums ached. Just as she thought she couldn't take any more, the screaming stopped. Harsh, metallic clatters followed. The soundtrack of her car being trashed. A *whoomph* as the fuel tank caught. The sudden flare lit the room, illuminating the outline of her father's body on the bed.

Another high-pitched scream, this one mercifully short. Cruel laughter followed, and then the voices faded as the mob moved on. Chrissie pressed her back against the wall. Rooting herself to the house until she could hear nothing but silence from the street.

Finally, when she was absolutely sure they had gone, she snuck a look outside. They'd left a body behind. A young woman, in the middle of the road, indecently well-lit by the flames. She lay on her back, clothes torn, face bloody.

Chrissie gazed at the body and wondered if the stories on the internet had been true. Social media had been ablaze with rumours. Pictures had been posted - people with chunks bitten out of their faces. It was sick. Too much to bear. The pandemic was bad enough. Nobody needed anything else on top of that. But the rumours persisted.

To begin with, the forums were full of stories about friends of a friend. Then it was, I know somebody who... Finally, the reports came first-hand. People were turning into zombies. Then the system crashed and there were no more reports about anything.

Feeling just a little crazy for doing so, Chrissie watched the body, waiting to see if it would get up and lurch around. But it just carried on lying there like a normal, everyday corpse.

Chrissie kept on watching. The corpse twitched. She caught her breath. The corpse stopped moving. Trying to catch her out. She told herself not to be stupid. The corpse didn't know she was there. Did it?

Chrissie stared, scared to blink in case she missed something. She stared until her eyes were dry and scratchy. Kept thinking the corpse was twitching, itching to get back on its feet. Doubting what she was seeing, telling herself it was a trick of the flickering light.

Shadows cradled the corpse as the flames died down. The streetlights were out. Soon Chrissie would have nothing to see it by. She didn't want to be left in the dark with her nagging doubts and fears. She had to go outside and check for herself.

The front door was bolted against the night. She was reluctant to change that, but did it anyway. Better to know what she was up against than lose her mind wondering.

Every sound was amplified. The scrape of the chain, the click of the lock, the creak of the hinge as she opened the door. Armed with one of her father's golf clubs, she went outside.

The remains of the fire glowed through the boundary hedge, the heat still fierce. The night air smelt thick and unwholesome. Cautiously, she walked the length of the short path to the gate and stared over it at the corpse. It didn't seem to have moved. Chrissie studied it for a few moments before opening the gate and stepping into the street.

Her heart thudded, She felt exposed, ready to take flight. There was a tremble in her legs. Out here, the golf club didn't feel like much of a weapon.

There was a gaping wound in the dead woman's head. Blood oozing from it had been cooked by the heat of the fire. Her hair was matted, her clothes filthy. She couldn't have been any older than twenty. Perhaps she'd been pretty once. Now she looked like road kill.

There was no twitching, no movement of any sort. Chrissie poked her with the golf club. Nothing. She poked again, harder. Still nothing. She jabbed the club sharply into the dead woman's side. Still no movement. She kept at it, jabbing and poking, trying to get a reaction. She was crying now, tears streaming down her face. She hadn't wept for anyone else, had been too numb, but she wept for her.

Her crying jag was brought to a sharp end. Something or someone was yowling. She swallowed a sob, her skin goose-fleshing in response to the drawn-out, strangulated sound echoing through the street. She couldn't tell if it was animal or human or how close it was, but as she stood there, wiping the tears from her face, she knew one thing.

She had to get out of the city.

2

When Chrissie woke at first light, the corpse was gone. There were stains on the road where it had been. She scanned the street. There was no movement, no sign of it.

She dressed quickly and packed a couple of holdalls with essentials - matches, candles, a torch, tinned food and a few bottles of water. She acted with a sense of urgency, refusing to let herself think about why she was doing it or where she was going. There was no time for it. Not here. Not now. She was working on instinct. Get out. Get away.

The bags were packed by the time she noticed the wine rack. Maybe drink was the answer. She sat the bags by the front door and helped herself to a couple of bottles of red.

Her father's keys were on the hall table where he always left them. She picked them up and, armed with the golf club, unlocked the front door and cautiously stuck her head outside. There was no breeze. The smell of her burnt-out car lingered in the air, but everything was still. There was no hum of distant traffic, no lawnmower buzzing, no sound of children playing. She paused, trying to take it in. The silence was unnerving. Still, she preferred silence to the hideous yowling she'd heard the

13

night before.

Her father's car was in the drive at the side of the house. Mercifully unscathed. With any luck, he'd have kept to his habit of keeping the tank filled.

Standing on the doorstep, ready to duck back into the house at the first hint of trouble, she unlocked the car with the remote. She cringed as the smart snap of the locks cut through the air. A quick glance around. Nothing stirred.

She gave it a moment. When nothing kept on happening, she took a step towards the drive. Then another. Eight paces in all. The thud of her own heart pounding over the silence.

When she got all the way to the car unscathed, she told herself to get a grip. Never mind zombies. She'd shred herself if she kept up this level of anxiety. It was cool. The end had indeed been nigh, but everything was cool.

She walked round to the passenger door, gravel crunching under her boots. She had a grip now, she really did. Even so, she took another look around. It was allowed. It was the sensible thing to do.

She helped herself to a big long scan of the neighbourhood. It informed her that there were no zombies shuffling along the street towards her. There was no anything. It was all still cool.

"Keep telling yourself that," she muttered under her breath.

She wanted the bags up front beside her. Everything to hand.

Safe in the knowledge that it was all still totally cool, she opened the passenger door, leant the golf club against the car, and went back to the house for her gear. Leaving the house for the last time, she took the time to lock the front door behind her before pocketing the keys. The house, her parent's home, was now a tomb.

She stowed the holdalls on the passenger seat, wedging the bottles of wine securely between them and shut the car door. Slammed it harder than she meant. The sound reverberated through the street, cracking the unnatural silence.

Another sound rumbled beneath the echo. Faint at first. It came again. Louder, more confident. A raw, guttural growl. Chrissie's skin prickled. The hairs on the back of her neck stood up.

Keeping instinctively still, she looked down at the wing mirror. Dogs. Behind her. Three of them. Large, radiating tension. Mouths dripping. The one at the front bared its teeth, took a step towards her. The others flanked it, growling. The sound vibrated through her. Turned her organs to jelly.

She had one chance and one chance only.

She grabbed the handle and yanked the car door open.

Behind her, a howl. Claws scrabbling on pavement. Churning up gravel.

Throwing herself into the car, she tried to clamber over the bags. The big one lunged. Fastened its jaws around the heel of her boot before she could pull her feet inside.

Sprawling over the bags, on her belly. Desperately kicking at the dog with her free foot. Wrong angle. No space to put enough force into it. It snarled, refusing to let go of its prize.

Still kicking, she twisted around onto her back. The dog held fast. Pink foam flecked its muzzle. It's thick, curly coat was matted. Its eyes rolled, whites showing as she lashed out. Kicking it over and over again. But the dog clung on tightly to the thick rubber of the boot's heel. Starving. Each of them as desperate as the other.

She scrabbled around trying to find something, anything, she could use to hurt it. Make it let go. A clatter as the golf club was knocked to the ground by the dog's hindquarters. Keys - she could jab it in the eyes with the keys.

Still kicking out, she tried to work her fingers into her pocket, but the material had twisted, knotting the keys in tight. The other dogs snarled and snapped behind their leader. They'd tear her to shreds if they got the chance.

Chrissie writhed and wriggled, working herself further inside the vehicle. The handbrake dug into her lower back. The big, curly-haired dog stuck with her. Edging into the car. Teeth fastened to her boot. Teeth that would soon be ripping into her throat.

She squirmed, desperate. Felt something dig into her side. Top of a wine bottle. She felt for the neck, gripped it hard, pulled the bottle out.

The other dogs were crowding at the door. Growing bolder. The big dog shifted its bite onto the boot's leather upper. She caught a glimpse of a name tag. *Sheldon.* Pain shot through her foot. Up her leg. She gasped. Now. She had to do it now. She twisted her arm around. Crashed the bottle onto its head. The dog yelped, lost its grip. Fell back on the others.

Scrabbling, twisting, she stretched over the bags, reaching for the door handle. Grasping it. Pulling it shut as one of them leapt. It thudded against the window, leaving behind a splatter of frothy saliva.

She clambered into the driver's seat. Stretching her legs out, she untwisted the pocket and retrieved the keys. Her hands were shaking. A tremble ran through her body.

The big dog recovered and threw itself against the car door. Another dog, a Staffie cross, hurled itself onto the bonnet, claws scrabbling for purchase. It was smaller than the others but looked powerful. Lips pulled back in a snarl, it snapped yellow fangs only a few inches from her face. It lunged. She screamed as it thudded against the windscreen. Pushed herself back against the seat. Expecting the glass to crack. It held fast. The dog slid off the bonnet, paws wheeling in the air.

There were at least six dogs out there now, prowling around. Snarling. Seeking a way in. A way to get at her. She fumbled the key into the ignition.

Thud, thud, thud. The dogs throwing themselves at the car. Testing it for weak points. She turned the key. The engine started. The radio blared white noise. Chrissie's heart pounded like it was about to burst.

She put the car in reverse and rocketed out of the drive. There was a piercing yelp followed by a grinding bump as the wheels rolled over one of the animals.

It was still twitching as she backed onto the street. Fake diamonds twinkled on its sky blue collar. Eyes rolling back as its insides oozed into its tangled fur. Two of its pack were already circling, making exploratory snaps at its broken flank as she sped away.

The rest of the pack went after her. Mean and lean, they ran alongside the car, snapping at the tyres. She pressed on the accelerator, moved up through the gears. Left them trailing.

Along the street, lying in the gutter, the remains of the young woman. She wasn't a zombie after all. Just dead.

A couple of Jack Russells snipped at the pile of bloodied rags the young woman had been reduced to. A collie and a lab fought over a long bone. Her thighbone, Chrissie realised. The knowledge unwanted but there all the same.

3

The tank was half-full. Not as much fuel as she'd hoped, but enough to get clear of the city and then some. Not that Chrissie knew where she was going. For now, it was enough that she was moving.

The dog attack had left her shaken. Her foot throbbed. Images of their slavering mouths flashed through her mind.

They'd been pets. Fed and watered, sticks thrown for them in the park. Now they were running wild. A feral pack. How long had it taken them to get into that ravenous, blood-thirsty state? How long had she been unconscious? She shook her head. No point in dwelling on it. What mattered now was staying alive.

She passed a sign for the police station. People in authority. Resources. Uniforms. If there was any place to get help it would be there. There had to be someone in charge. Someone who knew what was going on. What to do. There had to be.

She clung to the thought until she turned onto the Marketgait and was confronted by the sight of a smouldering, blackened building. She slowed. Stopped. Stared. She'd been clinging to dust.

She could smell the charred remains from inside the car.

There was no hope of help or rescue here.

It must have been burning through the night. Maybe for the whole day before that. But there was no evidence of anyone having tried to put out the blaze. No fire tenders, no ambulances, no rubber-neckers. No nothing. If anyone had been inside, they'd either scarpered or been roasted alive.

The glass had blown out of the windows. Chrissie gazed at the remnant of a scorched curtain stirring listlessly, like a fading pulse, in the light breeze.

Unruly mobs roamed the city at night. Feral dogs prowled the streets. Buildings burned. And no-one did anything to stop it.

She finally faced up to the fear she'd been pushing aside since she'd woken. There was no-one in charge. No law and order. Social constructs had been shattered. This was it. The real deal.

No one was coming to help.

She was on her own.

4

Now she was looking. Now she was seeing.

The city was a mess. Away from the quiet, residential area where her parents had lived, the devastation was much clearer.

People lay in the street, left to die where they'd collapsed. Chrissie recalled the sudden buckling of her own knees, the overwhelming desire to lie down. How weak she'd felt, as though the air had been sucked from her lungs. The strength sapped from her legs.

She'd seen it happening to others. Now it was happening to her.

She sat heavily on a chair, upper body slumping forward onto the kitchen table, head turned sideways so that she could feel its cool surface against her hot cheek. Her mother staring at her from what seemed a long way away. As if she was looking at her through the wrong end of a telescope.

Funny, she'd gone there to see Phoebe. To help. Now she was the one falling down and she didn't think she'd be getting up again. Not ever.

Her mother's mouth a dark O, her eyes wide. Chrissie wanted to tell her to close her mouth, that she'd catch germs. But even in that light-headed, feverish state, she knew it was too late. The disease had already got them.

People collapsed in shops, in their cars, in schools, at work. At first the ambulances came. Or the fire brigade. Or the police. But then no-one came, because they had it too.

Chrissie's parents had the good fortune to fall down quietly, in their own homes, but unlike her, they didn't get up again. For them the pain was over. They were the lucky ones.

It started very quietly, in another country, happening to other people. At first it seemed like the bird flu scare all over again. A non-event. Then all flights in and out of the country were cancelled. Suddenly, it wasn't happening to other people. It was happening to them.

Within a week the tabloids were calling it Falling Down Flu. The scientists said it wasn't a flu virus. It wasn't a virus of any description. It was a rogue prion. But that was too complicated to grasp. The people needed an enemy to rail against. A virus was ideal. Falling Down Flu stuck. FDF for short.

The internet was ablaze with it. A rumour started that it came out of China. The Chinese authorities denied it and blamed India. India blamed Pakistan and so it went on until the only continent left untainted by blame was Antarctica. Meanwhile people just kept on getting ill. This time round it wasn't the story that died. It was people.

There were riots in the streets. People protesting, demanding that the government do something about it. They did. They rounded up the Royal Family and herded them to the splendid isolation of Balmoral. They closed the ports, sealed the Channel Tunnel. Britain was in quarantine, but it was too little too late. FDF was already here.

Despite following guidelines about washing their hands and avoiding crowded places, people sitting in their own homes still got sick. There was a flurry of hysteria from the press. Faces of just-dead celebrities and politicians were splashed across front pages. Within three weeks the demonstrations stopped as the illness spread.

Television and radio stations went onto emergency broadcasts. Internet sites shut down. Handfuls of people in scattered council offices throughout the country became the prime source of information. Chrissie was one of them. The joke was, they were worse off than everyone else. By this time they had realised that nobody was going to come along and make this thing all better. Least of all the government. Most of them were already sick. Or dead.

Finally, the network died and the phones stopped ringing.

5

Chrissie drove through the city in a trance. Where streets were blocked, she changed direction. Reversing, doubling back on herself, twisting and turning through a maze of back-streets and alleys. Finally, more by luck than design, she came to the main arterial route through the city.

Normally a fast-flowing road, the Kingsway was haphazardly strewn with stationary vehicles. Some abandoned, others with drivers and passengers still strapped inside, bodies slumped.

There were smashes, one involving a couple of rolled army trucks. Chrissie wove her way around the wreckage, feeling emptier and emptier as she went. She headed west, her progress steady but slow. Several times she was forced to take a bone-jolting diversion over verges.

She passed a row of shops. Some had been boarded up. Others lay open, as if they'd been trading right up to the last minute. People had literally shopped till they dropped.

The dead were everywhere. Of the living, there was no sign. It was eerily still and quiet. No rumbling trucks or buses, no blaring horns, no cyclists, no people on the pedestrian walkways. All she could see was death.

She tried not to drive over bodies, but it couldn't always

be avoided. Then she tried not to think about the flesh and bones grinding and mashing beneath her car wheels, but she couldn't avoid that either. If the disease didn't get you, thinking about it would.

The suddenness of it was illustrated by the many bodies lying just beyond cars. People struck down in a feeble attempt to get help, doors hanging open behind them. No-one believing it would happen to them until it did.

Chrissie saw things she didn't want to see. A woman lying on the grass, her arm wrapped around a child.

She looked away, but the image persisted. Burnt into her retinas. The child dressed in pink.

How long before they were discovered by packs of scavenging dogs or rats? How long before the tragedy was rendered obscene?

A heavy shroud of guilt settled upon her. Guilt for surviving when they hadn't. Guilt for not doing anything - for not being able to do anything - to help. Guilt for being afraid.

She could have stood in the street and called out for other survivors, but she was too scared. She didn't even blown the car horn. She could have done that. But what if she found the wrong kind of survivor? Or the wrong kind of survivor found her. The screams from the night before still rang in her ears.

Even in the car she couldn't be sure of escaping them. There were too many hazards in the streets. They could petrol bomb her. Smash the windows, drag her from the driver's seat.

Before everything crashed, the internet had been rife with conspiracy theories and scare stories. FDF was only the start of it. There was a secondary disease following in its wake. The secondary disease affected the brain, causing outbreaks of irrational and violent behaviour. The crazier versions of the story - the posts on the forums - said that it turned people into zombies.

Turned out there was a whole world of people out there

who'd been waiting their entire lives for a zombie uprising. The survivalists were in their element. Just as excited, the religious fundamentalists grew more fanatical by the hour. Social networking sites were filled with tales of zombie encounters. People being attacked, their throats and faces bitten, bodies torn apart.

Whether they were actual zombies in the sense of dying before getting up and roaming around looking for a face to chomp, or just very sick and violent people, the end result was the same - bad news. After what she'd witnessed the previous night, walking dead or walking alive, these were the kind of survivors Chrissie had no intention of getting up close and personal with.

Deciding not to become a one-woman rescue party was absolutely justified. It was way too risky... but still, deep inside she felt like a coward for not even trying.

6

An overturned van brought Chrissie's guilt trip to an end. It blocked the grass-lined path to the left of the carriageway as well as the best part of both lanes. Several vehicles had smashed into it.

There were two cars on the central reservation. One had shunted into the other, both of them ending up broken and tangled in the shrubbery growing there.

Chrissie had to figure out how to get by the crash or go back the way she'd come. It had taken her long enough to get on the Kingsway in the first place. If she turned back, she could end up driving in circles, trying to find a way out of the maze of blocked streets, until night fell. She didn't want to be in the city after dark.

Leaving the engine running, she got out of the car. The sun was warm on her face. Death, destruction and carnage aside, it was a beautiful autumn day disturbed only by the low hum of electric cables overhead. Except that there were no electric cables overhead. The noise was coming from the bodies strewn on the road. With the unseasonable warmth came the bluebottles.

Swallowing her disgust, she studied the obstruction and tried to figure out a way through it. One of the car drivers, her head twisted on her neck at an unnatural angle, had a look of shock death-masked on her face. The van driver's head was spread across the windscreen in a slurry of blood, brain and bone. The only signs of life came from the feasting insects.

Her attention was snagged by a woman in a little blue Peugeot. She was flat back against her seat, head lolling, mouth hanging open. She looked as dead as dead can be, but all the same Chrissie had a sudden compulsion to make sure.

Maybe it was guilt working in her. Or maybe she wanted to check out the zombie theory. The woman was belted in. Even if she was a zombie, Chrissie would be safe enough.

The woman was dressed in a smart suit and crisp white shirt. Standards high right to the end. Chrissie peered through the half-open window.

"Hello - are you okay?"

What else was she going to say - *Excuse me, but are you as dead as you look?*

As the words left her lips, a fat, glistening bluebottle crawled out of the woman's mouth. She was definitely dead. And not a zombie. Chrissie gagged, her body convulsing with dry heaves. Eyes streaming, she turned away, concentrating instead on the vista of vehicular carnage.

Looking at it from the right angle, there appeared to be some space between the van and the cars on the central reservation. She got back behind the wheel.

So very recently, her father would have had a meltdown at the thought of what she was about to do to his beautifully waxed and buffed vehicle. That was then. This was now, and now, as Chrissie was beginning to realise, was a different time, a different world. Cleaning the car, mowing the lawn... those things didn't matter any more.

She bumped the outside wheels onto the verge and started nudging her way through. It was tight. Maybe too tight. The wing mirrors snapped off. She flinched at the scrape and screech of metal upon metal. But she kept on pushing it until she was jammed between the van and the cars. Couldn't turn back now if she wanted to.

Knowing there was no return made the job easier. She pushed and nudged her way through the narrow passage. Pumping the accelerator, crunching glass, grinding metal. And she was through.

She bumped back onto the road on the other side of the wreckage. Feeling pretty good now that she was moving again. She even smiled a little. Proud of her achievement. That she'd done *something*.

She passed a squadron of four-in-a-blocks. They were surrounded by a swathe of grass punctuated by play equipment. A set of swings here, a jungle-jim there, small bodies in brightly-coloured clothing scattered around them.

She tried not to look, but absorbed them all the same.

Children, taken ill, fallen on the spot with no-one around to pick them up and carry them to somewhere safe and warm. They'd died on the grass, or beneath the climbing frames. Died without a cuddle, without anyone to tell them that everything would be okay, because in all likelihood, everyone who loved them was also dead or dying, and nothing was going to be okay anymore.

A hooded crow alighted beside the head of one child - a boy of around seven or eight - and pecked at his eyes. It was soon joined by others. A murder of them, flapping and picking. They would do okay in this new world. They would survive and thrive. Chrissie felt hollow, as though part of her had already died.

A movement caught her eye. Smoke billowing into the sky. Another building ablaze. Maybe deliberately set alight. She was right to be getting out of the city while she still could.

She wondered how many mobs were running through the streets of Dundee and how much of it they would destroy before they fell down for the last time. Pictured the same thing happening in towns and cities across the country. Across the world.

Out by the industrial estate, Chrissie came off the Kingsway and swung on to a back road. It was narrow and winding, but it was the quickest way for her to get away from Dundee. There were only a few motionless vehicles scattered along the tree-lined road between the big country park and Templeton Woods, none of them blocking the road.

She thought, as she always did when driving this way, of the young women who'd been murdered and dumped naked in the woods all those years ago. Chrissie had only been a toddler at the time, but the story of the unsolved murders haunted the playgrounds when she was growing up.

She thought of the woman left dead in the street last night. No-one would investigate her death. No more law. No order. And no amount of warm sunshine dappling through the trees could stop the shiver running through her.

The road wound through a couple of small villages. Despite being so close to the city, there was little evidence of death and destruction here. Cars were mostly parked where they ought to be. There were no corpses on the pavements or in the gutters. It could almost have been a quiet Sunday from back when the shops were closed all day and all there was to look forward to was an episode of *Bullseye* on the telly in the afternoon. *Can't beat a bit of bully. Let's have a look at what you could have won.*

Past the villages, birds fluttered in the hedgerows. Chrissie relaxed into the drive, almost smiling at a pheasant standing on the verge. His head cocked, collar so white it looked as though someone had painted it on. Dead cows lay in the fields on either side of the road, unmilked bodies bloating in the sun. She'd once been told that dead cows could explode, but these were just plain dead and unexploded.

The road twisted and turned, climbing towards the heart of the country. The further away from the city she got, the safer Chrissie felt. The road was clear. She was finally able to move up through the gears and drive.

Hedgerows blurred as she picked up speed. She rounded a corner, taking it wide. There was a car. Silver estate. Broadside on the road ahead.

She slammed on the brakes. Tyres screeched. Smell of burning rubber.

She braced for the impact.

7

There was a massive jolt as she skidded into the other car. Her head snapped forward. Creak and crack of grinding metal. Cloud - like smoke - as the airbag deployed. Deflating almost immediately, it hung over the steering wheel like an oversized used condom.

The engine still running. More creaking and groaning of metal as she backed up, legs trembling just a little.

Two bodies slumped in the front seats of the estate. Both male, one a good bit older than the other. Maybe a father and son combo. Whatever trick of fate had put them in that position, they couldn't have blocked the road more effectively if they'd been dropped there by a crane.

Drainage ditches on either side of the road meant there was no way to drive around. No matter what, Chrissie was not going back towards the city. There was nothing else for it. She would have to move the estate.

The windows were closed. The interior of the car would be like an oven. Hot enough to cook the decomposing bodies inside. Before getting too close, she tossed a few pebbles at the windscreen. Zombie baiting. Just to be sure. Neither body stirred. The dead stayed dead.

Chrissie grasped the door handle. Trusting that it

wasn't locked, she turned her head away and pulled. The door swung open with ease. Despite the head-turning, she caught a blast of putrefied air. It unleashed an olfactory memory. *Dad, when I smell death, I think of you.*

She stepped back and let the stench clear.

The younger of the two was in the driving seat. Something to be grateful for. The older guy was bulky. It would take a bit of muscle to heft him but even for a dead kid, the driver looked undernourished. The kind school bullies hung up on coat hooks for fun.

Him being skinny didn't stop it being an awkward job. He was slouched over the steering wheel, seatbelt on. Chrissie stretched over him to reach the clip. The front of her rubbing against the back of him. Up close and personal, the smell was atrocious. But she was getting so used to it, it didn't even make her gag.

Belt undone, she grabbed him by his bony shoulders and hauled him out. There was no dignity in it. She dropped him a couple of times. Skinny he may have been, but it took brute effort to get his dead weight out of the car.

The second time she lost her grip, she stopped for a break. She didn't like to leave him with his upper half dangling out of the car like that, but she was running on empty. Feeling light headed. She would have to eat soon.

After a few moments, she had another go at him. Now that he was more out than in, it didn't take much to pull him clear. She hauled him to the verge and laid him on his back, autumn sun washing over him, his young face framed by wild flowers and grasses. There were traces of acne on his cheekbones. He looked barely old enough to drive. Probably still had coat-hook marks on his back.

She didn't relish the idea of getting into the car with Fat Dad, but as there was no way she was going to try to shift him, getting in is what she did.

Reaching for the key, she suddenly realised that all her hard work might have been for nothing. She should have checked that the car was going to start before shifting Skinny Boy.

Hindsight was a great thing but all this Omega Woman business was new to her. There were no guidebooks. Chrissie was making it up as she went along.

As it happened, the car started first time. Beginner's luck. It was hardly a classic three-point turn, but she was almost there when she hit the brakes a touch too heavy. It wasn't much of a jolt, but it was enough to shift Fat Dad.

She wasn't a natural born screamer, but when his head thudded onto her shoulder, she let out a good one. Images of his teeth tearing into her neck. Ripping out her carotid artery. Her blood spraying over the windscreen good style.

Her scream ran out of steam. She hadn't been bit. Fat Dad was properly deceased and rotting.

She shoved him off. He lolled right back on. They played the game a couple of times more but in the end she finished moving the car with him slumped on her shoulder. She couldn't wait to get out of there.

Her own car looked like it had been pulled out of the crusher in a wrecker's yard. The wing mirrors were gone, headlights smashed, front number plate hanging off, bumper cracked, doors gouged and buckled. But it still ran, and right now, that was all that mattered.

She put some miles between herself and Dead and Deader before stopping for food. She didn't know how many germs lived on the outside of a dead person. However many it was, she wanted to get cleaned up before eating.

A rummage in the glove-box was rewarded with a pack of Wet Wipes. She gave her hands a thorough clean, then wiped the steering wheel, gear-stick and hand brake.

She was starving. All caved-in. Opened the first tin she laid hands on. Tuna flakes in brine. Followed that up with a can of pineapple chunks. Wiped the juice off her chin on the back of her hand. Cleaned up the sticky with another Wet Wipe. Good old dad. Organised to the last.

She'd seen a lot of dead bodies since, but her father's was the first. That had been yesterday.

He'd been dead for some time. She'd watched the programmes on TV. Knew rigor mortis set in soon after death. But her father's body wasn't stiff and fresh looking. Rigor mortis had long since come and gone. His body was decaying. She knew that without having to look at him. The stench told its own story. He stank of shit and rotting meat. He stank of death.

She hadn't wanted to go into her parent's bedroom. Didn't want to discover what hideous secrets it contained. But as with the woman on the street - she had to see for herself. She had to know.

Standing in the hall. Her hand inside their bedroom. Feeling along the wall for the light switch. Breath caught in her throat. Waiting for something to grab her. Telling herself not to be stupid. Nothing in there could hurt her. Dead things didn't grab. But the Z-word was already lurking in the back of her mind.

A flick of the switch. Shoulders tensing at the abrupt *click*. Nothing grabbed her. No light either. She clicked the switch up and down. Sill no light. Nothing but the small sound cracking into the dark.

She stared into the room. No glow from the radio alarm. No background hum.

No power.

Swallowing the urge to retch, she fumbled her way to the bedroom window and pulled the curtains apart.

Daylight hit her widened pupils with a perfect stab. She blinked away the pain and opened the window. Sticking her face in the gap, she greedily sucked in fresh air before reluctantly turning back to the room.

The top of her father's head was poking out of a quilt cocoon.

She approached slowly, heart thudding, head filled with

a pulsing boom. She stood by the side of the bed for a moment before pulling back the duvet and exposing his face.

He was barely recognisable. His eyes were closed but had sunk into his skull. His mouth sagged open, trickles of fluid crusting on either side. His skin, tinged blue, had begun to split.

How long had she been unconscious? Was he already dead by the time she collapsed?

Her throat constricted, but no tears came. Surviving the wreckage of her marriage had toughened her up. Her husband's - ex-husband's - betrayal had led to the discovery of a new skill set. She could now efficiently stuff away her emotions. Box them up until she had time to deal with them.

Sometime in the future, she would drag them out and give them a going over. But not now.

Her father was alone. She glanced round at the door behind her, knowing that her mother was elsewhere in the house. Hoping that she'd pulled through. Chrissie had, why not her? Perhaps immunity ran in families.

Her mother could still be sleeping. Phoebe too. Still fighting it, their eyes gummed up the way hers had been. The silence enveloping the house was deathly, but there was always a chance, always a hope.

She took one last look at her father, feeling that she ought to do something. Perhaps hug him in a final farewell. But she was too aware of the process of putrefaction going on within his body. If she felt him liquid under his skin she would scream. If she started screaming now, she might never stop.

In the end, she simply pulled the quilt over his head.

She bunched up the Wet Wipes, stuffed them into the pineapple can and drove on. A mile passed. Two. Three. The city was well behind her. The sun was shining. There was food in her belly. She was alive.

Taking it easy on the gas, she rounded a bend onto a straight stretch. Up ahead, plain as plain could be, another car was blocking the road. Except, that as she drew nearer, Chrissie saw that it wasn't just one car - there were three of them.

8

Chrissie realised then that from now on, life was going to consist of a series of obstacles to be got around. She slumped at the thought, but she wasn't ready to give in. Not yet, although the idea of curling up into a little ball and pretending that none of this was happening to her did hold a certain appeal.

On closer inspection, it wasn't so bad. To get by, she'd only have to shift one of the cars. The driver inside it was on her own. Chrissie banged on the window a few times. The good news was that the woman stayed dead. The bad news was her size. She was one big corpse.

Holding her breath, Chrissie opened the door and stepped back. She was becoming a regular pro at the Dead Body In Car routine.

Once the air had cleared, she tried the engine. She wasn't going to make that mistake again. It coughed a couple of times before sparking into life. The wonder of modern cars. Chrissie contemplated her next problem. The dead woman had a solid look about her. Arms like boiled hams, the skin on them ripe for splitting.

This corpse was going to be much more difficult to heft than Skinny Boy.

She went around to the passenger side and unclipped

37

the woman's seat belt. She tried to simply push her out of the door but the hefty corpse had settled into the seat pretty well. She wasn't for moving. Chrissie sat for a while and contemplated her problem.

There was precious little space between the woman's belly and the steering wheel. The task would be a whole lot easier if she could slide the seat back a little. Trouble was, the lever was in the usual place. That is, under the seat. Chrissie had no choice but to get deep into the corpse's personal space.

Face crushed against nylon-clad, decomposing thighs and belly, she pushed her hand between puffy, liquefying ankles and groped under the seat for the lever. The combination of textures and smells was on a whole new level of bad. She finally got hold of the lever and pulled. The seat thunked back.

Chrissie had another go at pushing the corpse out, but this dame was stubborn. She had that look about her - pillar of the community type - more used to giving orders than taking them, but after the carnival of delights she'd just been through, Chrissie wasn't going to give up that easily.

In the end, she pulled the passenger door shut, wedged herself up against it, and kicked the bloated corpse out. This technique had the added bonus of her not having to touch the bare flesh of the arms. Still, it wasn't easy. She worked up a lather of sweat in the process, but finally, out the corpse fell.

The body was too heavy for Chrissie to drag out of the way, so she rolled it like a big, ungainly Easter egg. Liquid oozed and strips of skin peeled away from the corpse's arms, but it wasn't so bad once she got into the rhythm of it. In fact, she got the hang of it so well that she rolled the body right into the drainage ditch. It landed face down. Chrissie shrugged. Dead was dead and she wasn't going to waste any time weeping.

She moved the car out of the way, not worrying about

shunting the other two a little, cleaned herself up with a couple of Wet Wipes and got back on the road.

The wipes had their limit. Chrissie was so saturated in decay she could taste it. She opened her window. Air circulated around the car, gradually blowing the stench away.

Before long, she came to a roundabout on the outskirts of a market town. One of its exits led to a superstore. Chrissie slowed the car and eyed the building across the vast car park. It took her a moment to realise what was unusual about it. Then she got it. The lights were on. *Power.* The fuel pumps at the petrol station would be working.

She checked the fuel gauge. Less than a quarter of a tank. All that low gear driving had taken its toll. The thought of filling up was too tempting.

She drove round the circle and took the exit for the store.

9

There was a smattering of vans and cars. A small group of them clustered in the spaces nearest the store entrance. Otherwise, the huge car park was devoid of vehicles. She could see a few bodies, but a couple of plastic bags fluttering over the tarmac provided the only movement.

Chrissie cautiously drove into the filling station. There were four vehicles at the pumps - one van, two cars and a motorbike.

A passenger slouched in one of the cars, head against the window, mouth stretched in a silent scream, eyes open, seeing nothing. She looked all dried out. The back of the car was packed to the roof. They'd seen how things were going, were getting out before it was too late. The only flaw in their plan being that it was already too late.

The motorcyclist was on the ground beside his bike, helmet still on, body encased in a shroud of leathers. Another body on the pavement outside the kiosk. Male. Perhaps he'd been with the desiccated woman.

Skeletal hands stretched out from the sleeves of his fleece. His head was twisted to one side. Eye sockets empty and dark as depression. Soft tissue stripped from his head and arms.

Something had been feasting on him. Not dogs - they

would have torn him apart. Birds perhaps, like the hooded crow she'd seen pecking at the child's eyes. Insects then. Or rats. In the end, nature's scavengers would make short work of them all.

There was no-one else lying around outside. Maybe they'd died in the kiosk. Right in the middle of paying, loyalty cards still clutched in their dead hands.

The staff must be dead too. At any rate, there was no sign of life out on the forecourt and no-one was waving from the booth. Maybe there was no fuel either, but if she didn't get topped up soon she'd be going nowhere fast. She had to give it a go.

She pulled in at an empty pump, pressed the Pay At Kiosk button and put the nozzle into the tank. The fuel flowed just as if nothing had changed.

Withered flowers drooped in plastic buckets outside the kiosk. Through the windows she could see shelves stacked with sweets, crisps, fizzy drinks. Food of a sort. She looked across at the superstore. The kiosk hadn't been plundered. Maybe the store hadn't either. If not, there would be better pickings there.

She drove right up to the shop entrance and sat for a while, doors locked, engine idling. Up close, the scene wasn't as unspoiled as it had appeared from the filling station.

People had collapsed during various stages of the shopping process. Loading cars. Returning or fetching trolleys. Strapping in babies.

Bags of food - in trolleys, in open car boots, on the ground - had been clawed or chewed open. Likewise exposed flesh. A baby with its face eaten off. Tiny fingers curled. Grow suit splattered and stained. A woman, her hands reduced to stumps. A man in baggy shorts. Lying face down. Chunks of flesh and muscle torn from his calves and thighs.

Flies clustered on rotting flesh. Seagulls squabbled over

tasty morsels. Two of them pulling on what looked like a string of sausages. Someone's intestines. Smaller birds hopped and pecked around the edges, rising in a flutter whenever a seagull jabbed at them.

Dark shapes moved in the shadows beneath cars. No longer restricted to night manoeuvres, the rats were becoming bolder. There were no signs of dogs yet, or cats. Probably enough pickings in the town for them. But they would come. Chrissie was sure of that. Prowling, hunting, scavenging.

Bad though the scene of death and decay around her was, Chrissie couldn't help but think that it could have been so much worse. Perhaps they'd been struck down at night, when the store would have been quieter. Trying to stock up. Take care of their families.

No matter the whys and wherefores of it, the simple fact was, they were dead and she was alive and there was only one fact that could be changed in that statement.

She stared at the horn symbol on the steering wheel. She could give it a blast. See if there was anyone around who was still alive. But she might stir up more than she bargained for. Under these silent conditions, the blare would be heard for miles. No, better to just sit there awhile and see if the sound of the car engine was enough to draw anybody or anything out.

When several minutes passed and nothing had stirred, she switched the engine off and sat a while longer. There were bodies lying inside the store. Looked like they were in better condition than the ones outside, but nothing was moving.

Time to go shopping.

10

The doors parted with a satisfying *svisssshhh*. Chrissie pushed a large trolley between them, deftly steering it around the security guard. He was sprawled on the floor in his pseudo police uniform. Poor sod had died on the job. Most likely on minimum wages too.

As a sweet-toothed child, she'd often fantasised about being locked in the corner shop all night. Gorging herself silly from the sweet jars lining the shelves. And from the packets and tubes and fancy heart-shaped boxes behind the counter. Now that she had a bigger store than she could ever have imagined all to herself, the last thing on her mind was a fistful of Cherry Lips.

She helped herself to some bags for life. There was a display of them beside the dead security guard. She opened them up and sat them in the trolley so that she could pack as she went. When she was done, all she'd have to do was load them into the car.

Bags for life. She wondered, just for a moment, how long she'd get out of them. Then she got down to the business of looting.

No, she wasn't looting. All she wanted was a few things to help her stay alive. That wasn't against the law, was it?

Ha, what law?

The old rules were as dead as the security guard and as pointless as his clip-on tie.

She began her scavenging expedition in the outdoor and sports section. A wind-up radio, sleeping bag and mat went into the trolley along with a camping stove and a few tins of butane gas.

Wending her way around the bodies lying in the household aisles, she packed the bags with candles, matches, firelighters, batteries, a couple of spare torches and two packs of toilet rolls - the kind with a handle on the top of the pack that can be looped over the hook at the front of the trolley to save space.

J-cloths were next, along with antiseptic wipes, a first aid kit, painkillers, soap, washing up liquid, disinfectant, sanitary towels and three large tubs of petroleum jelly. Good for dry skin, cracked lips, minor cuts and abrasions. She'd read somewhere that it was even possible to eat the stuff.

The clothing department was next. Chrissie's jeans were hanging off her. A result of her enforced diet She needed clothes that fitted properly. Besides which, winter was on its way. Warm gear was going to be essential.

She strolled on by the shimmering party clothes. Nobody was going to be wearing those sequinned little numbers to the office party this year.

She rummaged around and found a pair of chinos that looked like they could take a bit of beating. She stripped off and changed into them, completing her ensemble with a cotton t-shirt, heavy grey sweatshirt and a pair of thick boot socks.

She put her old boots back on but chucked a pair of trainers on top of one of the bags. A few packs of underwear, a set of spare clothes and a waterproof jacket were squished into another. The bags were full. Time to load up the car before stocking up on food.

The occasional bird squawk aside, the car park was cemetery quiet. Working quickly, Chrissie piled her supplies into the back of the car, leaving the boot empty for food.

The in-store air conditioning system was effective at keeping the smell of rot at bay in the non-food departments. In the food aisles, the underlying stench of decay was much stronger. The reek wasn't just coming from the bodies on the floor. The meat counter, with its sickly, gut-clenching odour of ripe decay was grim. The fish counter was beyond rank.

Someone had collapsed in the fruit and vegetable aisle, taking a crate of oranges with them. The oranges looked temptingly bright and fresh on top, but when she toed a few of them out of the way they fell apart revealing their mouldy, blue undersides.

There were darting movements around her peripheral vision. Small creatures scuttling out of sight as she pushed the trolley by crates of grapes. The fruit turning to brown, liquid mush in its bags.

Blackened bananas had collapsed in on themselves. Filthy fur coats grew on rotten tomatoes. Carrots had softened and shrivelled like old men, black mould growing on them like liver spots. The bright spectrum of the regulation five-a-day was slowly reducing to a state of monochrome sludge.

A couple of boxes of apples looked remarkably fresh. Tempted, Chrissie picked one up and inspected it.

The fruit was firm, the skin unblemished. Her mouth watered. It had been a long time since she'd eaten any fresh fruit. She rubbed it on her sleeve and took a bite.

It crumbled, mealy, almost tasteless, in her mouth. She spat it out. Superficially, it looked fresh and good, but underneath it was as rotten as the corpses littering the floor. She threw it hard against a shelf, taking brief satisfaction from its splatter, and headed for the tinned goods.

Beans, meat, fish, fruit, vegetables. Curry, stew, soup,

haggis. Steamed puddings, all day breakfasts, hot dogs, burgers, chilli con carne, three bean salad. Every food group was available in a tin and each tin came with its own ring pull. Pineapples from Malaysia, corned beef from Argentina, beans from Heinz. The world was her tinned oyster.

Distracted by her bounteous haul, she pushed the trolley, *whack*, into a corpse. She said, *sorry*. The apology slipping out automatically. She laughed aloud at her foolishness, but the sound unnerved her and she choked it back.

She collected teabags, coffee, powdered milk, cartons of fruit juice, biscuits, oatcakes, slabs of chocolate, dried pasta, a sack of rice, soy sauce, dried herbs and spices, stock cubes, peanut butter, and, to top it all off, six boxes of red wine.

There were some tempting bottles on the shelves, but boxes were easier to carry and pack. For good measure she added a bottle of malt whisky. She'd never been a whisky drinker, but it seemed like a good thing to have. Medicinal.

The car boot was satisfyingly full when she'd finished loading it. It was a good haul. If she had to, she could eke it out for several months.

All she had to do now was find somewhere safe to hole up.

11

The sun was low in the sky. She'd got carried away in the store. Her shopping expedition taking longer than anticipated.

Part of her wanted to get into the car and go, but the headlights were smashed. She didn't fancy driving in the dark. Not in this world. It didn't help that she was tired and hungry. The clincher was that she needed to use the toilet.

Chrissie locked the car with its precious load and headed back to the store. There was a loud bang. She jumped. Turned around. Couldn't see anything.

It had come from some distance away. The town most likely. She looked at the car. Looked at the setting sun. Weighed up her options. Turned again and went back into the store.

She pushed the door to the Ladies. It thudded against a body. A ripe one. Its perfume as sickly sweet as the meat counter, but with a sour base note. There was the impression of sudden movement as something disappeared beneath it.

Chrissie let the door swing closed. With a touch more caution, she tried the disabled toilet. No bodies. No darting movements. Just the regulation, vaguely unpleasant smell present in every public toilet.

When she was done, Chrissie scrubbed her hands and splashed her face. Facing her reflection in the mirror above the sink was unavoidable.

She looked as weary as she felt. Her energy levels were low. Vitality sapped. She needed to eat and drink. Tinned tuna and pineapple chunks only got a person so far.

She would eat. She would sleep. She would get on the road at sun up. Having a plan, even a simple one, made her feel better.

Something hot in her belly would be good. With that in mind, she decided to check out the in-store cafe. Not something she would have willingly done in the past. Between lousy food and high noise levels, they were her idea of hell. Now, she could cook what she liked. Noise was hardly an issue. And she was developing new ideas on what constituted hell.

She walked the length of the serving counter, checking out the displays. Most of the sandwiches in the chiller were mouldy, but the odd one or two looked spookily fresh. Recognisable only by the labels, the cremated remains of shepherds pie, macaroni cheese and lasagne were still being kept warm under the heating lamps at the hot food counter. Shrivelled carrots and peas like ball bearings were strangely identifiable. Danuta was behind the counter.

She was on the floor, a name tag pinned to her uniform. *Danuta*. Perhaps a Polish name. She was blonde, early to mid-twenties. When alive, she must have been very pretty. Chrissie walked past her and pushed through the swing doors to the kitchen. Thinking she could use the facilities to cook up something hot and tasty.

The door hadn't swung shut behind her when the stench hit. She slapped a hand over her nose and mouth but the smell already had her reeling. She staggered sideways. Something crunched underfoot. She looked down, knowing that whatever it was, it wasn't going to be good.

She hated being right all the time. It wasn't good. She'd just cracked a cockroach. If it was a female, forty or so eggs had just been squeezed out of her.

After a day spent hauling the dead around, a crushed cockroach shouldn't be such a big deal. But Chrissie had a thing about cockroaches. It wasn't a phobia. Definitely not a phobia. Phobias were irrational. Chrissie's dislike of cockroaches was entirely rational.

For one thing, they spread disease. For another, they never came in ones. Or twos.

The kitchen was alive with them. Walls, floor, work-tops, stoves. If it was there, they were on it, over it, under it, in it. And they stank. She gagged and shuddered. They gave her the horrors.

She had been studiously ignoring the glimpses she'd caught of them since she'd walked into the supermarket. Now she'd unwittingly stumbled into the nest. She kept her mouth tightly shut, but inside she was screaming.

They were small, brown and shiny, with hairy legs and long, creepy-feely antennae. Two black marks ran along their backs. German cockroaches. She'd learned way too much about them and their kin at the close encounter sessions she'd taken Phoebe to. Phoebe holding a Madagascar hissing cockroach, laughing. Chrissie trying to hide her revulsion. Not wanting Phoebe to grow up scared of creepy crawlies. *Just wanting her.*

She shut down the thought before it could take hold.

Chrissie's presence hadn't exactly put the fear of God into the almost indestructible insects. One or two scuttled away, but most of them were unperturbed. They just carried on with the business of roaching.

One of the cooks, identifiable by his whites and checks, lay on the floor beside an overturned stool. Roaches crawling over his face. Another, a greasy looking, skinny dude, was lying by a bucket of mouldy vegetables. The contents of the bucket were roach Manna. Everything moving. The entire scene garishly lit by fluorescent strip lighting. It was the stuff of nightmares.

The door swung to behind her as Chrissie staggered out of the kitchen. It did a great job of sealing in the rank smell. Right now, she was feeling pretty rank herself.

A movement caught her eye. A roach, crawling on her arm. She flicked it off. It landed on Danuta's face, quickly scuttling under her head. Chrissie shuddered and looked away.

There was a microwave on the counter above Danuta. At least she could still get a hot meal. No matter how sick the roaches made her feel, she had to eat.

As she walked into the store to find some food, the realisation came that she had become an opportunistic feeder. Not much different from the cockroaches. Except that they had evolved into what they were eons ago, whereas Chrissie was beginning to feel that she was de-evolving. A process which had taken a remarkably short time to begin.

She chose some microwaveable food from the freezer section. Chicken balti and pilau rice. A fresh salad would have made an enjoyable accompaniment, but nothing in the store was fresh anymore. Not even the stuff that looked green and crisp. Especially not the stuff that looked green and crisp. Instead, she picked up a bag of steam fresh country veg. *From field to frozen in under three hours*. So went the blurb.

She had to move Danuta to get to the microwave. Hauling dead people wasn't such a big deal by now, but Chrissie didn't want to touch her. Couldn't stand the thought of the roach running up her arm. Funny that. Dead people, no problem. Well, relatively little problem. It was adapt and survive. But live roaches? What could she say - everyone had their limit.

In the end, she gritted her teeth and gripped the shoulders of the woman's uniform. She slid her over the tiled floor, out of the way.

While she was waiting for her food to ping, she fetched a bottle of lager from the chiller. Cold beer, hot curry. She might as well make a proper meal of it. Visions of living out of her car, like some kind of hobo, flitted through her head. There was no knowing when she'd next get the chance to sit at a table to eat. Might as well be civilised, while she still could.

She peeled the film lids from the curry and rice, pulled open the bag of vegetables and dumped it all on a plate. Yellow rice. Red curry. Green and orange veg. A culinary rainbow.

She sat at a table near the counter, just to the side of the big window looking out over the car park. It was twilight. The half world between day and night. As she chewed, she thought about the road she would take in the morning. North was the way to go. It was less populous. Less people meant less danger.

She took a long swallow of lager. Mmmm, tasty. And so refreshing. Felt like a treat. She was about to put the bottle back on the table when her hand froze, mid-air. She stared at the window. Body all seized up. Not even breathing.

A sound. Outside. It was urgent. Alarming.

The hollow pounding of feet on concrete slabs, matched the pounding of Chrissie's heart. Sweat prickled in her armpits. Cold sweat. Then came the screaming. Like the night before. Whooping and hollering. The excitement of blood lust.

A figure ran by the window. A blur of jeans and sweatshirt. A few beats later, a mob followed. Pounding behind him. Chasing him.

Chrissie put the bottle down. Willed them to keep on running right by the store entrance. But they didn't. Of course they didn't. Too much to hope for.

A sudden increase in volume heralded their in-store arrival. Along with the screaming and yelling came the crash and smash of displays being knocked over.

Chaos and death were within screaming distance of her.

Chrissie was a sitting duck.

12

Chrissie dropped to the floor and scrambled around the counter. She squatted beside Danuta. They hadn't seen her yet and she had to keep it that way.

Heart thudding. Body trembling from an adrenalin dump. Her instinct was to run, but she had nowhere to run to. All she could do was listen and try to figure a way out. At first, all she could hear was a jumble of screaming, yelling, and the pounding of feet. As they moved further inside the store, she was able to make out occasional words and phrases.

"Down there!"

"There you stupid fuck - go up there."

"This way."

"Get the bastard."

"Don't let him get away."

There was more of the same as they swarmed over the store. Instructions. Obscenities. Hollers of excitement as they spotted their prey. Harsh shrieks as they closed in on him. A piercing scream and she knew he'd been caught.

His excruciating cries soared over the triumphant cacophony before finally sinking into the melee. Now, Chrissie could discern only the odd rising scream and occasional swear word from the babble. An outburst of harsh laughter caused her skin to goose-flesh.

She couldn't see what they were doing to him. It sounded as though they were tearing, or kicking, him apart. Perhaps both. *Thud, thud, thud.* It could easily be the sound of booted feet kicking into a soft body. Gleeful squeals soared to the steel rafters of the store. Piercing screams faded to moans.

Hunkered down with Danuta, frozen in a foetal ball of fear, Chrissie realised that if she was going to survive, she had to move now. While they were still distracted. If not, she would be the next one making those terrible sounds.

She peered over the counter but couldn't see beyond the dividers separating the restaurant from the store. She'd be too exposed out there. The kitchen was her only hope. Maybe there was a way out - a fire exit, air vent - something.

She should have checked it out earlier. But that had been back in the good times, when she thought a room full of roaches was her worst nightmare.

About to make her move, she remembered her half-eaten meal. If any of the mob realised that the food was warm or the beer cold, they'd know for sure that someone was there. They'd tear the place apart looking for her. The only chance she had was if they didn't know she existed.

She peered over the counter again. She could hear them down at the other end of the store. Hoping none of them had strayed from the pack, she darted to the table. Keeping low, she grabbed the plate and the beer bottle. She scurried back behind the counter and stashed them on a shelf.

A burst of laughter from the other end of the store. The tone had changed. Their victim was most likely dead. She wondered why they'd been after him. If he'd been one of their own, or a random survivor like herself.

She crawled by Danuta and nudged the kitchen door open. Bracing herself for cockroach hell, she scuttled into the kitchen.

As soon as the door swung to, she stood up. A tremble ran through. Her worst nightmare was no longer her worst nightmare. One fear muted by a greater one. And she was fearful. Mad dogs and cockroach-infested kitchens were nothing compared to the bloodthirsty mob in the store. She couldn't think about what they'd do if they got hold of her. What she had to do was make sure it didn't happen. She was jolted by the sound of breaking glass.

Voices and crude laughter. Suddenly very close. Close enough to make out their words, even through the kitchen door.

"Look at this one."

"She's still quite fresh."

"Fresher than some we've seen."

"Fresher than some of the live ones."

"Look - she's wearing a name badge - Dan-what-the-fuck. She's a foreign cunt. Okay Dan-what-the-fuck - let's get a look at your tits."

The sound of fabric being torn sickened Chrissie. Nothing more than a swing door separated her from them. She didn't want to think about what they were doing. She didn't want to be next. She looked around for a way out. Saw a door. She jogged across the kitchen. Fat insects crunched underfoot. Eggs squishing from them. She turned the door handle. Pulled it open. Not a way out. A pantry. Nothing but a pantry. Harsh laughter pounding on the door behind her. She went into the store cupboard. Shut herself in. Heard the kitchen door bang open. Voices. Loud and aggressive. Close. Very close.

She was trapped.

13

"Bastard of a stink in here."

"Gross. Really fucking gross, man."

Chrissie lay on her belly beneath the bottom shelf, shielded by half-full sacks of soft potatoes and sprouting onions. She pulled empty vegetable sacks, reeking of earth and mould, over herself.

The cockroaches residing in the pantry darted out of sight when she yanked the door open. Now that it was dark again, they'd ventured out. Crawling over her face, through her hair. Crawling all over her. Over the backs of her hands. The nape of her neck.

She tried to ignore them, tried not to twitch. Told herself the sensations she felt - the tickling antennae, the bristling legs - were down to her imagination working overtime. Knowing she was lying to herself.

Empty sacks and half-bags of mouldy onions and rotten potatoes hardly made an impenetrable fortress, but the festering sacks were all she had. Ignoring the exploring insects as best she could, Chrissie pressed herself back against the wall. If anyone opened the pantry door at least they'd have to bend down to see her.

The intruders clattered and banged in the kitchen. She could make out two voices.

"Did you see the size of that bastard?"

"We should torch the place - watch the fuckers burn."

A new kind of fear radiated through her. All she had going for her was the fact that they didn't know she was there. If they set fire to the place that wouldn't matter.

"Yeah, let's have ourselves a bonfire."

Something jabbed at her left nostril. A leg? Antennae? Entire roach? She batted it away. Her skin was crawling but the roaches were the least of it. The thought of being roasted alive had her in another cold sweat.

She bit down on her bottom lip and breathed in potato dust.

Her breasts squished sore against the floor. Knees ground against it. The sacks itched at her face and neck. Her elbows were tucked into her sides, face resting on the backs of her hands. Her right arm was going numb. She shifted it slightly. Pins and needles prickled. The car keys dug into her hip. Roaches crawled all over her. Hairy legs pricking. Antennae probing.

"Yeah, let's torch it, but first I'm gonna get out of my box."

"Too right, man. Right out of our fucking boxes."

"And then we'll burn the bastard down."

"Yeah, then we'll burn the bastard down."

YES. Chrissie wanted to scream. Go back to the store. Get out of your boxes. Go now and do it.

She didn't know how much more she could take. She couldn't cry, couldn't yell, couldn't move. Her body was cramping and itching all over. She couldn't breathe properly. Felt as though she was suffocating.

She wanted to lash out, but if she made a sound - if she moved - they'd get her.

She tried to think of other bad situations she'd been in but nothing matched this. Not even giving birth matched this. But it had been bad. And she had worked her way through it. She'd sank into herself. Separated herself from the pain. She'd done it then and she could do it now. She could quash the panic rising within her. It would be alright.

She would live.

The pantry door swung open. Light ripped into her fortress. Scuffed trainers paced only a nudge away from her face. She was boxed in. Had left herself with nowhere to run. Stupid mistake.

"It's just a fucking cupboard."

Yes, but it's my cupboard. Get out.

She wanted to scream at them as they rummaged through the shelves above her. Moving stuff, knocking things.

"Whoa."

The exclamation a nanosecond before something hard. hit the floor. Glass shattered, releasing the acid tang of vinegar. Chrissie's eyes watered. One of the intruders kicked the potato sack. A fresh cloud of dust plugged her nose, turned to mud in her mouth.

"Fuck all in here."

"Yeah, let's go."

They left the pantry door open behind them. There was a blast of noise from the store as they banged out of the kitchen. Sounded like there was a party going on out there. A raucous one.

Chrissie desperately wanted to crawl out from her hidey-hole, but forced herself to stay where she was. It could be a trap. Maybe one of them was still in the kitchen. Best lie still and listen.

Beyond her own breathing, all she could hear was the discordant noise of the mob partying in the store. Screams, yelps, bangs and crashes. Her eyes streamed. The vinegar fumes. Or maybe she was crying. The state she was in, it was hard to tell.

No watch. No phone. No way to tell how long she lay on the floor under the shelf. Minutes? Definitely. Hours? It felt like it. The dust and vinegar fumes burned her eyes. They strained as she tried to glean information from the tiny bit of the world she could see from the back of the pantry.

She closed them. Only meaning to rest them for a few moments. But exhaustion overcame her. She fell asleep and, for a while at least, gained some respite.

14

Chrissie's leg cramped, the spasm jerking her awake. There was a dull thud as her foot kicked against the wall. Instinctively, she caught her breath. She listened, but there was no response from the kitchen.

Nobody there.

Time to come out.

Broken glass scraped against the floor as she pushed the sacks aside. Mindful of the shards and splinters, she cautiously emerged from her hiding place. Her kinked-up body felt about three hundred years old. She slowly got to her feet, and rubbed her neck, brushing off a couple of roaches in the process. A few more fell off when she rolled her shoulders. Her feel were all pins and needles. Feet throbbing in her boots. Her mouth was parched and her back ached. She'd had more refreshing naps.

When she figured she could move without falling over, she picked her way through the chaotic kitchen. Everything that could be knocked down or smashed up had been. Utensils, pots, pans, bowls, lay scattered, the breakable ones broken. The chefs had been kicked about and splattered with rotten food. A new smell in the mix gave her reason to believe they'd been urinated on.

Standing by the swing door, she listened, and listened

hard.   Hearing nothing, she pushed the door open a crack. Not a peep. Maybe her luck had changed. Maybe they'd left the store. There was always hope.

Taking a chance, she pushed the door wider. Danuta still lay on her back behind the counter but her overall had been ripped open, her bra yanked up to her neck. Her skirt had been pushed up to her waist, knickers torn off and her legs had been pulled apart, displaying her genitals. She was lying in a puddle. They'd urinated on her as well.

Chrissie had no doubt that they would do the same to her if they found her. Except she'd be alive. At least to begin with. She had to get of there and she had to do it now. There was nothing for it but to go through the store.

Listening so hard, her ears were buzzing, she skirted round the counter. Keeping low, she ran to the dividers separating the cafe from the store. So far, so good. No sound but the hum of the store and her own breathing.

The most direct route to the exit was by the long line of checkouts. She scanned what she could see of the store. It was as chaotic a scene as the kitchen. Stuff knocked from shelves, rotten food scattered and smeared. Paint splattered. Bags of flour thrown. But there was neither sight nor sound of the mob. Time to make a break for it.

Jogging by the checkouts, she was completely exposed in the flat glare of the fluorescent lights. She was near the end of the line when she saw their victim. At least, what was left of him. They had reduced him to a bloodied, pulpy mess. His clothing held what was left of him together.

Chrissie averted her gaze, instead looking out of the window. The sun was rising. She could see her car. Could practically feel the steering wheel grasped in her hands. Hear the steady growl of the engine.

One final sprint and she'd be there.

She grinned and ran right into the mob.

15

They had set up camp near the exit. She got the impression they were young. Late teens, early twenties. Mostly male, they were clad in scuffed streetwear. Looked like they'd come through a war zone.

They sprawled on sunloungers with reduced price tags dangling from them. And on piles of cushions and quilts. Empty cans and bottles were strewn around them. They were unconscious, some of them snoring. *Out of their boxes.*

Even asleep, they had a hard, hungry look about them.

Heart hammering, breath suspended, adrenalin shooting through her system, Chrissie crept around them. She had avoided two pools of vomit and was almost at the doors when a voice shrieked behind her.

"LIVE ONE."

She ran towards the doors, her step faltering as it slid slowly open. Sounds of the mob stirring behind her. As soon as the gap was wide enough, she launched herself through it without looking back.

She ran full tilt towards the car. Pandemonium unleashing behind her. If they hadn't been drinking, hadn't been hung over, they'd have been on her already.

Fingers in pocket. Fumbling for the key. Nerves made

worse by the clamour. By the knowledge that they were almost upon her.

Click. Car unlocked.

Get in the car get away get in the car get away get in the car get away.

Voices behind her. Hollering. High with excitement.

Thunk. Door closed. Key in the ignition. Hand shaking.

A glance at the store. A mistake. The mob, pouring out of the shop. Their number seeming more now that they were on the rampage

Start the car. Start the car.

Engulfed in fear, she couldn't stop staring at them. Thinking about the pulped body.

Don't think.

They were running towards her. Almost at the car.

Do something.

She turned the key. The engine roared. Their twisted faces contorted even more.

Lock the car. Start moving.

First gear. Moving. But they were moving faster. They had the same look about them as the dogs. Mouths foaming, eyes wild and rolling.

A hand slapped on the window. Another snatched at the door handle. They ran alongside the car. Chrissie shifted into second. They banged on the windows. Into third.

They screamed, tried to get at her. Angry faces, full of hatred. One of them ran in the road in front of the car. He was a kid. Just a kid. Chrissie swerved. Too late. He went under. The wheels churned relentlessly over him.

There was screaming. So much screaming.

She glanced in the wing mirror. Saw his arms flail above the bloody mash of his body. And still, they kept up with her. Throwing missiles now. Sharp cracks. Heavy thuds. She put her foot down.

She was going too fast as she approached the circle.

She squeezed the brakes. The car fish-tailed but she kept control. Got round. Onto the straight. Picked up speed.

Finally, they dropped behind her.

She shifted into fourth gear. Moving fast. Doing fifty, sixty, seventy. The mob well behind her now. But her speed wasn't safe. Anything could be on the road ahead. She hammered it anyway and wondered why she could still hear them screaming.   And then she realised.

It was her.

It was Chrissie screaming.

16

As the scream died in her throat, Chrissie eased off on the accelerator. The car gradually slowed to cruising speed. The world outside ceased being a blur and came back into focus. She opened the window, took in a blast of cool air and told herself to get a grip.

Driving like that was crazy. She'd been lucky. Barely touching the brakes, as she swerved through a chicane of smashed cars. Luck like that wouldn't last. Crossroads ahead. She slowed the car. Stopped. A decision to be made.

To the right, a maze of country lanes, passing through hamlets, dead-ending at farms. No way out if things got sticky. She wasn't about to trap herself again.

Straight ahead, another town. Larger than the last. More resources. More danger.

She stared through the windscreen as a plume of black smoke rose in the distance. A death pall hanging over the town. The decision was made. She turned left onto fifteen miles of twisting road which would eventually lead to the A9.

The longest road in Scotland, the A9 ran from the central belt to Scrabster, on the north coast, by-passing a myriad of cities, towns and villages along the way. Surely, somewhere on the route she would find a place she could bed down for the night, or maybe even hole up for a little longer. She needed time to get her strength back. Time to think.

Hay bales sat drying in yellow fields on either side of the road. Winter feed for livestock that was most likely deadstock. Washing hung limply from a line in a cottage garden. Toys scattered on the overgrown grass beneath it.

Chrissie instantly dismissed the cottage as a refuge. It was too near the road to be safe. Too easily come across.

She passed a deserted farmyard. A tractor, abandoned in a field. She swore under her breath as the road changed from double to single track, fearing a blockage ahead. But the way was clear. Seemed like the people in these parts had done their dying at home. Even so, she was thankful when it widened again.

Not far from the A9, she came to a junction. There was a sign - Feldybridge. It was a place she hadn't been for years. Chrissie narrowed her eyes. Though historically important, the village had gradually fallen asleep in the twentieth century. If the empty road she'd driven on was any indicator of safety, then Feldybridge was definitely worth a look.

A mix of buildings, newer on the outskirts, older towards the centre. Traditional high street with a butcher and baker but no candlestick-maker.

Chrissie noted a hardware store that looked like it might be worth exploring. A sign outside a cafe advertised locally made ice-cream. In the centre of the village, a picturesque stone bridge arched over the Feldy. The hotel, church and square were on the other side of the bridge.

The hotel would have been buzzing in the late Victorian and Edwardian periods. Palm trees in the conservatory, waiters in penguin suits dishing up silver service style while comedies of manners played out before them.

The church was medieval. Built to serve a thriving market town. Easy to picture horse-drawn carts clattering through cobbled streets. Cattle drovers herding their stock. But the noise and the bustle had long since faded. Feldybridge was already on its way to becoming a ghost town long before FDF struck.

Sure, tourists occasionally strayed off the main road to gawp at the quaint streets and the old church. They might even have bought an ice-cream to eat as they strolled over the bridge, but then it would be back in the car, back onto the A9.

It had been a long time since Feldybridge was a destination in its own right. It was a place you stopped off on your way somewhere more interesting. A forgotten wee place. In other words, it was perfect.

All the same, Chrissie had reservations about finding a place to stay in the actual village. There were few bodies lying in the streets, but that only meant that the houses would be full of them. And maybe they weren't all be dead. And if they were alive, they might be the wrong sort of alive.

After her ordeal at the supermarket, Chrissie's fears didn't start and end with bitey attackers. The pack there hadn't looked ill - like they might have the secondary disease - the zombie disease. They had been in rude health.

If they didn't have the disease, they were acting the way they did simply because they wanted to. The thought scared Chrissie more than the zombie rumours. Much more.

Dead bodies - properly dead bodies - wouldn't be much safer. They'd be gassing up and rotting, Stinking out the houses and attracting all sorts of vermin. She shuddered. She'd had all she could take of cockroaches and wasn't up for tackling rats or any other pests.

People, alive or dead, were best avoided.

She drove around the village, up and down streets,

moving further from the centre, until she was driving along a narrow lane. Rusting farm signs with hand-painted wooden notices staked in the ground beneath them stood guard at the ends of rustic tracks.

Private Property.

No Through Road.

Eggs For Sale.

She was not tempted to drive along those rutted trails. They would only lead to lonely farmhouses with decaying inhabitants, bloated, dead livestock and ravenous dogs. If anyone normal was still alive out there, they'd likely be armed with shotguns and prone to shooting on sight. She would if she was them.

Despairing of finding anywhere suitable, she had visions of ending up on the A9, pushing further north, sleeping in the car overnight. It was an idea she did not relish.

The lane twisted into a forest. Chrissie had the idea that she was in Birnam Wood, where Macbeth had met his violent end.

Whatever bloodlust and battle the woods had seen before, today it was peaceful. The leaves on the turn. Beautiful now in shades of red and gold, but soon they'd be brown and brittle, heralding winter's arrival.

Chrissie needed to find somewhere she could stay for more than one night. Was thinking that maybe she shouldn't have been so jittery about investigating the farmhouses.

She drove by the sign before knowing she had seen it. When it registered, she reversed the car. The sign was small, attached to an overgrown hedge. Almost covered by leaves. *Birch Cottage.*

She looked down the track leading from the road. After a few metres it veered sharply, disappearing into the woods.

There could be anything at the end of a track like that. Candy cane cottage, mad axe-man, three bears and a pot of porridge. A nest of zombies.

Or maybe a place she could stay for the night. Chrissie turned the car onto the track.

17

The stone cottage was a simple two up, two down affair. A weathered wooden fence bordered the front garden. There were two gates set into it. One, wide enough for a car to pass through, led to a gravelled drive to the right of the cottage. The other, smaller and coated in bright blue, flaking paint, opened onto the path leading to the front door.

Chrissie stopped the car in front of the blue gate and watched and waited.

The garden was overgrown. Weeds sprouted vigorously on the drive. The house looked empty and cold. No-one twitched at the curtains of the hollow-eyed windows. No-one opened the door.

She sat and waited.

When everything continued still and calm, she got out of the car. She stood beside it for a while more before opening the blue gate and walking slowly up the path. Though she had no prickling sense of being watched, she raised her hands.

Look, no weapons.
I mean you no harm.
I come in peace.
Please don't shoot me.

She tapped gently on the door. When there was no response, she gave it a hearty rap and then a robust pounding.

It didn't look like there was anyone at home. At least, no-one alive. she tried the handle. Locked. Chrissie peered through the letterbox. She couldn't see much in the dark hallway, but caught a whiff of closed-up mustiness. There was no hint of decaying flesh. All in all, it looked and smelled promising.

She went back to the car, switched off the engine and looked around. Trees, logs, mossy banks. Dappling sunlight, the sound of birds wittering and singing in the woods. It was a pastoral delight.

A key would be handy.

Chrissie looked underneath the door mat, lifted plant pots and felt above the door lintel. No joy. She waggled her fingers inside the letterbox in case there was one dangling on a string.

She looked under a couple of loose paving slabs and found worms, slaters and a millipede, but no key. She stuck her fingers into the damp, root-bound soil of the pots, filling her nails with earth, but the feel of metal eluded her.

Finally, in the overgrown flowerbed to the right of the door, she spied a smooth blue-grey stone, almost, but not completely, covered by withered fronds. She brushed the brown stems aside and prised the stone from the earth. There, in the soil, surrounded by worm grooves, an old, heavy key, like something out of a fairytale. She rubbed it clean on her trousers and unlocked the door.

The air inside the cottage was stale and thick, as if it hadn't been disturbed in some time. There was a hint of mildew, but no corpse stench. If anyone lay dead within, they had long since turned to dust.

The stairs, steep and narrow, creaked underfoot as she went up them to explore. Two bedrooms with sloping ceilings were separated by a cluttered box room. The beds were made up. The furniture hewn from dark wood, old and heavy. Dust motes swirled in the light. It felt as though no-one had been there for a long time.

There was an over-furnished sitting room downstairs. It gave the impression of being the good room. A place to sit with honoured guests. *More tea minister?*

Cushions sat primped and proper on the well-stuffed sofa and armchairs. Framed photographs and paintings crowded the mantelpiece, sideboard and walls. Faded flowers ghosted what could be seen of the wallpaper. The carpet, threadbare in patches, was of good quality.

The kitchen was almost as cluttered. A pulley dangled from the ceiling above a wood-fired range. An old two-seater sofa and an ancient armchair huddled around it. A Welsh dresser loomed on the wall opposite. The centre of the room was dominated by a heavy kitchen table and chairs.

A Belfast sink sat under the back window, a worktop running from the draining board to the wall, with cupboards below and laden shelves above. Peaty water flowed from the taps. The cottage most likely had its own water supply and septic tank.

What had once been the back door now opened on to an extension containing the bathroom and a small lobby leading to the back garden which was wildly overgrown. The weeds were hemmed in by a six foot stone wall which had a locked, wooden door set into it.

Chrissie kicked around in the undergrowth, revealing what had presumably been beds for a kitchen garden. Further inspection of the back garden revealed a rickety lean-to almost entirely veiled by weeds on a triffid scale. Knocking them aside, she discovered a bank of seasoned logs.

By sunset, Chrissie had unpacked the car and stowed away her supplies. A fire was burning in the range, the windows were closed, curtains drawn, paraffin lamps lit. It would take several hours for the back boiler to heat, and so she warmed a few pans of water on the stove and had a wash down at the bathroom sink.

Supper consisted of soup and oatcakes followed by a glass of wine.

She poured a second glass and curled up on the sofa, with the range door open so that she could watch the fire.

Exhausted and pleasantly fuzzy from the wine, she drifted into a comfortable sleep.

18

Chrissie threw herself into life at Birch Cottage and soon established a daily routine. She tended the range solicitously, keeping the fire at a low peep all day for the luxury of lukewarm water flowing from the hot taps.

Each morning she made new inroads into the vegetable beds. Within days, she had unearthed a few self-seeded carrots and potatoes, savouring the flavour of fresh vegetables with her supper. She found several packets of seeds in the Welsh dresser. Some were out of date, but even those packets were bound to contain a few viable seeds. If she pushed on with clearing the beds, she would have time to sow a new crop for spring.

Afternoons were spent foraging in the woods. She ate brambles, the juice staining her fingers, and collected deadwood for burning. An abundance of fungi grew in the forest. She suspected that much of it was edible, but would not take the risk of eating it. Even the discovery of a book on mushroom collecting did not assuage her fears. Better to live mushroom-free than risk poisoning herself.

Gaps in the day were filled by twiddling on the wind-up radio, small maintenance tasks, and housekeeping chores. She went through the radio bands slowly, ears straining for anything other than white noise. Only once did she pick up a human voice. It was tinny and seemed to come from very far away but she was so lonely, she almost wept at the sound of it.

The signal was weak and faded in and out, but she patiently tweaked the dial and managed to make out some of the words before it crackled and disappeared altogether.

Lord God... who is and who was... that you have taken your great power... have begun to rule...

She'd been hoping for something more practical, but as help wasn't coming from anywhere else, least of all God, she got on with it by herself.

The Parlour, as she had named it for her own amusement, contained a small library. As well as the guide to edible fungi, there were books on gardening, flower arranging, and a set of classics, which included *Treasure Island, Oliver Twist, Jane Eyre,* and *Wind in the Willows.* She read a few chapters each night. Losing herself on the *Hispaniola* with Jim or in Dickens' London, before going upstairs to bed.

The tribulations of the past were gone. It was all about food, warmth, shelter. There were no trivialities. No minor panics about wardrobe malfunctions or Phoebe's misplaced homework.

No hassles from the ex. No phones ringing, demanding to be answered. No credit card bills to be paid. No bills of any kind to pay.

No lunchtime shopping in overcrowded, overheated shops. No covering for absentee colleagues. No team building courses.   No TV, no internet, no social network.   No MOTs, no insurance renewals.   No birthdays to forget or friends to catch up with. Nothing but the business of survival.

Chrissie was down to the bare bones of life.

She carried a couple of knives with her at all times. They were everyday tools now, but she also carried them for protection.

Safe though she felt at Birch Cottage, she had not let

her guard down. She had dispersed a small arsenal of weapons throughout her refuge. No matter where she was in the house, there was something at hand she could use to defend herself. The poker in the Parlour. The wood axe by the back door. Knives by the bath, under her bed, beside the sofa. A hammer in the hall.

Fresh air was her friend. Being outside meant being physically active which meant falling into an easy sleep at night.

Inclement weather was her foe.

Light rain didn't keep her inside. She wasn't going to dissolve. But there were days when the rain was torrential, the wind fierce, and she was forced to stay indoors with only her solitude for company.

There were more dangers inside than out. There was only so much to do in the cottage. Tending the range did not require much in the way of time or brain power.

She made little mess, so there was little cleaning or tidying to be done. Only so much time could be spent fiddling with the radio or rearranging her supplies. There was just too much time for thinking and brooding. For feeling lonely.

She tried to distract herself by doing exercises. But she was already getting all the exercise she needed and sit-ups seemed pointlessly old-world.

Reading was a distraction that took her only so far. It was fine at night, after an active day, but during the day she couldn't settle to it.

One particularly bad storm lasted several days, forcing her to invent things to do. She cleaned things that didn't need cleaning.

She rearranged her collection of tinned goods several times. Sometimes alphabetically, sometimes by food group. She spent hours trying to pick up something on the radio, but there wasn't even a religious zealot to be had. Finally, bored and distracted, she turned to drink.

She drank until she passed out on the sofa.

The storm died that night. Chrissie awoke to a cold range, a well-dented wine supply and the hangover from hell. To top it all, she was virtually incapable of doing anything worthwhile on a fine and valuable day. Now she had a good dose of depression to go with her hangover.

A period of fine weather ensued. Her drinking jag behind her, she collected and chopped firewood, stacking the logs neatly.

She cleared the garden and sowed seeds for a spring crop of broad beans and peas. But as winter drew near, the days grew shorter.

Long nights meant more time than ever for brooding.

She tried to resist. Tried to keep herself occupied. But her mood became increasingly melancholic. Unable to concentrate on reading, she spent her evenings picking the scabs from painful memories. Her own mind a traitor as it turned in on itself, lingering painfully on the loss of friends and family, of the deaths of everyone she'd ever known.

Dwelling on hopes and dreams that would never be fulfilled. Ambitions never to be achieved.

But mostly she thought about Phoebe.

19

The first dead body Chrissie ever saw was her father's. The second was her mother's. Distressing of course, but in a way, natural enough. Parents should die before their children. But the third body was something different. Upsetting the natural order, it was the cruellest of all. It belonged to Phoebe.

Chrissie's parents lived in a Victorian semi, with high ceilings and deep cornicing. After Falling Down, she awoke in the guest room on the first floor. Her mother was obsessively house-proud and liked everything in its place. She wouldn't have liked Chrissie lolling around in the kitchen. Despite being a good head shorter than her daughter, she managed to hustle her upstairs and into bed.

Chrissie remembered being kissed on the forehead before the door closed. That part may have been a dream.

When she first woke up, Chrissie thought she was blind. In a panic, she flailed about, knocking a lamp from the bedside table. It crashed to the floor. She froze, listening for footsteps, the sound of voices coming to investigate. But no door opened. No foot tread on the stairs. She sat for several minutes, listening to the silence.

No-one was coming.

Her skin was stretched dry and tight across her face. Her lips were hard and cracked. Patches of dried saliva flaked at the corners of her gummed-up mouth. She felt across her eyes. A thick crust of dried matter had glued them shut. Hopeful that she wasn't blind after all, she rubbed and picked at it until she could prise them open.

While she was picking at her eyes, her father was rotting in the next room.

The dense, dead silence in the house told its own story, but part of her clung on to the desperate hope that they hadn't all died.

That she wasn't the only one who had survived.

She found her mother downstairs, lying on the living-room floor. She had soiled herself. In life she'd been a whirlwind of household efficiency. She'd have hated dying in a mess.

Chrissie knelt beside her dead body and tentatively reached out a hand. Her mother's face was cold and waxy. She'd been dead awhile, but the corpse was fresher than her father's. Not so obviously decomposing.

Feeling weak, and still disorientated with what she'd awoken to, Chrissie took a throw from the sofa and used it to cover her mother's body. She walked out of the living room, closing the door behind her, and never went back.

The room Phoebe slept in when she was staying over with her grandparents was beside the living room. Chrissie swayed as she stared at its door.

Scared of what she might find, she did not want to go in there. The silence was too deep, too thick. No, she wasn't scared of what she might find, she was scared of what she knew she would find.

When they closed the schools, Phoebe stayed with her grandparents while Chrissie was impelled to go to work and answer phone calls with reassuring lies.

She should have been with her daughter.

She had arrived at the house, knowing her father was ill. As soon as she saw her mother's face, she knew Phoebe had the sickness too.

Chrissie went straight to her. Caressed her face, kissed her on the cheek, told her that everything would be alright. More lies. But how she wanted it to believe that somehow her child would be spared.

Feeling helpless and inadequate, she watched over her daughter as she fell asleep. Quietly closing the door behind her, Chrissie joined her mother in the kitchen where she promptly fell down herself.

Slowly, she opened the door.

Phoebe was tucked up in bed. Just like the last time Chrissie had seen her, only now she too was cold and waxy.

Chrissie got better. Her little girl didn't.

Maybe it would have been different if Chrissie had stayed with her, but she don't know how.

Phoebe had died and she wished that she had too. What right did she have to life, when her child was dead. Better that she was dead instead. But when she thought about Phoebe waking up alone in this dangerous new world, she knew that wasn't right either. Why couldn't they both have lived - or died?

When she found Phoebe, she wished she had never wakened.

The pain was intense, and yet, she was calm, so amazingly calm.

She pulled the duvet over Phoebe's head and quietly closed another door behind her. That was it. No tears. No weeping or wailing.

Not yet.

PART TWO

20

Shaw watched, helpless, as life leached slowly from his mother, until finally, drawing her last phlegm-filled breath, she died with mucus still churning in her throat.

His father had died a few hours before. His body lay alongside hers. It was a strange scene, but they'd wanted to die together. In death as in life. Shaw pulled the bedcover over their heads and went downstairs.

Ironic that he'd been here, of all places, when it happened. Every time he came back it was like stepping into the *Twilight Zone,* each episode weirder than the last. Everyone still trying to squeeze him into a box that didn't fit. A box that had never fitted.

The soundtrack for the first twenty years of Shaw's life had been his father's constant gripes about working sheep. The tune for the next twenty was his profound disappointment at Jacob's refusal to follow in his footsteps.

Jacob. The village was the only place on earth anyone called him that. He'd always hated the name. Had been glad to leave it behind, along with the sheep, the clannish local mentality, and his mental ex-wife.

He quivered with unexpected weakness. A moment of surprise, before he collapsed, crashing into his mother's display cabinet.

21

He came round slowly, twitching on a bed of broken china, crystal shards grinding beneath him, head throbbing. His eyes were caked in crud and his mouth tasted like something had crawled in there and died.

He worked at his eyes, peeling off chunks of crunchy, congealed, crap. Slowly remembering. He cracked open his lips. The influx of air did nothing to improve the taste in his mouth.

He sat up, leaned against the sofa and wondered how long he'd been out.

Christ, his head hurt. It wasn't right feeling this bad when drink hadn't been involved. Falling Down didn't begin to cover it. He felt like he'd been whacked with a sledgehammer before being dropped from a great height.

He peered at the ancient clock on the mantelpiece. It had stopped at twenty past six. But when? In the morning - the evening - today - yesterday? He hauled himself onto the sofa. His joints ached, he hurt all over. Felt more like he was eighty-two than forty-two. Hell, maybe he was eighty-two. Maybe he'd done a Rip Van Winkle and been out for forty years.

He rubbed his chin. Stubble. More than one night's worth.

He pulled his phone from his pocket. Checked the time and date. It was seven minutes past eleven in the morning and he'd skipped two days.

There were two missed calls and a text, all two days old. He opened the text.

if you read this know that we will always love you

The missed calls were from the same number. He tried calling it. No network. As he was staring at the photo on the screen his phone bleeped and died. He tossed it onto the sofa and stood up, taking it slow and easy. There was a tremble in his legs. He'd seen abandoned lambs with more strength in them than he had now.

He hobbled to the front doorstep and looked up and down the deserted street.

"HALLLOOOOOO."

There was no response. He called out again. His cracked voice was rewarded by a feeble whimper coming from the back of the house.

The dog was lying in the run, her mouth cut where she'd tried to bite through the chicken wire. She was pathetically thin. Shaw pulled the gate open and knelt beside his father's collie. The old man had said Toby would be his last dog. He was right on that score.

Shaw filled the water dish and put it beside the dog. She twitched her nose but did not raise her head. He sprinkled a little over her muzzle. She licked up the drops. He sprinkled some more, continuing until the dog sat up and managed to lap some water for herself. Shaw grinned and, realising his own thirst, scooped a few reviving handfuls into his mouth. Toby gave him a playful lick.

"Hungry, girl?"

The dog thumped her tail in reply.

Shaw took her feed bowl to the shed where his father kept the dry dog food and piled the dish high. He was ravenous. Would have to get something for himself once the dog was sorted.

He took the dish to her, making noises about how she'd be fine now. The dog stood up and growled at him, teeth bared, hackles up. Shaw frowned.

"What's up, girl?" Wondering why the dog had turned on him.

A noise behind him. A footstep. The dog's growl deepened. Dropping the dish, Shaw whirled around. Barry Bell, his ex-wife's husband.

"Barry - are you alright?"

Barry didn't answer. Neither did he look alright.

His face was gouged and bloody and he had a wild gleam in his eyes. There was a moment of still as Barry glowered at Shaw and Shaw stared back. He'd never had much time for Barry Bell. The feeling was mutual, but they'd always kept out of each other's faces. Until now.

Barry lunged. Toby let out a volley of barks. Despite his degraded physical state, Shaw neatly sidestepped the clumsy attack. Barry stumbled. He had always been an oaf, but he was the kind of man who couldn't stand the thought of anyone getting one over on him. He took the craze and turned on Shaw, snarling at him.

Shaw stepped back. He was handy enough, but the ferocity on Barry's face startled him. Premonitions of being torn apart. He glanced around for a weapon. Barry swiped a meaty fist at him.

Shaw ducked, grabbed the kindling axe. He weaved in front of Barry.

"Come on Barry. Time to calm down."

Barry lunged again. Shaw smacked his temple with the flat side of the axe. Barry reeled. Shaw exhaled, relieved. Barry came right back at him, grabbed him by the throat, squeezed. Shaw's eyes bulged. He tried to swing the axe up, but black spots were dancing in front of his eyes. The axe slipped from his hand. A dull clang as it hit the path. Shaw, going weak. Slipping away.

A snarl followed by a yelp from Barry. Toby, fastening her teeth onto his ankle. The distraction enough for Barry to loosen his clasp.

Barry shaking his leg, kicking out at the dog. Now it was Toby's turn to yelp, releasing her grip as she did so. With one final, desperate, effort Shaw swung his head forward into Barry's face.

A bone-breaking crunch. Barry howling, staggering back, blood gushing from his nose. His big head slowly turning towards Shaw, murder in his eye as he let out a howl.

Shaw snatched up the axe as Barry came for him. He swung it round, catching Barry on the head. Barry screamed, but kept on. Shaw swung again. This time he caught Barry across the throat.

Barry clutched at his neck, eyes bulging. Gurgling. There was blood. Lots of blood. Pumping out of Barry's neck, flowing through his fingers, over his shirt. He slumped against the fence, landed in a heap.

Shaw approached cautiously. Barry looked up, still clutching his throat, bewilderment in his watery blue eyes. He opened his mouth, but all that emerged were a few bloodied bubbles.

22

Shaw didn't want to look at Barry's blood-soaked body every time he went out the back door so he took an old tarp from the shed and threw it over him. Job done, he went into the house in search of food. The dog stayed at his heels.

He had a powerful thirst. Breaking one of his mother's golden rules, he took a long drink straight from the kitchen tap. Then it was time for food.

The power was off so he ate baked beans cold from the tin. His mother would have had a fit at the sight. Would have insisted on a place set at the table. Cutlery laid out, plate warmed, bread toasted, kettle on, milk poured into a jug. Fussing and flapping. But she was dead and there was no bread, so that was that. His old man was dead. Barry Bell was dead. Seemed like most everybody was dead.

Although... Barry was only dead because Shaw had killed him. Barry had given him no choice. Even so, ending a man's life... no matter the circumstances, a deed like that left its mark. Taking a life, changed a life. Shaw felt it inside him. A twist that wasn't there before. But he'd make the same choice again, if he had to.

He'd been in a few scrapes, but he'd never killed a man

before. Never had any cause. He'd hunted deer and slaughtered sheep. Gutted, skinned and hung them too. And then he'd eaten them. He didn't much care for mutton. Had a belly full of it when he was growing up. His mother was an expert at spinning out the carcass. Every winter the rich, cloying smell of sheep meat radiated from the kitchen and the lingering, fatty taste hung on the back of his throat. A fry of venison was a different prospect. One that had him salivating. He tossed the empty bean can in the bin. Dropped the spoon in the sink.

He'd killed Barry, but he wasn't going to eat him. Funny thought to have. Must be the after-effects of being out of it so long.

After-effects - maybe that's what had been wrong with Barry. He had a big, old dose of the after-effects. Though it had to be said, after-effects or not, he'd always been a wanker.

He looked at the dog. "After-effects," he said.

She wagged her tail in response.

He took another drink from the tap before wiping his mouth on the back of his hand.

"Feeling better, girl?"

Another wag of the tail.

"What now?"

He looked around the kitchen. Despite a lick of paint here and there, it was pretty much the way he remembered it. The way it had always been. Always would be. The same cracks in the ceiling, the same scratches in the door, the same burnt spot on the counter. Out of all the places in the world he could have been when it happened - why here?

The second he arrived, he was counting the minutes until he could leave. Time stretched like elastic between every tick of the clock.

Every breath he took harder to draw than the last. The

brain-swelling pressure in his head. The urge to just get back in the car and drive.

It was the having to stay that killed him. Having to play it out. Having to force a smile on his face for his mother's sake. Small talk, making nice, playing the dutiful son. His mother's desperate need to parade him in front of the neighbours, to show how well he'd turned out after all.

The endless cups of tea. Every conversation exactly like the one before, each and every bloody one of them mired in the past.

Remember when Jacob did this, remember when Jacob did that...?

Remember? No-one was ever likely to forget. No-one was allowed to forget. You were shackled to your past, dragging it around like Jacob Marley. All your misdemeanours, big, small, real, imagined, clanking and rattling for everyone to pick over, time and time and time again.

Now, to add to the childhood shoplifting of a handful of fizzy snakes, getting drunk on Merrydown cider when he was fourteen, and breaking the heart of the prettiest girl in these here parts when he was nineteen, they could add the untimely and violent death of local big-noise, Barry bloody Bell. That ought to be worth a few more chains.

He gave in to a rush of anger. Lashed out with his foot. Kicked over a chair. It clattered on worn linoleum. The dog slunk into a corner. In a craze, Shaw upended the table. It wasn't enough, so he picked up a mug and smashed it against the wall.

Only then did he register the cowering dog. His anger ebbed as suddenly as it had erupted, leaving him hollow.

"Sorry, girl." He coaxed the dog to him, petted her, told her he was stupid. Promised not to do it again.

He righted the table and chair. Cleared the shattered remains of the mug. Thought about what, aside from trashing his parents' house, he was actually going to do.

The gun cabinet was fixed to the wall in the cupboard under the stairs. Shaw unlocked it and took out the rifle.

"Just to be on the safe side," he told the dog as he loaded it.

Could be a horde of villagers out there, each one as crazy as Barry and just as willing to have a go. No point in taking chances. Or maybe everyone was dead and he was the last man standing. Now that would be funny - him being the only survivor in a village he'd spent most of his life trying to escape.

23

Leaving the dog behind, he walked the streets alone. They were eerily devoid of life. No kids cycling or playing, no-one scurrying along to the shop, no-one yakking at the filling station, nobody driving a tractor or quad over a croft.

People always said they thought it must be peaceful living in a scenery-laden backwater like this, but in Shaw's experience there was always some bastard making a noise somewhere. Someone banging on something in a shed. A trail bike making an angry, high-pitched whine on the hill. A disembodied voice hollering at a kid or a dog, or swearing at a stubborn sheep. A radio blaring, the sound carrying for miles.

Today, it was peaceful. Quiet as a mortuary.

Hello, anyone there?

He called out as he slowly walked the road, scanning houses, watching windows for a curtain twitch, or a sign of movement.   Nothing. Maybe it was just him and the dog after all. Last man alive and his faithful border collie.

He wasn't even sure if he wanted to find anyone alive. Would have been happy never to set eyes on any of them again. But the only thing worse than finding someone alive was finding no-one.

Anywhere else, he'd have made do with the solitude, perhaps even embraced it - but here? He'd go round the twist in this place.

He'd have to get out. Head south. There would be people in the towns and cities. Stuff would be organised. Not like here, where it was just him and a village full of corpses. Village of the dead. Hell, now he was giving himself the jitters.

"Hey, you there!"

Shaw spun around, all jitters gone as he raised the rifle in a smooth, instinctive action.

An old man standing in the street. The gun aimed at his chest. Shaw's finger on the trigger. The safety off. One small, easy squeeze was all it would take. The old man waved his arms.

"It's me - Ben Gillespie - don't shoot."

Shaw studied the man. He was dishevelled, his hair awry, needing a shave, same as Shaw, but he didn't look crazy, just scared. Shaw lowered the weapon. Stood his ground as the old man approached, ready to crack his skull with the rifle butt at the first hint of crazy shit.

The old man walked towards him, arms still half-raised, hands bobbing, palms down, in a keep-it-calm gesture.

Ben was one of those guys who had always looked old. He'd looked about seventy years old to Shaw thirty years ago, and he looked about seventy years old now. He was within spitting distance before he let his arms drop to his side. He looked Shaw square in the face.

Shaw returned the old man's direct gaze, holding it beyond the point of politeness before letting his grip on the gun relax.

"Jacob?"

"Shaw will do."

The old man gave a slow nod, as though chewing over the statement.

No-one had ever accused Ben Gillespie of being a man in a hurry, but he had a steady character and was practical.

Shaw was suddenly relieved that he wasn't the only one left.

"You know of anyone else alive, Ben?"

Ben shook his head. "Mary's dead. I found her on the floor, cold as stone. That was last night. This is the first time I've left the house. I was too scared until I heard you calling. Heard some strange sounds last night - screaming and carrying on. You hear anything son?"

It was Shaw's turn to shake his head. "I just came round today. My folks are dead. So's Barry Bell."

"Barry Bell, you say?"

"I killed him, Ben. He went crazy - attacked me. I don't really know what happened." Shaw shook his head, still trying to figure it out.

"Strange times," Ben said. "I peeked out of the upstairs window when I heard all that commotion last night and by the light of the moon I swear I saw Barry Bell running about the place like a crazed dog. I closed the curtain over after that, kept myself out of sight until I heard you just now. Thought it was you from your walk. Just like your father."

"Did you see anyone else?"

"Didn't see anyone - but I sure as hell heard them. You didn't hear a thing?"

"No, I was out cold till today."

"What do we do now?" The old man looked at Shaw, wanting something from him, something Shaw didn't know if he could give.

He could take care of himself - he had no doubt about that - and the dog, if Barry hadn't done her a permanent injury. But now it seemed he was responsible for this old man as well.

Maybe he shouldn't have gone calling about the place. Maybe he should have struck out on his own, left the village, just got the hell out of there. Then he looked into Ben Gillespie's eyes and saw the fear there, saw that the old man was struggling not to cry, and he felt like shit for thinking the way he had. Hell, only a few minutes before he'd been relieved not to be the only one left.

"You got a gun Ben?" he asked.

"A .22, use it for killing the sheep."

"That'll do. Go fetch it and we'll check out the rest of the village."

By sunset, they'd picked up two more survivors - twelve year old Elizabeth Pierce and Howard Marsh, an out of condition forty-five year old who could pass for fifty on a good day.

Elizabeth's family had only been in the village a couple of years. Shaw didn't know her and he didn't recognise Howard until Ben hailed him by name.

Howard stumbled out of his house, slack-jawed and empty eyed. He mumbled at them but was yet to form a coherent sentence.

Ben peered at him. "Must've just come round," he said.

The girl was grubby but calm. All she'd said so far was that everyone was dead.

They headed back to Shaw's in the fading light of day. There were a few tins of food in the cupboard and they could get a fire going. It would do. For now.

"Hey!"

A shout from behind. Shaw spun round, rifle raised.

"Don't shoot, don't shoot!"

"That's Jamie Milton," Ben said. "Come on, Jamie. It's alright."

He beckoned the boy towards them, but Jamie stood rooted to the spot. Ben glanced at Shaw.

"For God's sake, Shaw, put the gun down."

24

Several long seconds later, Shaw slowly lowered the rifle.

Surprised at how quickly he'd become used to pointing a gun at people, he suddenly realised how much *everything* had changed.

The boy walked towards the small group, keeping a wary eye on Shaw.

"It's alright son," Ben said. He patted the fifteen year old on the shoulder. A tremble ran through the boy. Maybe his shakes were down to having a rifle aimed at his head or maybe it was the shock of waking up to find all his family dead.

Back at the house, Toby gave Shaw an enthusiastic welcome. He scratched her ears.

"You'll be okay girl," he said, not having any idea if she, or any of them, would be.

The rest of the group filed in behind Shaw and sat down. Shaw told them about Barry Bell.

"I'm sure you didn't have any choice," Ben said.

"No, I didn't," Shaw replied. "It was me or him."

Nobody said anything after that. The silence hanging eerily between them only served to emphasise the unnatural hush permeating the house. No clock ticked now. There was no hum from the ancient fridge in the kitchen, no tread of footsteps on the stairs. There was only the soft *thwack, thwack* of the dog's tail on the carpet.

Forgetting the lack of power, Shaw automatically flicked the light switch when they came in. Now, in the darkening room, he stood in front of the empty fireplace and looked at the four blank faces in turn. They were each staring into space, eyes unfocussed. The lines in Ben's face looked even more deeply etched in the gloom. Soon, Shaw wouldn't be able to see their faces at all, let alone search them for answers to questions he'd hardly begun to form.

A rummage in the bureau produced his mother's emergency supply of candles. He set them up on the mantelpiece and lit them. That brief flurry of activity over, he turned back to the group and cleared his throat. Eyes flickered towards him.

"I think we should stick together," he said.

Ben nodded. The others stared, but no-one disagreed.

"Okay." He glanced around, trying to think what to say next. "We'll make do here for tonight, but tomorrow we'll move somewhere more suitable. Somewhere secure and with a place for everyone to sleep. Everyone okay with that?"

This time Elizabeth and Jamie nodded along with Ben.

Encouraged, Shaw continued. "There are probably other people alive in the village - either too scared or too weak to come out earlier. We'll do a house to house search for them."

"Sounds like a plan," Ben said. "A good plan."

Howard's face creased into a frown.

"Problem, Howard?" Shaw asked.

Howard's gaze, now sharply in focus, slid up to meet Shaw's. "I was just wondering who put you in charge, *Shaw.*"

"You want the floor Howard? Be my guest - let's hear what you've got to say."

Oh, this was perfect. The end was bloody well nigh and he was holed up in his mother's over-furnished living room with two kids, a guy old enough to be Methuselah's grandfather, and a self-important windbag with a big gut and a bad attitude. And now the windbag was eyeballing him. Hell yeah, he *really* wanted to be in charge. It was like all his dreams had come true.

Despite his welling anger, Shaw's voice was low and calm.

"Come on Howard, we're all waiting."

Howard's mouth pursed into a cat's arse as he gathered himself, but Ben piped up before he got a word out.

"Seems to me that Shaw here is the only one at least trying to do something about the situation we're in. What were you doing before we found you, Howard? Trembling under your bed?" Ben snorted.

Howard's lips pursed up tighter. The old man continued before he could slacken them enough to get anything out.

"Let's be clear, Howard. This isn't one of those committees you and Barry Bell were so fond of setting up. Bah, committees for this and committees for that, committees for blowing your nose and wiping your backside. This is a *bad* situation Howard, and it seems to me that Shaw is coming up with some good ideas. But if any of us disagree with him or come up with any ideas of our own, I'm sure we'll speak up - I know I will at any rate - and when that happens, I'm sure Shaw will be ready and willing to listen. Isn't that so Shaw?"

"Absolutely." Shaw grinned.

He'd enjoyed the old boy's performance and felt ashamed of himself for thinking him a burden. Howard Marsh wasn't the only one who had to get over himself.

But Howard wasn't going to give up so easily.

"Think you've got it all figured out - don't you?" He sneered at Ben, "But before you get carried away, let's have a look at the facts. For example, has it slipped your

98

senile mind that our friend *Shaw* here killed Barry Bell. *Murdered* him, in fact. What's to stop him killing the rest of us?"

"Nothing much in your case, Howard." Shaw tossed the remark off without thinking.

Before today, he hadn't spoken to Howard Marsh in years. Seemed he hadn't changed at all in that time. He'd been a wanker then and he was a wanker now. Hardly surprising he'd been so palsy-walsy with Barry. He wondered if there was a collective noun for wankers - cluster-fuck? Yeah, sounded about right. Howard Marsh and Barry Bell - a cluster-fuck of wankers.

"Did you hear that?" Howard looked round at the group incredulously. "He just threatened me."

Nobody seemed unduly disturbed on Howard's behalf.

"Let's have a vote."

Four heads turned to look at Elizabeth Pierce. She looked like she could do with a clean-up and a good night's sleep, but her eyes gleamed in the candlelight. It was clear her brain was engaged.

"Why don't we vote for a group leader then you two can stop bickering about it?"

She smiled sweetly at them both and Shaw burst out laughing. Soon Ben was hee-heeing along and even Jamie cracked a smile.

Howard sneered, "Listen kid-"

Ben cut him off, "I think that's an excellent idea Elizabeth. I'll start - I vote Shaw for leader."

Jamie put his hand in the air. "Shaw," he said.

Elizabeth raised hers. "Shaw."

The three of them looked at Howard. He pursed his lips so tight they looked like they'd been stitched together. His gaze slid around their faces before he finally let out a long exhalation. With his lips unpuckered, his face looked like a burst balloon. Wanker he may be, but he wasn't stupid. He knew when he'd been beat.

"Right then, if that's the way it's going to be." He

rolled his eyes. "Shaw," he muttered.

Ben hee-heed again. "Looks like you're it, Shaw."

Shaw struggled to keep a straight face. Who knew there was so much merriment to be had in a situation like this.

"Okay - who's got an idea for where we can stay?"

Howard harrumphed. "I thought you were the one with all the answers."

"Shut up Howard," said Jamie.

"Don't you tell me to shut up you little-"

"Howard!" Shaw barked. "That's enough. Let's say we lay out some ground rules. Rule number one - everyone gets a say in what we do. Number two - if anyone has got any ideas about anything, let's hear them. Number three - nobody behaves like a wanker."

Elizabeth and Jamie stifled giggles.

"Anyone got a problem with that?" Shaw continued. "No - well let's get on. Anyone got any ideas for where we can stay?"

After a brief huff, Howard slipped in a stealth boast by suggesting either his or Barry's places as they were both big houses. But once the group had established that each home came complete with dead families they decided against the idea. Everyone had had their fill of dead bodies for the time being.

Though he played it cool in front of the group, Shaw was as squeamish as anyone about using Barry's place. He had no desire to see the body of his ex-wife or her children. Somewhere more neutral, preferably with no dead bodies, was required.

The local hotel was an obvious choice, but it was big and sprawly and would be too hard to heat, let alone defend in the event of any more crazies like Barry coming out of the woodwork.

It was Elizabeth who suggested Kelnamara Lodge. It was a big old place down by the sea, with open fireplaces and even better, the couple who owned it were abroad when the disease struck. Plenty of bedrooms, no dead bodies and it was vacant.

Better still, Elizabeth's mother cleaned the place when the couple were at home, and kept an eye on it for them when they were away, meaning there was a set of keys for the Lodge at her house.

"I've been there with my mum," Elizabeth faltered a bit at this, but then, "There's a gas hob in the kitchen and an Aga so we'll be able to cook."

"Excellent," Shaw said. "We'll bed down here for the night and go to the Lodge in the morning."

25

With the plan for the next day settled, they got organised for the night. Coal was fetched, the fire lit. Food heated over it, the flames blackening the bottoms of the pans. Howard grumbled at having to do such menial work but got busy with the dustpan and brush. He made short work of clearing up the devastation Shaw had wreaked on the display cabinet.

Steadfastly ignoring the closed door of his parents' bedroom, Shaw went on the hunt for quilts, blankets pillows and anything else he could find for them to bed down with.

Finally, they settled by the fire. Surprised, and maybe a little embarrassed, by their hunger, they devoured a supper of unevenly heated baked beans and corned beef.

Shaw shovelled the food down like he was stoking an engine. When he took the time to glance around, he realised that everyone else was doing the same.

When the meal was over, sleeping arrangements were discussed. There were two spare beds upstairs, but no-one wanted to use them. Why go upstairs to a cold room when the fire was blazing downstairs? The living room was warm and cosy - it seemed daft not to make the most of it.

Though nobody said it out loud, Shaw understood the truth of it. None of them wanted to be alone. Himself included.

At Shaw's insistence, Ben slept on the sofa. Being small enough to make a comfy bed of it, Elizabeth was given his dad's recliner. The rest of them fashioned beds for themselves on the floor.

It was early autumn, but the dark hours were already stretching. Like everyone else, Shaw was exhausted and soon fell asleep. Several times, he woke up - edgy, feeling that something had roused him but not knowing what.

Each time, Toby was sitting up beside him. He could feel the tension in her. The embers of the dying fire giving off enough light so that he could see her ears were pricked.

Shaw listened hard, but all he could hear was Howard's heavy breathing and Elizabeth's gentle snores.

After a while, his eyes grew heavy and he began to drift. He was in a twilight haze of semi-sleep when he heard it. Someone outside was screaming.

If it had been a scream for help Shaw would have been on his feet in a heartbeat. But it wasn't that kind of scream. It wasn't the kind of sound that attracted you to it. It was the kind that made you want to run hard and fast in the opposite direction.

Shaw wanted to cover his ears, shut it out, but even though it curdled his blood and brought a chill to his heart, he forced himself to listen. It barely sounded human, but he didn't know of any animal that could make a noise like that.

Stories from his childhood sprang at him from the dark shadows of the room. Tales of banshees screaming in the night, their wails foretelling violent death.

Shaw was shocked to realise that he was scared.

26

Shaw looked around the kitchen while Elizabeth sorted through a jumble of keys hanging on hooks. She'd stared straight ahead when they walked into the house, as if on a tightrope with no safety net below. Now there was a look of intense concentration on her face, as if the keys were the only thing that mattered.

Clutter lay on the counters. Pens, elastic bands, tea lights, a couple of shrivelled lemons. There were colourful magnets on the fridge, drawings and paintings taped to the wall. Curled underneath the table lay the lifeless form of a young boy. Elizabeth didn't say anything. Neither did Shaw.

"Here they are," she spun round, a bunch of keys in her hand, a too-bright smile fixed to her face, "the keys to The Lodge."

Shaw glimpsed a photograph on the pin board behind her. Blue skies, smiling man, laughing woman. Elizabeth in a floppy, yellow hat. The boy from under the table holding an ice-cream as big as his head.

"Do you want to collect anything before we leave?"

She replied with a stiff shake of the head. Eyes glassy, smile tight, ready to snap.

"C'mon then, let's get out of here."

As Shaw turned away, she snatched the picture from the board and stuffed it into her pocket. He pretended he didn't notice when she wiped away a tear.

Ben and Jamie were waiting with the dog by the side of the road.

"Where's Howard?" Shaw asked.

"Gone to get his vehicle," Ben replied. "He's going to drive us down to the Lodge."

"Will it take us all?"

"Oh, it'll take us alright."

Right on cue, a black Range Rover came roaring down the street, Howard at the wheel.

"He doesn't do understated, does he?" Shaw asked.

"Nope. Sure as God made little green apples, there is nothing subtle about Howard Marsh."

Shaw grinned. The old boy was growing on him.

The Lodge had the familiar fusty air of a home unlived in, but there was space aplenty and the kitchen cupboards contained an abundant supply of dried and tinned food. Best of all, there were no dead people anywhere.

"Looks like we've got ourselves an excellent base, thanks to Elizabeth," Shaw said. The group had gathered in the kitchen.

The girl blushed, delighted with the praise.

"Are we gonna do the search now?" Jamie asked.

"Yes," Shaw replied, "but first there's something we need to talk about."

"You heard it last night, didn't you?" Ben asked.

"I can still hear it." The hairs on the back of Shaw's neck prickled at the thought of the screams.

"Heard what?" Howard asked.

"Screaming. Someone was screaming," Ben said.

"Screaming?" Howard raised his eyebrows.

"I think maybe it was someone who went the same way as Barry," Shaw said.

"So you say."

"For God's sake Howard - can you not get it through your head - I've told you - he was in a craze. I killed him because I had to. It was him or me."

"Shaw's right," Ben said. "I saw him the night before. Your friend looked like a mad dog."

Howard looked from Shaw to Ben, his refusal to believe them written all over his face.

"Do you think there are more like him?" Elizabeth asked. The blush drained from her face.

"I don't know. Maybe," Shaw said. "Look, I'm not trying scare anyone, but if there's any danger, we all need to know about it."

"There were stories..." Elizabeth spoke tentatively, "on the internet - before everything shut down. They said there was another disease. One that turned people into zombies."

"Oh for goodness sake!" Howard sneered. "Zombies? You've got to be kidding me."

Shaw stared at Howard. The man was a pain in the arse, but on this occasion, Shaw hoped he was right. He hoped the stories were rubbish. But hope as he might, the screams from last night lingered in his mind and he could not forget the look in Barry's eyes. Whether he had been a zombie or not, Shaw didn't know, but he didn't have any other word for it.

Shaw and Ben were armed with their rifles. Jamie had a shinty stick he'd found, Howard and Elizabeth had a large kitchen knife apiece.

The girl's eyes widened as Shaw handed it to her.

"Just in case," he said. "Don't worry, we'll be sticking close together."

"I want to be with you," she said. Shaw nodded his agreement.   "Howard, Jamie - you go with Ben."

They banged on each door, calling their presence as they entered. It was the same story, over and over. Dead body after dead body, most of them already decomposing. Suddenly, Jamie came hollering for Shaw.

"Quick, you need to come and check this out." The boy was goggle-eyed..

They stood in a circle, looking down at the woman's contorted body lying on the swirly carpet. Her face was twisted beneath a mask of congealed blood. However she had died, it had not been peaceful.

"Who is she?" Shaw asked.

"My teacher." Elizabeth was trembling.

"Lena Duncan," Ben said. "Leastways, this is her house so I assume it is - was - her. Kind of hard to tell, though."

"What happened to her?" Jamie asked.

"Maybe the same thing that happened to Barry Bell," Shaw said.

"You mean you killed her?" Howard raised an eyebrow at Shaw.

"Jesus Christ, Howard! You know what I mean. Will you stop being so obtuse and accept what's in front of you?"

"She was a zombie, wasn't she?" Jamie said, staring at the body with renewed interest.

"Do you think she was the one screaming last night?" Elizabeth asked.

"I don't think so," Shaw replied. "It looks as though she's been dead for a while."

"But there might be more like her," Ben said, "I mean ones who are still alive."

"Zombies," Jamie said.

"No," Elizabeth said, "Not zombies - Screamers."

"Screamers," Howard repeated. "Very droll."

"Whatever we call them, let's be careful," Ben said.

Closing the door on Lena, they split into two groups again. Shaw didn't like the idea of the twelve year old girl searching through the houses with him, but everyone had to muck in. Besides, she'd already proven she had back-bone.

Shaw checked the downstairs of the next house while Elizabeth went up to the bedrooms.

The kitchen was empty. He opened the door to the living room. The smell punched him in the face. He gagged, turned away, dry heaving.

A gut-wrenching smell like that couldn't mean anything but death and decay, but he had a duty to check.

There was a foot sticking out at the end of the sofa. Someone lying on the floor in front of it. He stepped forward for a better look, willing himself not to gag. Then a scream from upstairs. *Elizabeth!*

Something came at him before he could respond. It hurled itself across the room, snarling. Shaw raised the rifle and fired. The blast filled the room. Made his ears ring.

The thing thudded to the floor. He stared, incredulous. A poodle. He'd just shot a bloody poodle. That explained the smell. Death, decay and poodle shit. He looked at the body on the floor. The poodle had been chowing down on its owner's face and legs.

A heavy thud from upstairs cut through the ringing in his ears. *Elizabeth! he'd forgotten about Elizabeth!*

He took the stairs two at a time. She was lying on the bedroom floor.

No, no, no.

27

Elizabeth raised her head and smiled at him.

Shaw let out a long breath. "What-?"

She put a finger to her lips to hush him then put her head to the floor and spoke under the bed.

"It's okay - it's only Shaw," she spoke gently. "He won't hurt you. You can come out now."

His ears had cleared enough for him to hear a murmured reply, but he could not make out the words.

The walls were painted pink. There were posters of ponies and puppies. A shelf laden with soft toys. This much he understood: he was in a kid's bedroom. A girl's room. Some poor kid had been hiding under the bed while her mother was having her face chewed off by the family poodle.

Elizabeth looked at Shaw.

"She wants to see what you look like."

Shaw nodded, like it was what he had been expecting. He dropped to his knees beside Elizabeth and peered under the bed.

A little girl was huddled against the wall, surrounded by empty crisp and biscuit wrappers. There was a strong smell of stale urine.

He tried giving her a reassuring smile but it felt twisted

and unnatural.

"What's your name?" he asked.

The girl stared at him, unsmiling. She was five, maybe six years old. He got the feeling she was weighing up the situation. Stay under the bed with the biscuits and the damp patch or take a chance with the guy with the twisted grin?

"Her name's Lucy." Elizabeth said, "Lucy Kirk."

"Okay Lucy, here's what we'll do," Shaw said, "I'll move away and you can come out whenever you're ready. Okay?"

He thought she gave a slight nod.

Shaw stood up and waited by the door. Elizabeth reached under the bed and gently coaxed Lucy out.

The girl looked warily at Shaw. She was thin and pale. There was a grub of sugar crust around her mouth. Her hair was in a knotty tangle. The stench of stale urine coming from her was eye-watering. She hadn't been drinking enough water. Was most likely dehydrated. But she was alive, and right now Shaw figured that was as good as it got.

"Okay Lucy," he said. "We're going to go outside now and meet some other-"

"Shaw, Elizabeth!" Jamie yelling.

"Up here," Shaw yelled back. "We're okay."

Toby bounded upstairs to Shaw.

"Okay girl," he said, settling her down. "It's okay."

"I've got a dog," Lucy said.

Not any more you don't, Shaw thought.

28

By the end of the day they had found three more survivors, but no more pets snacking on dead owners. The other three had all woken up that day and were still disorientated.

Back at the Lodge they gathered by the fire in the living room and told their stories. All except Lucy, who had attached herself firmly to Elizabeth's side but hadn't said a word since telling Shaw her dog was called Princess.

Each had a similar tale to tell.

"It happened so quickly," Marjory Mackay said.

She was a retired nurse. Sturdy, with short grey hair.

"I had an overwhelming urge to lie down," she continued. "The next thing I remember is you people," she nodded towards Ben and Howard, "standing over me and saying that I was alive. I was glad to hear it - but this," she flapped her hand to include the entire village, "it's beyond belief."

"Believe it," Shaw said.

"How far has it spread?" she asked.

"We don't know." Shaw replied, "The only thing we do know is that before the broadcasts stopped, it looked bad, like it was everywhere."

"Could be the whole world." Robbie Mackenzie spoke

quietly, his green eyes wide with shock.

"What's your story then Robbie?"

Ben spoke gently, trying to coax the nervous young man out of himself.

Robbie shrugged. According to Ben he was twenty-two. Shaw would have put him closer to seventeen. His face still bore traces of confidence-sapping acne.

"Everyone was ill," Robbie said, "Mum, dad, my sister, Julie... they were dying and I got it too. I crashed on the sofa and thought that was that - I was done for. The next thing I heard you guys yelling... Is it true - is everyone else in the world dead?"

Ben leaned over and squeezed Robbie's shoulder. "I don't think so son. There will be others out there - other survivors. Bound to be."

Shaw wondered who he was trying to convince - the kid or himself. He nodded at the third survivor.

"What about you?"

"Fell down, woke up, same as the rest of you," Darren replied.

He looked at Robbie. "Is Julie dead?"

Robbie stared into the fire and nodded.

"We were engaged," Darren said.

Silence crept up and shrouded the group after that. The only sound was the occasional crackle from the fire. The survivors either cast their gazes downwards at nothing in particular or stared into the flames. Around them, shadows lengthened and deepened.

The newcomers were still coming to terms with what they'd woken up to, but Shaw's shock had worn off. He was adapting, as they would all have to do if they were to survive. The problem he was wrestling with was what he had done to survive.

Ben stretched in his chair, the movement pulling Shaw from his thoughts.

By mutual consent, they all decided to bed down in the

living room. Seemed that nobody wanted to be alone.

"Tomorrow," Shaw said, to no-one in particular, "we'll get organised."

He didn't know what he meant by organised, but fortunately, no-one, not even Howard, who had been particularly quiet all evening, asked him.

The screams came again that night. The Lodge was set slightly apart from the village and the screams were further away than the night before, but there was no mistaking what they were. No chance of pretending the wind had got up and was whistling around the eaves or through the trees.

Shaw lay stiff, not moving, holding his breath. No-one broke the silence in the room. There was no snoring, no heavy breathing, no rustling of quilts. Everyone was listening.

When the screams finally faded into the night, no-one said a word.

The curtains were drawn and the fire had long since died. Shaw stared into the dark until he didn't know whether his eyes were open or closed.

29

Howard lay in the dark listening to the small sounds around him. The screams he could no longer deny had long since faded and, gradually, people had managed to drift off to sleep. They weren't all asleep though. There were others awake. He could sense it in their breathing, in their movements. It was unusual for him to be so aware of others. His lack of empathy was, according to his wife, only one of his many shortcomings.

She constantly berated him for his selfishness and sneering cynicism. Her attitude struck him as ironic, as it was these very attributes that had served him so well, thus providing her with a large, well-appointed house, a new car every two years and as many clothes as she could crush into her expansive, fitted wardrobes.

Well, she wouldn't be berating him any longer. The thought didn't comfort him as much as he thought it might. Truth be told, he had been touched by the sight of her lying dead on her bedroom floor, hand clutching at the edge of the counterpane, too weak to pull herself into bed.

He had been even more affected by the sight of his dead children. The boy tucked in his bed. The girl curled up like a kitten on the bear-shaped bedside mat.

The three of them had been a constant demand on his

time and wallet. He'd received precious little in return, particularly from his wife - it had been a long time since they'd shared a bed - but, strangely enough, now that everyone was gone, he missed them. Wife gone, children gone, and, thanks to that waster Shaw, even his best friend, Barry, gone.

Howard lay on his back, staring into darkness, thinking about what he'd had and what he'd lost. Very soon, a pair of fat tears welled up and trickled down his face.

The next morning was almost unbearable. Shaw trying to pretend he had a clue about anything. The fat nurse taking charge of the kitchen with her let's-put-the-show-on-right-here, vomit-inducing jolliness. Ben Gillespie irritating him with his pithy old-man sayings. Worst of all, that annoying little girl who kept staring at him all the time. At least she didn't speak. That was all they needed on top of everything else - her squawking and making a racket.

Shaw wanted to head south. Had it in his head that there would be more survivors there, that things would be better organised. Though what he based that on was anybody's guess. It was Howard, as per usual, who cut through the bullshit.

"How do we know things will be better anywhere else? Look at this." He took his mobile phone from his pocket and threw it onto the table. "I don't know why I was still carrying it. It's useless."

The fools stared at it, utterly clueless.

"The battery is dead and even if it wasn't, there's no network. There are no networks of any kind. Don't you get it? No television. No internet. Nothing to tell us what's happening out there. Oh yes, Shaw here might be right. There might be more survivors out there, but for all we know, the world is over-run by *Screamers*, and I, for one, do not want to go hurtling headlong into a city full of them."

Saliva had flecked at the corners of his mouth, the way

it always did when he was having a rant. He wiped it away. They were staring down at the phone. Looking back at him. He'd won the argument, as he knew he would. Okay, maybe he'd been cynical to start with, but they'd all heard the screams last night.

"Maybe there's another way," The Spot said.

"What do you mean?" Shaw, trying to reassert himself.

"We could try using Raymond's VHF

"Raymond?" Shaw asked, once again proving how little he knew about anything.

"The man whose hospitality you are currently enjoying." Howard took pleasure from putting him back in his place.

"He keeps it in the shed," Robbie said. "It was kind of a hobby of his. Mine too." The boy blushed at the revelation, until his entire face was spot coloured.

Having no desire to be bossed around by the fat nurse, Howard went to the shed along with Shaw, Ben and The Spot.

The old man stopped in his tracks on the way down, almost causing Howard to collide into him. Ben harrumphed as he gazed at the sky.

"What is it now?" Howard expected perhaps a rescue helicopter on the horizon, but saw nothing but a few clouds.

"Looks like snow," Ben said.

"Looks clear enough to me," Howard said. "Besides, it's only October."

"We'll see."

Barry had a shed, but it was nothing like this one. Barry's shed was a gentleman's retreat with comfortable chairs and a well-stocked bar. He expected Raymond's to be even classier, but surprisingly it was a dump.

A large worktable covered with half-finished projects sat in the middle of it. Bits of dismantled clocks, model aeroplanes, and broken china lay in piles. A stack of crossword puzzles was weighed down by a large polished stone. A whisky bottle, one third full, and a sticky glass sat beside it. The whisky a cheap blend.

Two low shelves running along one length of the shed were laden with different sized tins. A smaller table sat against the opposite wall, and on that table was a radio. Shaw, Ben and The Spot crowded around it, looking at it as if it held the answer to life itself.

"I don't want to burst anybody's bubble," Howard said, "But doesn't it need electricity to run?"

"Nah." The Spot shook his head. "It runs on a 12 volt battery." He sat down and connected crocodile clips before turning the radio on. "I guess I should try channel sixteen," he said, "the distress channel."

He spoke into the handset. "This is Kelnamara. Kelnamara. Is anyone receiving me?"

Surprisingly enough, The Spot actually seemed to know what he was doing. Despite himself, Howard shared a frisson of excitement with the others. Robbie repeated the call, listened and repeated again. The excitement of the group deflated with each repetition.

Suddenly, he held up his hand - "I think I've got something." He adjusted one of the dials and a voice came through.

"Kelnamara, it's Laxford here. Are you receiving me Kelnamara?"

"Laxford!" Robbie exclaimed, "I'm hearing you loud and clear. Who am I speaking to? Over."

"Billy Grant speaking. Who's that in Kelnamara? Over."

"Robbie Mackenzie. There's nine of us here - what about you? Over."

"Three of us... but there are some others, but -" Muffled voices could be heard. "Alice just came in - she thinks we should join you folks. Over."

To Howard's annoyance, The Spot agreed at once. Surely this was *exactly* the kind of thing that should be discussed beforehand?

"We're at The Lodge. Over."

"We'll be there as soon as we can. Over and out."

"Well done son," Ben patted The Spot on the shoulder. Of course Shaw just had to join in. Robbie' face reddened with the praise and attention.

"Yes, good job Robbie," Howard said, "Just a pity you couldn't come up with something more useful than a few strays from Laxford."

He didn't care that he was pissing on the boy's chips. They were a pathetic group to start with - too many weak links - and he doubted that anyone from Laxford would bring anything to the party apart from more mouths to feed.

30

Half an hour later, Howard was sitting in the cab of Darren's pick-up. The Spot was in the back, the three of them on a food-gathering mission.

"Where to first, Howie?"

"The shop. And don't call me Howie."

"Sure thing Howie- Howard." Darren grinned at him.

Howard had never rated Darren. He was a fish farm worker, not management, obviously. Spent his days in oil skins and went home to an ex-council house owned by his employers. As far as Howard was concerned, Darren was not someone worth socialising with. He was strictly background material. Now that he'd come to the fore, he was proving himself to be an irritant. However, he did manage to park efficiently at the shop, with the tail end of the truck backed up to the door.

By the time Howard heaved himself out of the cab, The Spot was spluttering by the shop door.

"It's ripe in there." His eyes were watering. Looked like he was going to throw up.

Howard pushed his way past the boy and opened the door. The Spot hadn't lied. The smell was indeed ripe. Gagging, Howard pulled a couple of bags of kindling in front of the door to wedge it open.

"We'll let it air for a minute."

Several minutes and one quick look-see in the shop later, the source of the smell was apparent.

Cheese and Onion was lying dead in front of the post office counter, her corpulent body now one big sack of liquefying putrescence.

Howard stared at her dispassionately.   Real name Shirley, Barry had nick-named her Cheese and Onion on account of her habit of continually snacking on strongly flavoured crisps. Between eating and spreading gossip, the woman's mouth was in continual use.

"Poor Shirley." Darren gazed down at the woman.

"Yes, quite," Howard said, "But let's not allow her to spoil our shopping experience."

Before Darren could respond, he was already examining the shelves.

"There's not much here," he said. Hardly surprising. Efficiency had never been one of Cheese and Onion's strong points. You could barely rely on the woman for a box of cornflakes.

Tweedle Dee and Tweedle Dum trailed around behind him. The contents of the freezer had thawed and turned to bags of mush. The fridge was a mouldy disaster zone and the fresh produce, which was never of top quality when it arrived in the first place, was either soft and wrinkly or covered in blue fuzz.

"We'll just have to take what there is," Howard said. "Fill these with whatever you can find." He kicked a couple of empty cardboard boxes towards them.   "I'll check the back store."

Darren muttered something under his breath as Howard turned to go. he suspected it was *arsehole*, but he let it ride for now. He'd been called worse by better, but he wouldn't forget. Darren's card was marked.

There were two unopened cases in the back.   One containing own-brand tomato soup, the other tinned cling peaches in syrup, neither of which caused Howard to break into a song and dance routine.

Howard cast a critical gaze over their haul as they stowed it in the back of the truck. Undoubtedly, they had picked up some useful items - matches, firelighters, soap and so on, but there was nothing exciting. The bottles of spirits were low-end, he hadn't eaten tinned peaches since he was a boy at his granny's house and the tomato soup was, at best, pedestrian. He didn't think he'd ever eaten a Fray Bentos tinned pie and he wasn't sure that the end of the world as he knew it was a good enough reason to start now. He sincerely hoped they would fare better at the hotel.

They passed Shaw and Jamie on the way to the hotel. They were on quads, towing trailers loaded with logs. Darren honked his horn at them and received big waves in return. One big happy family. Howard felt the sudden need for a sick bag. Happy families... he knew all about those.

"Go round the back," he directed Darren, "to the kitchens"

Howard called out a cautious *hallo* at the kitchen door. There was no reply. They entered. Carrying a roll of bin bags, Howard led the way. There were no dead bodies. No bad smells, only the faint lingering aroma of cooking oil.

He had high hopes for the hotel. For obvious reasons the season had ground to a premature halt which meant the larders should still be well-stocked. More so than the shop, he hoped, or else they'd be dining on tinned fruit and cheap tomato soup for a long time to come.

"You seem to know your way around pretty well," Darren said.

Howard shot him a look.

"The Walkers are good friends of ours," he replied.

"Yeah, so I heard."

Howard narrowed his eyes. Darren's grin confirmed his

suspicions - the jungle drums had been beating. Well, his wife was dead and no doubt Kate and Grant Walker were dead too, so it should hardly mattered any more. But somehow it did matter. What's more, Darren Grubb's barely concealed mockery enraged him. He longed to wipe the knowing grin from his weasel face.

Howard yanked open the pantry door. His heart swelled at the sight, the sudden influx of joy sweeping away his resentment at Darren's cheap jibe.

There wasn't a tin of cling peaches or tomato soup in sight. Just lots and lots of delectable goodies - canned, pickled and preserved - everything from caviar, capers and chutney to stuffed olives, venison pate and gentleman's relish.

"There's real food in the other cupboard," The Spot, standing unnecessarily close, peered over his shoulder into the pantry.

Howard flapped his hands at him.

"Do something useful then -" He tore a few bags from the roll before thrusting it into The Spot's hand. "and get it packed. I'll take care of this."

Ignoring the glance exchanged between the Tweedles, Howard turned back to the cupboard and began filling the bags. Oh, he was happy in his work. Practically singing as he pictured the feast he would have tonight.

Three bin bags later, a sizeable dent had been made in the pantry stores. There were still plenty of delectable pickings to be had, but they would keep for another time. For now, Howard had horizons new in mind. He lugged the bags out to the truck.   Credit where credit was due, the Tweedles hadn't been slacking. They were busy loading sacks of vegetables and containers of dry goods - flour, sugar, lentils and the like. The sight gladdened Howard's heart. They would eat well tonight, and for some time to come.

"Don't forget these." Howard added his bags to the pile.

"You going to give us a hand?" Darren asked.

"In a minute." He was already turning back to the hotel.

"Where are you going now?" Darren called.

"To the bar, Mr Grubb," he turned to face them. "I take it that neither of you gentlemen would be averse to a drop of the amber nectar this evening?"

The Spot's grin threatened to tear open a couple of ripe pustules on his cheek.

"Well, now that you mention it... ," Darren replied.

"Thought not." With that, Howard went back into the hotel.

Through the kitchen, into a small corridor and thence to the bar where he took a moment to savour the glorious sight of the gantry. The top shelf was of particular interest, hosting as it did, a line-up of exquisite malts. He'd have a quick snifter now before deciding which to take back with him and which to squirrel away for his private enjoyment. No point in wasting the good stuff on the ravening hordes. Which to try, the *Auchentoshan* or the *Lagavulin*... which was he in the mood for..?

The pleasure Howard derived from his deliberations was disturbed by a dawning realisation that he was not alone. It was the same sensation he'd experienced through the night... he could feel a presence in the room.

Slowly, he turned. His eyes widened.

"Kate?" Howard could hardly believe his eyes. "Thank God you're a-"

31

"Slopey-shouldered bastard," Darren said as the door swung to behind Howard. "Did you see the crumbs on his chin? Greedy sod was stuffing his face in there."

"No wonder he's so fat." Robbie giggled.

"Have you clocked the way Shaw looks at him? I wonder how long it'll be before he lands one on him."

"I'd like to see that."

"Man, I'd pay. Right, that's it, we're done here. Better go and get Howie before he gets tanked up on the *amber nectar*."

Robbie held the door open for Darren. "Do you think he knows he's going bald?"

"Well if he doesn't, it'll kill him to hear it."

A high pitched scream cut through their laughter. They stared at each other. A second, frozen in time. Fingers of icy fear clawed at Darren's spine.

"What the fu-"

Another scream broke the tableau.

They ran towards the sound.

Darren frowned, trying to take in the scene. Howard, lying on the bar floor. Arms raised, trying to protect his face. Kate Walker sitting astride him, clawing at him, snarling and hissing like a wildcat.

"Mrs Walker!" Darren yelled.

She looked up at him and every instinct in his body told to him to get out of there. To run and not look back.

Howard stared at him from behind defensive hands.

"Help me," he pleaded.

He moved his arms revealing a raw, bite-sized wound on his cheek.

It was Kate Walker on top of Howard. Darren was sure of that. But he'd never seen her - never seen anyone - look the way she did now. The Kate Walker he knew was a well-groomed woman. Meticulous to the point of obsessive. Now her face was all screwed up. Distorted by fury. Her hair a tangled mess, her make-up streaked and smudged around blazing eyes. Blood leaked from her mouth, dribbled down her chin.

In a heartbeat, she was on her feet, launching herself at him. Howard scrabbled into a corner. Kate was slender, but her sudden onslaught took Darren by surprise. He staggered backwards, into the bar. She came at him, a rabid frenzy of teeth and nails.

He pushed her away. Hard. She came right back at him, scrabbling at his face with dirty, broken nails. She grunted and squealed, trying to get to him, excited, desperate. Wanting to take a chunk out him the way she'd done to Howard.

He tried to get a grip of her. He wanted to pick her up, throw her against the wall, but it was like grappling with a sack of rats. Every time he thought he had a hold of her, she squirmed out of his grasp. Robbie - where the hell was Robbie?

Finally, he got a hold of her by the neck. She gasped and spluttered, still trying to bite him. He dug his fingers into her throat. Her nails gouged wildly at his cheeks, trying to get to the soft pulp of his eyes. Ignoring the pain, he balled his free hand into a fist and smashed it into her face.

She staggered back, howling. Blood erupting from her pulped nose. She put one of her clawed hands to her face. It came away dripping red. Darren watched as she stared at it for several long seconds. She turned her hand, examining it as the gore dripped through her fingers. His breathing was heavy, his heart thumping. *Fight or flight?* She looked up at him. His body tensed.

The rage had gone from her eyes. Her brow was furrowed. She looked confused.

"Darren? Darren Grubb?" She looked at him liked he'd just dropped out of the sky.

"Mrs Walker?" Darren took a step towards her, horrified now that he had punched her in the face. Thinking that somehow he'd got it all wrong. He glanced at Howard, sitting in a corner, clutching his cheek. Staring intently at nothing Darren could see.   Shock. Must be shock.

He turned his attention back to the woman he had punched.

"Mrs Walker, are you -"

Even as the words left his mouth he could see the transformation come over her. She screamed, lunging at him. He tried to side-step her but she twisted, came at him again. Flecks of saliva foamed at the corners of her mouth. She threw herself at him. They fell to the floor. She was on top of him. A scrabbling mass of teeth, nails and limbs.

One arm trapped under a shelf. He tried to defend himself with the other, but she was bearing down on him, teeth exposed. He tried to squirm away, but she had him pinned. He screwed his eyes against the inevitable bite.

There was a sickening thud.

She slumped onto him. A dead weight on his chest. Crushing the air out of his lungs. He opened his eyes.

Robbie staring down at him, vodka bottle in his hand.

"Where the hell have you been?" Darren gasped.

"Sorry, I er..." Robbie's face was milk white.

"Never mind - just get her off of me."

Robbie put the bottle down and dragged the woman off by the arms. Darren stood up. He examined himself for bites. Found none. Relief.

"Is she dead?" Robbie asked.

"I don't know if I want to get close enough to find out."

Howard lumbered up to the bar. He leaned over and gazed down at Kate's body, the raw-meat wound on his face glistening.

"No." The word came out in an elongated moan.

He staggered around the bar and fell on his knees beside her.

"Oh Kate, not like this." He raised her head onto his lap and stroked her gore splattered face. "Never like this."

He looked up at Darren and Robbie, mouth hanging down, eyes lost in his sagging face.

"I'm sorry, Howard," Darren said.

He guessed the rumours about Howard shagging Kate Walker were true after all. He'd have credited her with more taste. Robbie quivered beside him.

"It's okay mate," Darren told him. Robbie looked like he'd been de-boned, was ready to collapse in a puddle of jelly.

Howard whimpered over Kate, caressed her face, tried to smooth her matted hair. Fat tears rolled down his cheeks, into his wound.

Darren looked away, bile rising in his throat. Any sympathy he felt for the man was quashed by Howard's self-indulgent wailing. They'd all lost people. Howard had lost his own kids, yet here he was blubbering over the married woman he'd been banging like she was the only dead person in the village. The sight gave Darren the creeps.

"Come on, Howard, there's nothing more we can do here. Time to go." He spoke quietly, keeping his disgust to himself. Feeling he'd aged ten years in as many

127

minutes.

"I'm not leaving her."

Howard looking up at him, face awash with tears, snot flowing into his gaping mouth.

"Well, you can't bring her with you."

Howard let out another wail. Darren sighed. Kate's eyes flicked open.

"Kate!" Howard's cry of joy, gurgling in mucus.

"Howard - no!" Darren yelled.

Too late. Kate raised her head. Howard was still smiling when she sank her teeth into his arm. He screamed. She twisted her head, tore out a chunk of flesh. Howard's scream went stratospheric. Darren snatched up the vodka bottle. Brought it down hard on Kate's temple. She let out a small *oh* of surprise as her skull caved in. Still screaming, Howard pushed her from his lap. Her head thudded on the floor. He rolled away from her, sobbing as he mashed his face against the wall.

Darren sat the vodka bottle on the bar. It was smeared with hair, blood and brain matter.

"Is she dead now?" Robbie asked.

Kate stared up at them, eyes unseeing.

32

Shaw wasn't convinced that staying in the village was the right thing to do, but the decision was made. For now. In the meantime, there was enough to be getting on with.

Whilst it was true they needed food and fuel, what they also required was to be kept busy. The less time any of them had for brooding the better. There would be more than enough time for that with the onset of long winter nights.

What Shaw hadn't shared with anyone - not even Ben - was the inner fear that Howard was right and he was wrong. That there was nothing to head south for. This was all that was left. Oh, there were undoubtedly others, but maybe those others were just like them - bewildered pockets of survivors trying to come to terms with a new world. The rest - law, society, order - all gone.

It wasn't something he'd ever imagined mourning the loss of, but without those structures they were reduced to a hand-to-mouth existence. There was plenty of food around now to scavenge, but when the remnants of the twenty-first century bounty ran out they'd be back in the middle ages.

He hefted another log into the trailer. More scavenging.

"Oh no!" Jamie's exclamation broke through Shaw's thoughts.

"What is it?"

"The road's blocked," he said. "Don't you remember - it was before anyone here got sick - to stop the disease getting in."

"Fat lot of good that did - anyway, I thought that was just pub talk - flaming torches and pitchforks."

"No, they did it - but the ones from Laxford -"

"They won't be able to get through - we'd better get up there now."

They unhooked the trailers and drove the quads out of the village to the blockade, which turned out to be an old Massey Ferguson tractor parked at an angle across the road. There was a road barrier on one side, with a steep drop to the loch beyond it, a ditch on the other. Impossible to drive around, it was simple, yet effective.

Jamie clambered onto the tractor.

"Damn, no key."

"Wouldn't be much of a barrier if there was one."

"Guess not," Jamie grinned down at him.

"Know where to get one?"

"Sure do."

Several minutes later they were raking through an extensive key collection in Jimmy Gunn's kitchen. Jimmy's wife lay dead below a sink full of dishes, a broken mug shattered on the floor beside her. There was no sign of Jimmy, though the usual tell-tale stench of death and decay permeated the croft house.

"This is it." Jamie waved a key with a piece of twine attached to it at Shaw.

"You sure?"

"Yup."

"Maybe we should take the rest, just in case."

"Nope, this is it," Jamie said before disappearing out of the back door.

Shaw shrugged and followed him. The kid seemed to

know what he was doing. At least his mood had lifted. He'd been quiet for a while after they picked up the quads from his old man's barn.

Back at the barricade, the boy climbed onto the tractor. He put the key into the ignition, gave Shaw a wink and turned it. The tractor rumbled into life.

Shaw laughed as the boy expertly manoeuvred it to one side of the road.

Jamie switched off and jumped down, a broad grin on his face. Shaw's laughter ceased. He cocked his head.

"Do you hear that?"

They looked out to the steep hill of the Glen Brae.

"Yeah, I hear it," Danny replied.

A Land Rover sped into sight at the top of the hill.

"It's going too fast for the bend," Shaw said.

The vehicle took it wide, but managed to cling on. It came hurtling down the hill, disappearing from sight as the road dipped. Reappearing as it came fleeing round the head of the loch.

"Somebody's in a hurry," Shaw said.

The vehicle picked up more speed as it came along the straight.

Shaw waved his arms. "Slow down, slow down."

The vehicle thundered towards them.

"Oh shit." Shaw pushed Jamie into the ditch, and dived in after him.

The smell of burning rubber rose into the air as the Land Rover screeched to a halt. Shaw and Jamie clambered out of the ditch. The driver's door opened. A woman stumbled out.

She was wild-eyed, young, no more than eighteen or nineteen, long hair plastered to her pale face. Blood beaded on a long, angry, scratch on her cheek.

"Are you okay?"

She screamed as Shaw approached her. Tried to scramble back into the Land Rover.

"Are you Alice?"

She turned towards him.

"I'm Shaw, this is Jamie."

"We know each other," Jamie said. "Hi Alice."

"Hi Jamie. Sorry, I..."

"It's okay," Shaw said. "Where are the others?"

She shook her head. "They didn't make it."

33

Shaw passed a mug of sweet, black tea to Alice. She nodded her thanks.

"We'd already broken into the shop," she said, "yesterday, I think. Maybe it was the day before. It felt wrong, but we had to get food."

She looked round the table at them, awaiting judgement. The range was lit, the kitchen warm. Alice, wrapped in a blanket, cradled the mug in her hands. Howard, Darren and Robbie hadn't returned yet, but everyone else had gathered to hear her story.

"It's okay, Alice." Ben caught Shaw's eye as he spoke. "Things are different now. We've all had to do things we wouldn't have done before."

She stared into her mug and nodded. "There didn't seem much point in leaving it behind - we joked about not turning up empty handed - " she looked up and smiled wanly "- so we decided to take what we could. The boys were loading it on, and I was in the back, stowing it away. That's when they attacked."

"There were three of them. Our next door neighbour - Donnie MacLeod - was one of them. We knew the others as well, and they knew us, but it didn't stop them attacking. They fell on Billy and Kevin like wild animals and tore them apart."

"Kevin?" Jamie asked, "Your brother?"

Alice nodded. "I tried to get out and help them, but there were too many bags and boxes in the way. By the time I got to the tail-gate the boys had stopped screaming. It all happened so fast... they were lying on the ground... Kevin's eyes had been gouged out. Their throats had been ripped open. They were young, fit men, but they didn't stand a chance."

Shaw glanced around the table. Everyone's eyes were on Alice. Everyone's that is, apart from Elizabeth's. She'd taken the photograph from her pocket. Was holding it in her lap, staring at it.

"Donnie saw me then. I was still in the back of the truck, on my hands and knees. He looked me right in the eye and his gaze wasn't human. He lashed out, caught me on the cheek."

She touched the scratch on her face with tentative fingers.

"I clambered to the front of the Land Rover. Someone grabbed my foot, but I kicked out and kept kicking and kept on going until I was in the driver's seat. They tried to get in after me, but they fell out when I put my boot down. I kept it down all the way here."

"I can vouch for that," Shaw said. "She was driving like her arse was on fire."

She almost managed a smile. "The tailgate was still open - I think I lost most of the supplies."

"Never mind that. You're safe now." Marjory rubbed Alice's arm through the blanket.

"Am I?"

Alice's question was still hanging in the air when the door burst open and Darren and Robbie staggered in, supporting Howard between them. Shaw stood up, pulling his chair out. Howard slumped heavily into it.

"What happened?" Shaw asked.

"He's been bit - Kate Walker did it," Darren said.

"She's dead now."

"Kate," Howard moaned the word.

"Alice?" Robbie stared across the table at the newcomer.

"Hello Robbie." Her voice was as flat as her expression. Looked like everything had been sucked out of her and then some.

"Is he okay?" Shaw's attention back on Howard.

"Let's just take a look," Marjory said. "Elizabeth, fetch me the first aid kit - it's in that cupboard."

"No." Elizabeth stood up. "You're not my mother. You can't tell me what to do."

She stormed out of the room. Marjory moved to go after her, but Shaw held her back.

"Leave her," he said.

Marjory looked at him. Opened her mouth to say something, thought better of it and fetched the first aid kit herself.

Howard whimpered as Marjory set about cleaning the wound.

"This will sting a little, Howard, but you'll be fine."

Ben stood up. "Getting dark in here," he said, and set about lighting the candles and lamps.

Avoiding eye contact, Elizabeth slunk back into the kitchen and quietly assisted Marjory. Lucy stroked Toby. Robbie stared at Alice. Alice stared into her mug. Darren told Shaw about what had happened in the bar with Howard and Kate Walker. In return, Shaw told Darren about Alice's arrival. Jamie listened.

"Howard was right," he said. "There are Screamers everywhere."

34

A knot tightened in Shaw's stomach as he pushed open the door to the bar. Darren and Robbie insisted Kate Walker was dead, but Shaw wanted to be doubly sure. They didn't need a crazed-up, bitey-woman freewheeling about the village.

The door creaked open, releasing familiar pub smells. The fabric of the place ingrained with beery fumes and whisky breath. The smell of burning tobacco lingering on in dusty corners.

He stepped inside, Darren and Marjory close behind. All was still. Darren pointed to the bar. Shaw nodded and looked behind it, expecting to see Kate Walker lying there, her head stoved in. She'd been there alright. The bloody matter on the floor was testament to that, but of Kate, there was no sign.

Darren's eyes widened. He opened his mouth to speak, but Shaw hushed him. Backs against the bar, the trio looked around. The shadows of the bar conspired against them. Too many dark corners. She could be anywhere.

"Kate?" Shaw called out gently. "We want to help you."

There was a sound, a whimper. Darren pointed to the alcove where the pool table was kept. Shaw nodded. They moved cautiously towards to the sound.

She was huddled in a corner, her bashed skull exposed to them, something white gleaming in the dripping mangle of hair, blood and skin.

"Dear God," Marjory whispered.

Shaw realised he was looking at Kate Walker's brain.

Kate looked at them. Opened her mouth. "Ga-ga-ga-"

"What did we do to her?" Darren, horrified.

Marjory opened her bag on the pool table and pulled on a pair of nitrile gloves.

"Be careful," Shaw warned.

"She needs help," Marjory replied.

Kate made the ga-ga noise again. It was a sick sound, made Shaw feel queasy.

"It's okay," he said, "We're here to help. Marjory's a nurse - she's going to take a look at you."

He kept his gaze on Kate. She looked dazed and confused, which was hardly surprising, given that her brains were poking out of her head. Marjory knelt beside her.

"Now, Kate, I'll just-"

Kate's eyes suddenly focussed as Marjory leaned in. She snarled. Lunged at Marjory.

"Look out!" Shaw yelled.

Darren leapt forward. Grabbed Marjory by the arms. Hauled her away from Kate, but she came after them. Nails clawing at Marjory's legs, teeth snapping. Marjory screaming, kicking out.

Darren stumbled. Fell back. Kate bearing down on Marjory. Ready to bite out a chunk. Shaw firing a kick. His foot connecting with Kate's jaw. Kate flying back. Slamming into the wall. Sliding to the floor, leaving behind a skid mark of blood, brain, bone and hair.

She lay in a slump. Not moving. Not breathing. He approached, still on full alert. Felt for her carotid artery. No pulse. Just to be sure, he checked again.

He stood up, turned to the others. "She's dead."

"You sure?" Darren asked, getting to his feet.

"I'm sure."

"Third time lucky."

"I'll drink to that."

They helped Marjory up, led her to the bar. Shaw poured three stiff measures of brandy. Marjory gulped hers down in one. Shaw poured another. She took a sip, sat the glass on the bar.

"That," she said, "was almost as bad as a Saturday night shift in A&E."

35

The night was cool and clear. The waxing gibbous moon bright enough to cast shadows behind the trio, but it would be dark inside the medical centre. They clicked on their headlamps.

"Ready?" Shaw asked.

The lights bobbed as Darren and Marjory nodded. Shaw opened the door. They reeled back from the smell, coughing, retching, fanning their faces.

Shaw thought he was used to it by now - he'd barely screwed up his nose in Jimmy Gunn's house - but this was a whole new level of concentrated bodily corruption. He staggered back into the night air after the others.

"My God," Marjory said, "How many people are in there?"

After wedging the door open, they found out.

The waiting room was full of people. Some had died where they sat, heads sagging forward on their chests, or lolling back against the wall, but most had collapsed onto the floor. They lay in a death-tangle, across each other's arms and legs, gas-bloated bodies rapidly decomposing in the warm building. A mother lay atop her dead baby, it's blue face peering over her shoulder, scrunched in a silent, death-mask scream.

A web of cracks radiated from the centre of the security screen at the reception desk. A man lay beneath it, hands still grasping the chair he'd used as a weapon, desperation etched on his dead face.

"Where are the drugs kept?" Shaw asked.

"Through here." Marjory led them to a door at the side of the reception.

"Do you know the code?" Darren asked, looking at the security keypad.

Shaw grasped the handle and turned it. The door opened. "No power, no security," he said.

They entered the room behind the desk. Marjory went straight to the drugs cabinet and started picking through the contents.

"Take everything." Shaw opened up the holdalls he'd brought from the Lodge. "I don't want to come back here."

Darren opened the door to the surgery. "Dr. Harvey's in here," he called, "I think she killed herself."

Shaw stepped over the receptionist, who was face-down on the floor, and joined Darren in the surgery. The doctor was lying on the examination bed, staring dull-eyed at the ceiling, a tourniquet on her arm, needle sticking out below it.

"Poor Fran," Marjory said. "She could see what was coming."

"I think she was a coward," Darren said.

Marjory narrowed her eyes at him. "I suppose you think that makes you brave?"

"No, I think it makes me alive, and I intend on staying that way. What do you think?" he asked Shaw.

Shaw looked towards the bodies piled in the waiting room.

"A doctor would have come in handy. No offence," he said to Marjory.

"None taken," she replied, still glaring at Darren.

36

"Is he going to be okay?" Shaw spoke in a low voice.

They'd moved Howard to one of the bedrooms. He was sitting in a chair by the window, rocking back and forward, moaning quietly to himself.

"I don't know," Marjory admitted "normally a wound like that would be dealt with in a hospital. Human bites are dirty - even when the biter isn't carrying a disease there's a high risk of infection."

"You mean Howard might end up like Kate?"

"It's a possibility." She looked beat, all traces of her earlier spirit now gone. Even the soft light from the hurricane lantern could not disguise the weariness evident in her face. "I've cleaned and dressed the wound as best I can. I've given him a tetanus jab and started him on a course of antibiotics. He's in God's hands now."

Shaw didn't believe in anything much, least of all God, but maybe Darren was right, maybe the doctor was a coward. Maybe she had taken the easy way out. Or it could be that she had played it smart. She'd seen how things were, knew how bad they were going to get. Maybe she didn't want to hang around for the after party.

He knew just how unappealing the idea of spending the apocalypse holed up with a bunch of randoms was.

Neither was there much charm in the thought of either slowly starving to death or having your face chewed off by a crazed local. Or maybe suicide had been on the doc's cards for a long time and she had simply fulfilled her own destiny. Jolly good timing, in that case.

One thing Shaw did agree with Darren on - he was alive and he wanted to stay that way. He didn't know why he felt like that, why he wasn't tempted to go the way the doctor had, but the feeling was intense.

He wanted to live and he'd do whatever it took to make sure that happened.

37

Rules evolved. No-one went anywhere alone. All doors and windows were secured at night. Everyone took their turn at the daily chores. Howard was watched at all times. A sense of order had settled over the Lodge - it was beginning to feel less like a refugee camp and more like home.

There were two roads leading to the village - one from the north, the other from the south. They had reinstated the tractor barricade on the north road with a similar set-up on the southbound using a couple of cars. Ideally, Shaw would have liked to have someone on watch at either point, but they couldn't afford to spare anyone, besides which, the more immediate threat came from within the village. The make-shift barriers would have to suffice for now.

They had hoped the nightly torment would end with Kate's demise, but the banshee wails had continued after her death.

A night of silence had given them hope, only for the howling to start up again the following evening. However, the wails had lost much of their gusto lately, becoming more of a pathetic lament than blood-curdling scream. It seemed their resident Screamer was dying. Shaw felt little in the way of sympathy. He just wanted the caterwauling to end.

They had shelter, they had fuel, they had water. With winter on the way and ten mouths to feed, plus one dog, food was the immediate priority.

Ben had put a couple of sheep in the pen the day before, starving them before slaughter. Howard raised an imperious eyebrow.

"With no fridges or freezers, just how do you propose to keep the meat from going off?"

"Well we have a few days of fresh meat and then we go back to the ways before fridges and freezers were invented - we salt it," Ben calmly replied.

Howard gave a theatrical shudder. "Ugh, salt mutton."

If Ben was bothered by his attitude, he didn't show it.

Howard was kept under Marjory's beady eye at the Lodge. She had recovered from the wobble she'd had after Kate's attack and had taken a stern, matronly tone with Howard which, despite his protests, got results. Under different circumstances, watching her boss him around would have been comical. Even under these circumstances, there might have been some amusement to be had if Shaw didn't suspect that there was something wrong with Howard.

He hadn't turned, as they'd feared, after Kate's bite. He *seemed* to be on the mend. He *seemed* to be getting back to his old self, but Shaw had caught sight of him when he thought no-one was looking. Stroking the bandage on his cheek, a peculiar expression on his face. An expression Shaw didn't like. He couldn't explain it, he just knew Howard had to be watched.

Darren, Alice and Robbie had gone to the fish farm. Some of the salmon would have died, but Darren reckoned there would be plenty still alive in the cages. They were going to feed them and net a couple for dinner.

Everyone else was on Ben's croft. Jamie, Elizabeth and Lucy at the bottom of the field with the dog, digging up

144

carrots and potatoes, loading them into the quad trailer.

"Fresh salmon and potatoes straight from the ground - we'll be eating like kings tonight," Ben said.

"It'll make a change from tinned soup."

"Yup, sure will. You ready?"

Shaw eyed the sheep in the pen. Despite his antipathy towards mutton, he could see that they were fine specimens. Besides which, he had a feeling that he was going to be very grateful for fresh meat in the coming weeks.

"As I'll ever be."

"Let's get started."

Shaw helped Ben, much as, once upon a time, he'd helped his old man. He turned the first sheep on its back, holding it between his legs while Ben made short work of trussing it. He then loaded it into a wheelbarrow and took it round the corner to the hard standing in front of the barn. There were those who had no qualms about slaughtering one sheep in front of another, but Shaw was glad Ben wasn't one of them.

"Do you want me to...?" Shaw pointed at the gun.

"No son, I'll do it."

Ben aimed the .22 at the back of the animal's head and shot it swiftly and cleanly with one bullet.

"Hate that part," he said, "but I never duck out of doing it."

Shaw held the head of the dead animal while Ben cut the artery in its throat. They let it bleed outside the barn, where the mess could easily be hosed away. When the blood stopped flowing Shaw wheeled the carcass inside. Ben untied the legs and they lifted it onto a table.

"Do you remember much about this?"

"Some," Shaw replied. "I definitely remember the smell."

"There's no mistaking it," Ben grinned.

The air was thick with the distinctive aroma of warm mutton as Ben began removing the head. He cut all round the flesh of the neck with a knife then finished the job with a saw.

"I remember that bit," Shaw said as Ben tied off the top of the gullet. "The old man drummed it into me."

"He knew what he was talking about - you don't want bile getting out and spoiling the meat. Right then, you can give me a hand skinning it."

Ben cut open the skin on the front legs and pushed his hands in as far as he could to the backbone to loosen it off while Shaw held the legs open for him. Starving the sheep for twenty-four hours beforehand helped to loosen the skin, but it was still a laborious task.

The process was repeated with the hind legs until the skin was slackened as far as possible all the way round the sheep. He then cut the wool away from the animal's belly before carefully slicing it open.

"Got to be careful not to cut into the stomach. Hell would probably smell better."

Vile though the inside of the sheep's stomach may be, Shaw didn't think it could come close to the rank corruption in the health centre.

"Hope you're paying attention," Ben said as he pulled apart the flaps of the belly, "you're doing the next one."

He removed the guts, liver, heart and lungs and dropped them into a bucket. The kidneys were left to hang with the mutton. He removed the skin then Shaw used the block and tackle to hoist the carcass.

"How long are you planning on hanging it?"

"Weather's cool and getting cooler," Ben said, "I reckon we'll be eating mutton chops in seven days."

The second sheep done, they stepped from the dim barn into golden October sunshine. It was true what Ben said, despite the sun, there was a chill in the air. It was too cold for flies at any rate, which was something to be grateful for.

"You still reckon we're in for snow?"

"I can practically taste it," Ben said.

Shaw looked but couldn't see anything but blue sky. Not a snow cloud in sight.

"What have you got there?"

Shaw turned. Lucy was running up to Ben, giggling, holding something in her hand. Shaw raised his eyebrows. This was a breakthrough. Though they had managed to coax the occasional smile from her, Lucy was still only talking through Elizabeth, whispering in her ear if there was something she wanted to share with the group. These giggles were the first sound Shaw had heard her make since she'd told him the poodle's name.

"Is it a potato?" Ben asked.

Still giggling, Lucy nodded, holding out a lumpy tuber in her grubby hand. Elizabeth came up behind her, a grin plastered across her face. They looked the way Shaw thought kids ought to look - happy and carefree.

Lucy handed the potato to Ben then whispered in Elizabeth's ear.

"She says to tell you that it looks like Howard."

Ben turned the potato in his hand, examining it.

"Why so it does," he laughed. "Shaw, take a look at this."

Shaw looked and laughed. The potato did bear a striking resemblance to Howard.

Jamie arrived on the quad, Toby riding pillion.

"Did you see it?" he asked.

"We certainly did." Ben held the potato up, admiring it. "Tell you what," he said, "We'll give it to Howard for his supper tonight."

The kids returned to the Lodge with their harvest. Ben and Shaw decided to take a ride around the village. Ben wanted to check out the livestock and make plans for moving the animals into more easily managed locations in preparation for winter.

"We're fine for fresh eggs, not to mention the odd chicken for the pot but we should take a look at Angus

147

Black's cows. I've never killed a cow, but I dare say the basic principle's the same. A couple of sides of beef wouldn't go amiss."

Visions of juicy steaks danced in Shaw's head.

"You know," Ben continued, "there are a lot of resources right here on our doorstep."

Shaw nodded. Maybe he had been too hasty in wanting to leave immediately. Ben was right - there was a lot here. They were already in the process of organising themselves. Getting their food supply sorted would give them space to think. Then they could make plans for the future.

Along with his entire family, Angus Black was dead, but Falling Down Flu had had no impact on his highland cattle. There was plenty of rough grazing in their field and the burn running through it provided them with water.

"Fine beasts," Ben said.

Shaw leaned on the gate. He had to agree. They were fine beasts and they looked particularly magnificent now, their auburn coats highlighted by the autumn sun as they grazed. The field was still green, the sky blue, the sea sparkling beyond.

He had felt a great sense of achievement when both sheep were hung. They had done something real - food had been provided for the group, and he had enjoyed the physicality of it. He felt as if they were doing more now than just trying to survive - they were pushing ahead.

He took a deep breath, filling his lungs with pure, clean air. In that moment, it felt as though his restlessness had evaporated. He almost felt content.

Ben spoke, as if reading his thoughts. "We can do it here, Shaw. We can make it."

He regarded the old man. "Maybe we can, Ben. Maybe we can."

Gunshot cracked through the air shredding the tranquillity of the day. Startled, the cows stampeded to the bottom of the field.

"Which direction?" Shaw demanded.

"South."

38

Darren winked at Alice as she jumped nimbly onto the pontoon. She favoured him with a smile as he tied up the boat. He stood beside her as she gazed around. The sea loch was completely calm, mountains perfectly mirrored in the water.

"It's beautiful."

"Yes, it is." She glanced at him, catching him gazing at her instead of the scenery and laughed.

"Everything looks different from the water," she said.

Darren smiled, enjoying her happiness. She'd looked like a frightened deer when he'd first seen her in the kitchen, pale-faced, trembling, wrapped in a blanket.

Seeing her that night, he'd have put money on her losing it. But she hadn't broken down. She'd rallied round, realising that it was what it was and she had to get on with it.

What Darren was beginning to realise was that even though a terrible thing had happened and even though everyone he cared about was dead, not only did life still go on, incredibly, it was still possible to experience moments of happiness. Like now. He was happy now. Temporarily at least, the horror of what he had seen and done, had lifted. He felt light. He thought he might be falling in love.

"Let's get on with it."

Robbie dumped a sack of fish food by - almost on - his foot. He'd been his usual goofy self at breakfast, but as the morning wore on, his mood had soured.

"What's eating you?" Darren asked.

"Nothing."

Robbie slit open the sack and threw a handful of oily pellets into one of the fish cages. The surface of the water suddenly boiled with long, silver bodies as the salmon surged for the food.

"Look at them all," Alice said. "Can I feed them?"

"It's what we're here for, isn't it?" Robbie snapped.

Alice put a hand on his arm. "Have I done something to offend you?"

Robbie looked at her hand, looked up at her face. The blush that spread across his was of volcanic proportions.

"Got out of bed the wrong side this morning," he mumbled.

"We all have bad days." She smiled at him. He smiled back, his teeth stark white against the blaze of colour on his face.

"That's better," she said.

Against the odds, his blush deepened until it was almost purple.

"Alice... I'm sorry about Kevin -," he stuttered the words out, "he was my best friend at high school."

She peered at him, a quizzical look on her face, followed by realisation.

"I remember you!"

"You do?"

"Yes - you were the quiet one - you never said a word to any of us. It was funny, because Kevin was always so noisy."

She flung her arms around Robbie and hugged him close. Darren couldn't help but notice that Robbie put up no resistance.

151

"I'm so glad you're here," Alice said.

Robbie beamed at her words, the smile fit to crack his face in two.

"It's like having a part of my little brother here."

Darren's burgeoning pang of jealousy died a sudden death as Robbie's beam stuttered. Little brother! No luck, Robbie. A big, old grin spread across Darren's face.

"Now that you two have figured out who you are, can we get on with feeding the fish?"

Give him his due, Robbie hid his disappointment well. In the end, the three of them had a good time out on the pontoon. They made tea in the hut and shared a packet of Hobnobs someone had left there. Later, they cheered Alice as she netted a couple of salmon for dinner that night, then laughed at her screwed-up face when Robbie clubbed them, using what he indelicately referred to as the Killing Stick. Darren gutted the fish, threw them into the boat and they headed back to shore.

The three of them sat squished up in the front of the pick-up as they drove back to the village, laughing and joking, spirits high. It was almost as if the bad stuff hadn't happened.

"Uh-oh," Darren stared at the wing mirror.

"What is it?" Alice asked.

"We've got company."

Alice and Robbie turned in their seats and looked out of the rear window.

"Motorbikes," Robbie said.

"How many?" Darren asked.

"Two - no, three - there's three of them."

"Maybe they're friendly," Alice said.

"We'll soon find out." Darren stepped on the gas.

"They're gaining," Robbie said.

"I see them."

Darren floored the pedal. The bikes kept up, began closing the gap.

"I don't think they're friendly," Alice said.

"What are we going to do?" Robbie's voice rising with his panic.

They passed through the open barricade cars, on the edge of the village now.

One of the bikes roared right up behind them.

"He's got a gun!" Alice screamed

"Get down!" Darren yelled.

The rear window exploded. Darren lost control. Alice screaming. Robbie screaming. His ears singing with the blast. The pick-up swerved. Bounced over the kerb. Hit a wall.

Everything went black.

39

When he came to he was breathing grit. Felt like his tongue had been pebble-dashed. He tried to spit it out but he had no saliva. He started realising. Slowly getting it. Where he was. What was happening. None of it was good.

He was lying face down on the road in the middle of Mitchell Terrace. Felt like he'd been shredded. That the only thing holding him together was the clothes he was wearing.

They said you could only feel pain in one part of your body at a time. It was a lie. Everything hurt. All over. At the same time. He didn't know if he'd been dragged out of the truck and left for dead, or if he'd been thrown out. Alice - where was Alice?

He raised his head a little. It was enough.

She was scared. Robbie too. It wasn't right. She'd been scared enough already. They all had. No need for any more.

They weren't Screamers. Even from this distance, he could tell they didn't have the disease. They just were what they were.

One was fatter than the others, eyes small, like piss-holes in the snow, but they all looked mean. Men you would cross the road to avoid.

He wanted to tell them - there was no need for it. They were all just trying to survive. But his mouth didn't work. He didn't think it mattered. Didn't look like they were the kind of people who would listen There was no small talk going on here. No conversational gambits. No one-liners. Plenty of laughter though, except it was all the wrong kind.

He watched through the slits of his swollen eyes.

Alice and Robbie, back-to-back. The bandits circling them, like hyenas testing a wounded animal. Throwing jabs at Robbie. Grabbing at Alice. Copping feels. He didn't like that. Didn't like the way they were groping at her.

She tried to repel them. Twisting her body, pushing at their hands. They laughed, enjoying the sport. He could see the way it was going. Tried to yell at them. Exhaled dust.

Robbie lashed out at one of them. Got a kick in the balls for his efforts. He doubled up. They laughed all the harder. Made repeated snatches at Alice. Grabbing at her breasts, her crotch.

He. Had. To. Do. Something.

His body felt all smashed up, but he forced his muscles to work. He inched towards them, on his belly, like a broken snake.

Alice slapping them away. She was crying. Tears of outrage. One of them grabbed at her jacket, pulled it off. The others egging him on.

Robbie shouted *no*. He was grabbed by the hair. Pulled down. Kneed in the face. He staggered, blood spurting from his nose. They gave him a couple of kicks. He fell over. They gave him another couple of kicks. Darren close enough now to hear the air expelling from Robbie's lungs.

They turned back to Alice. She was on her own now. Exposed on all sides. They circled her. Salacious grins dripping from their faces. The fat one grabbed her by the arms. She struggled. Yelling. Kicking out.

Darren yelled *no*. It came out as a broken-glass howl.

They turned towards him. Heads cocked. Eyebrows raised. The fat one kept a hold of Alice, but his attention was on Darren.

One of the others strode towards him.

"Well, well, well. It's still alive."

"Not for long," the fat one quipped.

"Ain't that the truth."

He stopped in front of Darren's head, standing so close, Darren could see every scuff mark on his heavy leather boots. Reckoned he'd be able to smell them too, if it wasn't for the fact that his nose was choked with blood and grime. One of the boots swung back then swooped towards him, filling his vision.

The heavy leather connected with his face. Alice screamed. Pain exploded in his head. Pain so excruciating it was ridiculous. Beyond belief to feel like this yet still be alive. The boot swung back. Darren laughed. Looking up at his attacker through puffed-up eyelids. Seeing the puzzlement on his face as the laugh emerged as a throaty gargle. The boot hesitated.

"Again," Darren said, "Do it again." The words mangled. The meaning clear.

His attacker looking at him as though he was mad.

He felt as though he probably was mad. As though the pain had unhinged something inside him.

He was going to die. That much was clear.

May as well have some fun while he was at it.

"Kick me you bastard," he gargled.

His attacker grinned. "Ask and ye will receive."

He swung his foot back.

Darren kept his eyes open. When death came, he wanted to watch it come.

The boot swung back. *Bring it on, baby.* A clap of thunder.

Darren watched, amazed, as the kicker's guts exploded out of him. Just as astounded, the kicker looked down at the hole in his belly. He died with a look of almighty surprise on his face.

Not thunder, Darren realised. Gunfire.

The cavalry had arrived.

40

Keeping a tight hold of Alice, the fat one wheeled around, trying to figure where the gun shot had come from. He pulled her hard against his body. Looked like he was trying to wear her.

The other was already at his bike, pulling out a sawn-off shot-gun.

"I wouldn't do that if I was you."

Shaw stepped out from behind one of the houses, his rifle aimed squarely at the bandit's head.

The bandit paused, his hand still on the gun.

"No problem, boss. We don't want any trouble, do we, Janko?" he called over his shoulder.

"No, not us. We don't want no trouble at all," the fat one replied. He edged back, towards his bike, dragging Alice with him.

She tried to resist, but he had a meaty arm hooked around her neck, squeezing so tight she had to use both hands to keep from choking. She gasped, eyes bulging, feet barely touching the ground.

"Tell you what, boss," the other said. "Howzzabout we just get on our bikes and go. That's a deal, right?"

A slow grin spread across his lips as he eyed Shaw. The grin told Shaw everything he needed to know.

The bandit snatched up the gun and fired. Shaw instinctively fired back. Knowing, even as he squeezed the trigger, the shot had gone wide. He juked behind the house, as shot splattered the building. Glass imploded. Someone let out a long scream.

The sound died. Shaw stayed flat against the wall.

"Come out or the girl gets it."

He peered around the corner. The fat guy was weaving a machete in front of Alice's face. She stared at the long blade, mesmerised.

"All the way out, boss," the one with the gun ordered.

Shaw stepped into view.

"Throw down the rifle."

Shaw heard the order, but his fingers didn't want to yield the weapon.

"Drop it."

The bandit's eyes were cold, unflinching. They showed no fear, no doubt. If Shaw didn't do as he was told, Alice would be filleted.

Shaw dropped the rifle on the scrubby lawn..

The bandit raised the shotgun. Shaw, staring down the barrel. The fat guy sniggering. Robbie lying in a crumpled heap. Robbie on his feet. Throwing himself at the gunman.

The fat guy yelled a warning. The gunman spun around. Shaw made a grab for the rifle. The gunman cracked Robbie on the temple with the gun butt. He dropped like a sack of lead.

"Hold it right there, boss."

Shaw froze, his fingertips on the barrel of the rifle. Figuring if he had time to snatch it up, take aim, fire. Feeling the black eye of the shotgun on him. Knowing he'd be dead before the rifle was in his hands.

"Okay, boss. Let's say we do it old school. Hands in the air. Come on, gettem up."

Shaw straightened up slowly, raised his hands. The gunman was toying with him. Had no intention of letting him - of letting any of them - live. He could shoot him right there and then, but he was dragging it out for kicks.

He walked towards Shaw, until he was in point-blank range. Shaw was a dead man standing and he knew it.

Someone screamed. Shaw glanced at his friends. Took less than a second. Darren lying in a pool of blood, face like a pound of raw steak. Robbie, skull cracked, unconscious. Alice could barely breathe, let alone scream. His own puzzlement reflected in the gunman's face.

The answer came hurtling out of the house beside him.

An old woman in a torn, stained nightdress. Feet bare. Blue veins marbling her skinny, milk-white legs. Hair a shocked frizz.

The gunman laughed. Called to his comrade.

"Hey, Janko - your girlfriend's here."

"Fuck you," came the reply.

The gunman still laughing as the Screamer launched herself at him. He tried to bat her away. Underestimated her frenzied strength. His eyes widened as she bit into his throat, tore out a chunk. She chewed on it then spat it in his face. Still going at him. Relentless.

He wrestled her. Wrangled the muzzle of the shot-gun under her chin. Pulled the trigger. Blasted her face up into the wide blue yonder. Blinded her. Took off her lips and nose. She had no face but she didn't let up with the screaming.

Trying to stem the blood coming out of his throat with one hand, he used the other to club her with the gun. She collapsed, still hollering, still clawing at him. He kicked her head until the sound died then folded on the grass beside her.

Shaw picked up the rifle.

The gunman was kneeling, sitting back on his heels. Blood pumping through his fingers. He reached out a supplicating hand.

Shaw walked over. Looked down at him.

"There's nothing we can do for you. You're already

dead,"

The gunman gargled. Collapsed across the body of the dead Screamer. He died, still staring at Shaw.

Shaw snorted. Turned his attention to the fat one.

He'd manoeuvred himself and Alice onto the bike. Her, half-strangled, perched astride it, between his legs. Fine cuts criss-crossing her face where the machete had got too close.

"Don't come any closer or she gets it in the neck." Knuckles tight and white around the machete handle. Jabbing the point at her jugular, piggy eyes bulging.

Shaw stopped dead, holding the rifle casually in two hands.

"You okay?" he asked Alice.

A short nod in reply.

"What about you?" he asked fat boy. "You must be feeling pretty lonesome right now, with your buddies all dead."

"Don't you worry about me, cunt face. I'm out of here," he said. "Gonna ride out the road and have a party to myself with your girl here."

Shaw stood, impassively, and listened as fat boy ranted on.

"I'm gonna fuck her inside out, *boss*. And when her pussy's all tore up, I'm gonna fuck her in the ass till she bleeds and then I'm gonna fuck her some more. And when I'm done fucking her, on account of what you did to my brothers, I'm gonna cut her. I'm gonna cut off her titties and I'm gonna cut up her cunt, and-"

"You don't want to be doing that, son."

Ben, standing behind fat boy, the muzzle of his .22 pressed into the bandit's skull.

"What kept you?" Shaw asked.

"Old bones," Ben replied. "Drop the knife," he ordered the bandit.

"I was just joking around," tiny eyes popping, gibbering at Shaw. "I wasn't really gonna do those things. It was all talk. I'm not like them, honest. I was just gonna get out of here and drop her a few miles down the road. I didn't hurt you girl, did I?"

"Let her go and we'll talk," Shaw said.

"If I let her go, you'll kill me." The flat edge of the machete pressed against Alice's cheek, enough pressure on the razor edge to create a thin bloodline.

"We're not like that."

"Then tell that bastard behind me to get the fucking gun out of my head."

A look passed between Shaw and Ben. A nod from Shaw. Small exhale of tension from the fat one as the pressure from the .22 was relieved. Time for one small look of surprise as Ben relocated the muzzle under fat boy's ear and shot, diagonally, through his head.

His brains, what he had of them, arced and splattered across Shaw's boots. The machete clattered to the ground, taking a sliver of Alice's cheek with it. She pressed the back of her hand against it to stem the blood. The other rubbing at the red marks on her throat.

Superficial wounds. She'd live.

Shaw wasn't so sure about Darren and Robbie.

Ben put the safety on his gun and looked, weary eyed, at Shaw.

"They made killers of us."

"They didn't give us any choice."

41

Howard watched as Tweedle Dee and Tweedle Dum were carried into the Lodge. Fuss ensued. Lots of fuss. There was hooing and hawing, and weeping and wailing, and oh yes, you'd better believe it - there were tears before bedtime. Streams, rivers, nay, floods of tears shed over the plucky - or should that be *plooky* - youths.

He didn't recall any tears being shed when half his face was bitten off. There wasn't any breast-beating going on then. No, he'd had to suck it up. Take it like a man. Not so, the Tweedles.

They were fawned over, caressed. Cool hands wiped their fevered brows. They were cleaned and stitched, bandaged and bound, then laid on soft beds, heads cushioned by layers of marshmallow pillows. And, despite all the doom-laden prophecies about one or other, or neither of them, making it through the night, they both woke up to a new dawn. And the one after that, and the one after that, ad nauseam.

Three cheers for big old, fat old, nursie for fixing the Tweedles. Clap hands, sing hallelujah. Praise be, oh yes.

She'd stitched the girl up too. If Alice was upset about having her looks marred by the scar running the length of her face, she didn't show it. She'd barely winced as the needle ran through her skin, time and time again, knitting the flapping edges together.

Howard admired her stoicism. What's more, he didn't grudge her his admiration, not one bit. No, he gave it willingly. She'd been badly hurt, scarred too. But she was strong, uncomplaining, intelligent. He looked at her and recognised a kindred spirit.

He intuited that she, like he, was growing the tiniest, teeniest, ickle-wickle bit bored with the retelling of the tale. Whenever they were gathered, out it rolled. Round the kitchen table. Gathered by the fire. The merest lull in the conversation was all it took, more often than not, provoked by the piping voice of the hitherto Silent One.

Yes, dearest Lucy had found her tongue. What a delight for them all, to listen to that sing-song, cutesy-wutesy, little voice from dawn till dusk. Wittering and twittering, sharing the knowledge she had amassed during her six years of being. Asking questions, making demands - her favourite one being, tell us about the bad men, Shaw. The same demanded of Ben and Alice, then of The Spot when he joined them and, finally, of Darren, when he at last arose from his bed Lazarus-like and joined them at the table.

Five of them, telling the same story, from every which way. Left to right, upside-down, inside-out, until he felt like he'd been there himself. Five minutes after it happened, it had already reached epic proportions, a legend in the making. A ready-made history for this newly-birthed post-apocalyptic world.

However, tales of heroism aside, there was one aspect of the narrative Howard enjoyed immensely, even, perhaps particularly, on the retelling, as with each retelling of the tale, some extra detail was added.

This was the part in which Molly MacAulay came a-running out of her house, nightdress flapping around her skinny shanks. He'd have liked a ringside seat for that show.

She'd been a self-righteous prig in the previous world. An ostentatious church-goer, pillar of the community, professional nosey-parker. Forever sticking her nose in where it had no right to be. Well, she wasn't anything now but dead, her face splattered over her front lawn. It was no better an ending than the crone deserved.

Yes indeed, Molly MacAulay had it coming to her, but Kate didn't. Poor, lovely, prickly, sexy Kate.

Howard raised a hand to his face and stroked his bandage, as he always did when he thought of her. Poor Kate, why had she died while the likes of The Spot lived on?

Yes, they'd cried and wailed for the Tweedles, but nobody had shed a tear for his loss. He was all alone in his anguish and grief.

Fat Old Nursie certainly didn't care. It was all a front. The only thing she really cared about was where her next shot of brandy was coming from.

Ha, he had her there. She thought nobody knew, but he'd seen her slugging straight from the bottle when she thought there was no-one around.

The best laugh was, *they* thought that they were spying on Howard, when all the time, he was really spying on them.

Funny, funny, funny. They were watching him, waiting to see if the bite turned him like Kate or Molly MacAulay. They thought he didn't know. People had been underestimating him all his life. On the one hand, it annoyed him. Stung his ego, pranged his pride. On the other, well, he did what he'd always done - he turned it to his own advantage. Used his time under surveillance to gather information on them. Information that, at one point or other, he would use to his own advantage.

So far, he knew that Fat Old Nursie was a drinker. That her preferred tipple was brandy, but she'd down practically anything she could get her hands on - as long as they weren't shaking too bad. He knew where she stashed the bottles - he'd had a bit of sport moving them around and replacing the odd half-filled one with an empty. Oh, the look on her face. Priceless. And he knew that she needed a shot first thing in the morning, just to get her going.

He knew that The Spot was infatuated with Alice. Probably fancied himself in love with her. Always tried to sit beside her at the table. He'd had a bit of sport with that as well, taking the seat just before The Spot could get there. Acting as if he was completely oblivious to the situation.

Oh, he knew all sorts. But the best thing he knew was that Shaw was not a leader of men. It wasn't just his feet that were made of clay, he was mud all the way up to his armpits. Dubbed a hero after the shenanigans up at Mitchell Terrace, but sooner or later he was going to reveal himself as the wreck of a man he truly was and that's when Howard would step forward and finally - finally - be recognised.

But not until this infernal pain went away.

He touched the bandage. Pressed it, pressed it hard into his cheek, trying to subdue the pain. Fat Old Nursie had given him pain killers earlier, but they had worn off. The throb was rich and intense, and impossible to ignore.

"I need more tablets."

Nursie turned around from the sink, where she was scrubbing carrots. Carrots, carrots, endless bloody carrots, night after night. Ben Gillespie had a whole field of the buggers growing and they were on a mission to eat every last one of the pointy-ended roots. Boiled carrots, roast carrots, carrot sticks, carrot soup, carrot bloody cake. It was a wonder he wasn't pissing orange.

"Are you sure?" says Nursie. "It's not been that long since the last lot."

"I need them," he said.

Throb, throb, throb, the bandage practically pulsating. Why wouldn't the woman listen?

She wiped her hands on a tea towel. "Let me get cleaned up and I'll take a look at you."

Howard nodded curtly as she bustled off. Good grief, she was irritating. Now she'd be prodding and poking at him and she'd only end up giving him the damn tablets in the end anyway. Why wouldn't the bloody woman just do as she was told in the first place?

He pushed aside the turnips he'd been peeling and sat by the table. She reappeared with her bag a few minutes later and made a great show of cleaning her hands with anti-bacterial gel, the smell of which, Howard noticed with some relish, was not strong enough to offset the brandy fumes coming from her mouth.

He flinched as she peeled back the dressing from his cheek.

"Is it painful?" she asked.

"Christ almighty, yes!" he exploded, "that's what I've been trying to tell you."

She drew back from him and gave him one of her Nazi commandant faces.

He muttered an apology.

"Manners cost nothing, Howard."

He said sorry again, but she was already poking at the wound. She was none too delicate about it either. Howard bit his lip. If that's what it took to get his tablets, let her have her fun.

"Hmmmm."

He didn't like the sound of that.

"Yes, it's a little red around the edges. I think an infection might have set in, but the antibiotics should take care of that."

Howard rolled his eyes. Finally, she was paying attention.

She applied a fresh dressing and checked his temperature.

"It's a little high," she said, "but nothing too alarming. We'll increase the pain killers for the next twenty-four hours, and I think you should lie down and rest for a while."

At last, some respite.

She doled out the painkillers and he gobbled them greedily before climbing the stairs in buoyant mood. Joy of joys, a morning free from the indignity of menial tasks.

The painkillers were already kicking in as he stretched out on his bed. There was to be roast chicken for dinner that night, served with the obligatory carrots and mashed turnip to be sure, but perhaps there would be a glass or two of a nice white to go with it. He would take it upon himself to suggest it if no-one else did. No need to give in to barbarity.

The pain in his cheek was melting away, there was a good meal to look forward to, and in the meantime, there was peace and quiet. No Nursie small-talk, no wittering from the child, or cheek from the youth, just blissful solitude.

A creak on the landing.

They were checking on him.

Howard smiled and drifted into a pleasant doze.

He slept longer than he'd intended, and they had been willing, it seemed, to let him do so. Perhaps his period of rest gave them some respite from constantly watching him. He was woken by a rap on the door. It opened, Lucy's head appeared around it.

"Dinner's ready," she said.

The child spoke the truth. A delicious aroma tantalised his taste-buds as, freshened and spruced as best as he could mange in these circumstances, he entered the kitchen. What's more, his cheek was barely throbbing at all.

His convivial mood improved further as he spied two bottles of wine on table - Pinot Grigio - not what he would have chosen, but at least they'd made the effort.

Even better, two painkillers already laid out at his place.

There was something of a celebratory air around the table that night. The talk was mainly of food - what they already had in store, what they could get. Ben spoke of going out on the hill for a stag, a suggestion Howard heartily supported. Venison, now there was a tantalising prospect. Not to be outdone, The Spot suggested collecting whelks from the shore, an option Howard found rather less appealing.

Another bottle of wine appeared. Howard surprised even himself by raising a toast to Fat Old Nursie for looking after him so well. He even remembered to call her Marjory. His toast was heartily seconded by the Tweedles.

They sat around the table for a long time, chatting by candlelight. It almost felt like a normal family meal. Except that none of them were related and all their families were dead. Heigh ho, thought Howard, as he climbed the stairs to bed. Can't have everything.

In the morning, he awoke to a strange light. He went to the window, pulled the curtains aside and peered out at a white world.

Winter had come early.

42

At first the snow caused great excitement. There was sledging and there were snowball fights, marshmallows toasted on the open fire and instant hot chocolate to drink. The kids behaved like kids again. It transformed their world. Concealed the horror of what had gone before beneath a blanket of hushed white. It gave them a chance to forget, at least for a while. The problem was, the snow kept on coming.

Every day Shaw stood by Ben's side as he inspected the sky. Shaman-like, the old man had predicted the coming of the snow and no-one had believed him. Now they believed in his magic and wanted him to predict when the snow would go away. The novelty of it had long worn off. But every day Ben shook his head. "More on the way," he said. They believed him now, and they were right to do so.

After the first fall, they could still make it around the village in the four-wheel drives, but with subsequent snow showers, the roads disappeared and not even the four-by-fours could cope with the soft, deep, drifts.

They tried spreading salt and grit. The snow melted where they scattered it and froze up overnight, creating ice sheets, more hazardous than the snow. Gradually the village disappeared beneath a silent shroud.

They had stores enough in the Lodge to easily last a month. They could probably eke them out for two, but if the snow lasted longer than that... They would be in the heart of winter by then, spring a long way off.

At least they could feed themselves for now. The livestock was another matter.

A few of the barns had bales of hay and sacks of bruised barley and oats left over from the previous year, but there had been no time for anyone to buy in feed for the coming winter before the disease struck. Besides which, getting to the barns was a problem in itself, let alone getting the feed to the animals.

Shaw looked to Ben for answers.

"We can't save them all," Ben told him, "and we can't shoot the ones we can't save - at least not all of them. Even if we did have enough bullets, we can't get to them."

Shaw knew it was true, but it didn't stop him feeling sick inside.

The highland cattle were hardy beasts, bred to withstand severe Scottish winters. They were good foragers, though whether even they'd be able to find anything to eat in this snow-bound land was doubtful. At any rate, they couldn't be brought inside.

"Guaranteed they'll get pneumonia if you try," Ben assured him. And so the cattle were left to fend for themselves. If they made it through the winter, they'd be bone bags come spring, but there was nothing else to be done.

The hens were already dead by the time they got to them. Either frozen to death outside the henhouses, or blocked inside and starved to death. No more fresh eggs, and none for the pot.

The sheep had no chance of surviving outside without extra feed, but as they couldn't feed and house them all, a dozen healthy specimens were picked out and put in Ben's barn. Of the rest, they slaughtered six.

When they'd been hung and butchered, they wrapped the meat in bin bags and buried it in the snow at the back of the Lodge. It was hard going, but they thought they were being smart, making use of the deep freezer nature had provided. Turned out, they'd got it wrong.

On blue sky days, despite being buried in the snow, the black-wrapped packages absorbed the sun's rays. There wasn't much heat, just enough to raise the temperature inside the parcels by a few degrees above freezing. Just enough for the meat to defrost and begin to decay.

Of course they didn't discover any of this until they unwrapped one of the packages and defrosted the refrozen meat. The stench of rotting mutton filled the kitchen. A tin of corned beef was stretched out between them that night, mashed through the potatoes to make hash.

The second parcel of mutton was the same. It took the third attempt before they figured their mistake.

The rest of the sheep were left outside in the snow to fend for themselves. Shaw wasn't sure how much better off the ones in the barn were. Perhaps all they were doing was prolonging their suffering.

They struggled to fetch the feed from the isolated barns. Jamie ditched a quad bike trying. Two of the sacks he'd been carrying were ripped in the crash, scattering the precious feed over the snow. He suffered a split lip and was black and blue down one side, but miraculously did not break any bones. Two days later, Robbie plunged the tractor into a deep drift, leaving them with no means of transport other than a slow trudge by foot. All they could do now was eke out the animal feed already stored in Ben's barn.

The strain of walking through the snow day in, day out, took its toll on Ben until, finally, Shaw insisted he stay in the Lodge. Now Darren accompanied him on the heavy trek to the barn to feed the sheep. They walked in silence, the creak of icy snow beneath their feet the only sound, the slate-grey sky matching their mood.

"It's going to get worse," Ben told them, before they left the Lodge. The twinkle had long gone from the old man's eyes, his mouth now set in a permanent grim line.

A small group of red deer, driven down from the hills by the weather, scattered as they approached. Starving, they'd been nibbling at the ice encrusted oats spilled when Jamie lost control of the quad.

Deafening bleating greeted them in the barn. The sheep already looking much leaner than when they'd brought them in. Shaw checked that the water was still running through the hose into the trough. They put out a couple of square bales of hay and trickled a thin trail of bruised barley along the feeder. The animals clambered over each other to get to it, butting heads, pushing in, mouths in the trough, gobbling up the grain. The only thing that mattered was getting something into their bellies. How long, Shaw wondered, before they were reduced to the same state?

In the first few days, when the snow was still a novelty, Elizabeth said maybe they were entering a new ice age. They'd laughed and teased her about hairy mammoths and sabre-toothed tigers, but no-one was laughing now.

The mood in the Lodge was muted. Aside from looking after the sheep, feeding themselves and keeping warm were the priorities. There were no more snowball fights, no long, chatty meals, and precious little laughter.

They dressed in layers of clothing raided from the wardrobes in the Lodge. Any fresh snow was cleared from the log pile every morning and a supply brought into the house. The fire in the living room and the range in the kitchen were kept going all day. The rest of the house was unheated. Elizabeth and Lucy doubled up in bed, wrapping themselves around hot water bottles and each other. Some of the others were sleeping in the living room again. Craving solitude, Shaw still went upstairs to bed where he slept fully clothed under a thick duvet, the dog snuggled beside him.

Of them all, it was Howard who seemed least affected by their predicament. If anything, he had flourished.

Marjory had sunk into herself. Though he'd never mentioned it, Shaw frequently smelt brandy on her breath. *Purely for medicinal purposes*, she joked, embarrassed when he walked in on her taking a large shot from a glass. At least she wasn't slugging it straight from the bottle. Yet.

He could see the attraction of alcohol himself, which was why he mostly avoided it. He doubted he'd have Marjory's self control. No, if he went down that route, a wee tipple here and there would not suffice. He would have to do it good and proper. He would lose himself in the bottle with the intention of never sobering up.

As Marjory deteriorated, Howard thrived. Without anyone noticing until it was a done deal, he gradually took charge of the kitchen. He turned out to be a surprisingly good cook so when the new regime was finally apparent, no-one complained.

Howard was now fully occupied and making himself useful. He discovered a latent talent for making bread and beamed at the praise the others bestowed upon him. He even laid off with the snidey comments.

His soups, stews and baking were a distraction from the daily battle for survival, and with a hot meal the only pleasurable thing they had to look forward to, he became something of a hero. In a strange way, Howard was now the glue holding them all together. Howard the Great. Howard the Good...

But no matter how hard Howard tried, Shaw could not shake off his sneaking suspicion of the man.

His thoughts were not pleasant and he had nothing concrete to base them on and so he kept them to himself, mulling them over at night when he was on his own, or at times like this, when he was with someone but they were both locked in their own silence.

Yes, Howard was feeding them and, given the circumstances, feeding them well. But Shaw very much doubted he was doing it for love of his fellow man. Howard had created a warm, cosy world for himself in the kitchen, and, given these lean days, his waistline remained suspiciously thick.

Shaw had visions of them all growing thinner and thinner, whilst Howard grew fatter and fatter. Him growing stronger, while they became weak. Howard picking them off one by one. Turning them into stews and pies. Roasting them, eating them, chewing on their bones, sucking out the marrow.

Christ Shaw, get a grip. It was the cold getting to him. The cold and the pathetic sight of the sheep locked up in the barn. It was also seeing Elizabeth and Lucy getting skinnier by the day. It was thinking about what it was going to be like for them in this hostile world. Wondering if they would get to grow up. Whether any of them had a chance. Thinking maybe losing himself in the bottle didn't seem like such a bad idea after all. That maybe the doctor had gotten it right. All she'd done was take a short-cut to where they were all heading anyway. *Bloody hell*, his feet were numb. The cold biting into his cheeks, nipping at his eyes.

It was snowing again. The trudge back from the barn an endurance test. Within minutes, the wind was up, whipping the snow into a blizzard. Leaning into each other, they stumbled on, finding their way by instinct. The Lodge invisible until they were almost in touching distance.

They stumbled into the front porch, brushing snow from their clothes, wiping their faces. Skin tingling, ringing from the cold.

They stamped their feet, shaking snow loose from their boots before going inside to the hall. They unzipped their jackets, shook them out, hung them up.

"Glad that's over," Darren said.

"Until tomorrow," Shaw replied. *And the day after that.* He kept that thought to himself. No point in spreading the misery.

His thoughts were riven by a high-pitched scream.

Inside! It came from inside. There was a Screamer in the Lodge!

43

Howard grabbed Lucy by the upper arms. She didn't put up any resistance.

"Thief," he roared into her face.

Her open mouth was a dark silent circle. Behind him, Elizabeth screamed. She screamed and screamed and screamed but the sound seemed to come from a long way off.

They were constantly in his kitchen, warming themselves beside his range, looking in his pots, poking around, pretending to help. But he knew what they were really up to.

He'd been watching them. Finally caught the little one red-handed. Grubby fingers wrapped around a freshly scrubbed carrot.

"Put that back," he bellowed.

She froze, carrot clutched in her hand. He snatched it from her, threw it into the sink to be rewashed. Grabbed her by the arms. He'd only meant to give her a ticking off, but the red mist descended. He shook her. Shook her like a rag doll. He shook her and he couldn't stop. The fear on her face... it just made him want to hurt her more. Shake her till her insides came loose. Shake her till her brain rattled. Shake the life out of her. One less mouth to feed. More to go round.

Suddenly, the sensation of moving backwards. Realising he'd been grabbed from behind. His hands involuntarily releasing the thief. Someone's arms around his chest like a steel band. Pulling tighter and tighter.

He struggled against his captor. Broke free. Swung around. Balling his fist. Punching him in the belly.

"Oof!"

A cartoon noise. All the funnier because it was Shaw he'd punched. Not such a big man now, doubled over with his lips all pursed up.

Double lucky. He'd caught the thief *and* he'd taken Shaw down a notch or two. Oh happy days.

The bastard came back at him. Smashed his knuckles into Howard's nose. Squelch and crunch of bone mashing into cartilage. Streaming eyes. Searing, blinding pain. He staggered back, clutching his gushing nose.

His vision clearing. Blurry image of Shaw. Raising his arm, creating a punch. A hand coming from behind him. Grabbing his arm.

Shaw spinning around, fist still raised. Looking for somewhere to land the punch. Looked like it was going to land on Darren but he pulled it back in time. Pity. Howard would like to have seen that. Would have taken the edge off his pain, seeing them all turn on each other. Rip each other to shreds.

It was not to be. Shaw spun back around to face Howard.

"*What were you doing?*"

His voice a crazy falsetto. Shaw was losing it. Ha, ha, ha. The others crowding into the kitchen behind him, faces agog. About to witness the demise of their leader.

Howard pressed a clean cloth against his nose, then calmly pulled out a chair and sat down.

He'd never been a physical man. The thought of pain terrified him. He'd spent his entire life, from school onwards, avoiding any situation in which he might get hurt. Now, in the space of a few short weeks, he'd had a chunk bitten out of his face and his nose broken by a punch.

There was no denying it - in both cases, the pain was extreme but, strangely enough, it wasn't all that bad. Turned out, that after all these years of slinking his way out of trouble, he could take the pain. Better still, not only could he take it - he could give it.

"I caught her stealing food."

Aware of all eyes on him, he dabbed at his nose, whilst gazing steadily at Shaw. *Feel the power.*

"What food?"

"A carrot."

"You attacked a child because she took a carrot?"

Shaw's eyes looked like they were about to explode out of his head.

"It doesn't matter what it was - the fact is that it was food meant for everyone."

There, that ought to do it. Thanks to him, they were getting three meals a day, but with the way he had to eke things out, no-one left the table feeling entirely sated. Wasn't quite the same for him of course. What with having to taste things as he went along. A nibble here, a soupcon there. Fairly took the edge off.

For the rest of them, there was always that little bit of hunger lingering on. And now he'd laid it out bare for them - the girl had virtually taken food out of their mouths. They would all have been that little bit hungrier if it wasn't for him. He wouldn't be surprised if they turned on her. Tore the greedy little bitch to pieces.

Two sharp strides and Shaw was standing over him. Filling his vision. Veins on his neck in bas-relief. A quiver running through the muscles on his face.

When he spoke, his voice was low, controlled. All traces of the outraged falsetto gone. He towered over Howard, anger emanating from his body, filling the room with its crackle.

Howard shrank back in his chair. He wasn't feeling the power any more.

"She stole it," he squeaked.

"It was a carrot, Howard. A carrot."

Disgust written all over Shaw's face. His eyes burning into Howard. Finally, he shook his head and turned away. He walked out of the kitchen, the mob parting for him like the Red Sea before Moses.

Howard looked at the rest of the group, his gaze going from face to face, seeking solace, but he found no comfort in their stony expressions. Even Alice's face had calcified. He shrivelled under their scrutiny, growing smaller by the second. He hardly noticed them drifting away until suddenly realising he was by himself.

He sat for a while, stricken with self-pity. Tears pricked at his eyes. He wiped them away with the back of his hand. Short, rough strokes. Punishing himself. His hand banged against the wound on his cheek, setting off a new pulse of throbbing pain.

He stood up, lurched to the sink, thinking to get himself a glass of water. He saw the carrot he had taken from the girl. Snatched it up, threw it on the floor. Stamped on it. It splattered underfoot. He stamped on it again. And again, and again.

"What are you doing?"

Alice standing in the doorway, a peculiar expression on her face.

He blushed, stammered an answer, tried to make light of the situation.

"Making carrot juice."

He smiled at her, demonstrating that it was a joke, but between his pulsating cheek and mashed up nose it felt all wrong on his face. Twisted.

Judging by the look she gave him, it looked that way too. He tried a different tack.

"How is the girl?"

Alice's eyes narrowed. "*Lucy* has got bruises on her arms

and she is terrified but other than that, I guess she'll be okay."

"I'm sorry," he said, his voice small. "I don't know what came over me."

They didn't exactly send him to Coventry, but no-one spoke to him unless they had to. His *good mornings* were greeted with non-committal grunts. His attempts at conversation rebuffed. His meals acknowledged with perfunctory thanks.

He had mocked them, loathed them, despised them, but he had done all those things from within the safety and comfort of the group. Now that they had shut him out, he felt cold and lonely and he desperately wanted to get back in.

The girl was the key. If she forgave him, everyone else would have to.

At first he tried to appease her with some treats he had squirreled away. Biscuits, a few squares of chocolate. She cringed from him like he was the bogeyman, hiding behind Elizabeth who glared at him with pure, adolescent hatred. Intuiting that it would not help his cause any, Howard resisted the urge to slap her. Perhaps a more roundabout method was required.

Darren had stopped Shaw from hitting Howard again, which in Howard's eyes, made him a reasonable man. Two reasonable men ought to be able to straighten things out. He waited until he could speak to him alone and made his pitch.

They had so few fresh vegetables left - what there was had to be eked out - shared by everyone. She had stolen food from them all. He had lost his temper. He realised he shouldn't have done what he did, but he'd been thinking about the group, and after all, the girl was fine. No real harm had been done.

The look of disgust on Darren's face as he spoke shocked him. Here he was, being reasonable, opening himself up, seeking a way forward, and he had been snubbed. To come in friendship and be treated thus was an outrage.

He slunk back to the kitchen, angry and humiliated. Fine, if that was the way they wanted it, they could have it. There would be no more friendly overtures from him. No more attempts at a rapprochement. From now on, it was him and them, and Howard was looking after Number One.

So, they didn't care about people helping themselves to food? Didn't give a damn about the precious few fresh vegetables they had left being used up? That being the case, why should he care? Why should he be the one doing all the eking? Let someone else have the responsibility. Let that bastard Shaw feed them.

He tossed carrots, turnip and potatoes into the sink and washed them under a stream of ice-cold water.

In an effort to discard as little as possible, he had been scrubbing vegetables where possible. Now he peeled them, the peelings curling from his knife deliberately thick and wasteful.

He dumped the peeled vegetables onto the big wooden chopping board and, disregarding the chopping knife he usually used, took a cleaver from the drawer.

One clean, satisfying swipe split the turnip in two. Howard smiled and brought it down again, and again and again, keeping time with the throbbing in his cheek.

"Oh, Howard, this looks delicious," Fat Old Nursie exclaimed.

"It's just a simple vegetable broth," he replied.

A dull throb persisted in his cheek but his rage had been vented on the chopping board as he reduced the vegetables to pulpy nothingness. He watched with interest as they tucked in before finally trying a tentative sip himself. Not too bad considering he'd had to make it from peelings.

"It's very good," Marjory said. "Has lots of body.

Don't you all think so?"

She looked round the table, eliciting a few mumbled words of assent. She gave Howard a too-bright smile. He managed a grimace in return. Taking this as a sign of encouragement, she began prattling on about soup she'd once eaten on holiday.

She was drunk, he soon realised. Dear old Nursie was way past the tipsy stage. Properly drunk, as in blotto, sozzled, sloshed, plastered, smashed. That explained her sudden loquaciousness, her misplaced sense of bonhomie - she had forgotten that he was Mr Big Bad. That she wasn't supposed to be talking to him.

He glanced around the table to see if any of the rest of them had noticed Nursie was in party mood. He guessed from their grim faces that it was only too apparent to one and all.

He encouraged her loose talk with little interjections - *Really? That's fascinating. Do tell me more.* And she did. She garbled all the way through the meagre meal, slurping her soup, laughing too hard and too long at things that weren't funny in the first place until finally, her laughing jag became a crying jag.

As both states involved various gulps, snorts and much heaving of her rounded shoulders, it took Howard several moments to register the change. When realisation dawned, he regarded the wailing woman with some distaste and more than a little amusement.

A smirk danced impudently across his lips as some of the others fluttered around her, embracing her, making soothing sounds, trying to calm the huge sobs wracking her body.

Nursie's bubble had finally burst.

44

Shaw sat in the kitchen in front of the range, the door open so that he could watch the embers. Toby lay at his feet, basking in the heat. He took another sip of the whisky he'd been nursing for the past half hour.

Everyone else was sleeping - either in the living room or upstairs in bed - but he couldn't settle. He thought the whisky might help. Funny that, because Marjory's brandy habit hadn't done her any favours. She'd not been a pretty sight when drunk. All tears and snot. His guess was her affiliation with the bottle was a long-standing affair.

He wished he could get pissed and forget it all. But what was the point - he'd only wake up the next day with a hangover and it would all still be there. There was no escape. No hopping on a plane or train. No getting into a car and driving away. Guilt had dragged him back to see his parents but this time he couldn't escape at the end of the visit.

Something touched his shoulder. He jumped like a prawn on a hotplate.

"Whoa, steady there."

"Bloody hell, Ben, you almost gave me a heart attack."

Shaw gave a small laugh, embarrassed by his jumpy nerves.

"Didn't mean to creep up on you like that." Toby's tail thumped lazily as Ben bent down to scratch her ear. "Mind if I join you?"

"Be my guest," Shaw said. "You want a drink?"

"Don't see why not."

Shaw fetched another glass, poured Ben a generous measure and topped up his own. They sat side by side, contemplating the fire.

"I was beginning to think we could do it," Shaw said. "Make a go of living here, I mean."

"It was looking good."

"It's all gone to hell now."

"Don't lose your faith yet."

"Faith in what - God? I've never been one for the church, Ben."

"Well that's between you and the man upstairs, but what I mean is, don't lose faith in yourself." Ben leaned towards Shaw. "It's looking grim, I'll give you that - but the only way any of these people here are going to survive is if you lead them ."

Shaw shook his head. "I didn't ask for that."

"You got it all the same - and you've done a good job up until now."

"Now I know you're kidding. Good job how? Take a look around you - we're falling apart."

"We'd be in a worse state if it wasn't for you."

"Persistent old sod, aren't you?"

"Yup."

"Persistent or not, if you're looking for a noble leader, you're looking in the wrong place."

"We don't need noble, we need you. You're smart, you're practical. There's a strength in you that gives the rest of us hope - and what we need more than anything right now is hope."

Ben swirled the remains of his whisky around the glass before swallowing it in one go.

"You want another?" Shaw asked.

"No, I'm going to hit the hay. I meant what I said about needing hope..."

Shaw regarded the man beside him. The man who had become his friend. There had been a vitality about him when they were out working on the croft together. A twinkle in his eye, good humour running through the age lines on his face. Now his face sagged and he looked worn. Like something had been sucked out of him these past few days.

"What's worrying you, Ben?" he asked.

Ben replied with a question of his own.

"Have you looked out of the window in the past hour or so?"

Shaw shook his head.

"I think we're in trouble, son."

There had been other blizzards. Short, frenzied outbursts, soon losing their vigour. This one was different. It didn't let up. It went on and on and on.

Individual snowflakes swirled close to the windows, beyond them there was nothing but blank white. Gradually the snow built up against the glass until finally, the world beyond the panes disappeared altogether.

Wind whooped, sighed and moaned around the eaves. Fetching in wood for the fire and stove was difficult. Getting to the barn to feed the sheep impossible.

They all moved back into the living room to sleep, huddling against each other for warmth. Despite their best efforts, the pipes finally froze up. Water was at a premium. Snow was loaded into buckets, pots, pans and brought into the Lodge to melt. The resulting water was then boiled before use.

Leftover washing water was used to fill the cisterns of the two toilets they kept in use, both of which were on the ground floor. Only two used, only two to be cleaned. To Lucy and Elizabeth's disgust, the rule was, if it's yellow, let it mellow. If it's brown, flush it down. Toilet paper was rationed. Food was rationed. Water was rationed.

Shaw allocated tasks every day. Cooking, cleaning, fetching logs, gathering snow, boiling water, filling the cisterns, keeping the fire and the stove going. Keeping busy. Keeping it together. But every day they grew hungrier, dirtier. Tempers frayed, jealousy flared. Despite his efforts, the group was turning on itself and still the snow fell.

One morning, tasked with fetching logs, Jamie opened the back door only to be faced with a wall of snow.

"Maybe we could tunnel through?" he said.

"We could try," Shaw dug his fingers into the drift, "but it's a lot of snow to shift and it's soft. I don't think we'd get far before it collapsed. We'll go out by the front and see if we can get round the side. If that doesn't work, we'll dig."

Jamie by the porch, feeding out rope as, happed up and roped up, Shaw led the way through the thick blizzard, followed by Robbie.

Staying within touching distance of the wall, they slowly waded through thigh-deep snow. With his arm fully stretched in front of him, Shaw could just see his hand through the whirling snow, and only then because he was wearing a fluorescent yellow glove.

The snow was packed more solidly at the gable end of the house and had frozen over. They were able to clamber on top of it and walk on the crust. Clinging to the wall, they made their way to the back of the Lodge. Shaw's heart sank as he turned the corner.

Snow was piled far above the lintel of the back door. It had to be twelve or fifteen feet deep. He took a few exploratory steps forward, but, as he'd feared, the snow here was soft. After a few steps he floundered, began sinking.

Robbie hauled him back to the wall.

"It's no use," Shaw said, raising his voice to be heard

over the wind.

They were never going to be able to dig down to the logs. He signalled for them to return. Robbie leading the way this time, they lumbered back through the blizzard.

The going, hard to begin with, got harder with every step Shaw took. Feet either slipping on ice or sinking into snow. Exposed skin on his face stinging. Legs heavy. Body heavy. Stumbling into each other. Rasping against the wall. All his thoughts focussed on making it back. Getting inside. Away from the biting wind, the searing cold. Trying not to think about what next and what after that. There would be time enough for that when he was inside.

Robbie turned to him. Yelled something. His words muffled, lost in the wind.

"What?" Shaw yelling back.

"The rope - it's gone slack."

Scraping against the wall, they struggled through the last few feet of snow to an empty porch, the inner door lying wide open, Jamie nowhere to be seen.

Shaw stumbled into the dark hall.

"Jamie?" he called out.

"Shaw - look out."

Jamie's voice. Shaw turned. Felt a sudden, intense flash of pain. Then nothing.

45

Screaming. Yelling. Feet pounding.

Shaw opened his eyes. He had been hit on the head. He sat up. Sent tentative fingers creeping round his scalp, feeling for damage. Tender. Bruised. A swelling egg. Nothing broken. His hat had cushioned the blow.

A commotion down the hall. He stood up. Staggered towards the noise. Still stunned. Trying to gear up. Trying to go faster. Trying to run. Bouncing off the walls. Unsteady.

His legs gave way. He slid down the wall, dizzy. Head pounding. Ahead of him, two figures grappled in the gloom. Robbie fighting Howard. No, Robbie fighting off Howard. Howard snarling and snapping. Robbie clumsy in his layers of clothing. The same layers protecting him from Howard's biting teeth.

Darren and Jamie came running from behind. Armed with golf clubs, they started laying into Howard. Beating him. He dodged them again and again, batting them off, grappling with Robbie. Using him as a shield. His strength bewildering. Darren finally got in a good one. Whacked Howard around the head.

The club crunched into Howard's temple. Snarling, Howard cast Robbie aside, turning the full force of his fury on Darren and Jamie.

Shaw yelled. "Don't let him bite you!"

Howard hadn't just lost the plot. He'd turned. He was one of them now.

Shaw tried to get to his feet. He had to help Darren and Jamie. Had to stop Howard. Hands came from behind. Helping him. Pulling him up. He glanced around. Alice and Marjory.

Marjory puffed sour breath on him. Tears streaming down her face. *She's got a secret stash.* The thought flashing through his mind. Already dismissing her.

He spoke to Alice.

"Get the .22 - quickly."

Alice already responding. "Don't forget the bullets," called at her retreating back.

Feeling steadier now, he pulled off his cumbersome jacket. Darren and Jamie were still fending off Howard. Robbie edging around him.

"Where are the girls?" Shaw snapped at Marjory. "Where's Ben?"

"We're here," Elizabeth's voice came from the bottom of the stairs. Lucy at her back.

"Get back up," he ordered. "You go with them," he told Marjory, "Lock yourselves in one of the bedrooms."

She turned to go, but Shaw grabbed her by the arm, hissed in her ear. "Pull yourself together."

Her face quivered.

"He got Ben," she said.

"Wha-"

Alice came back, thrust the .22 at Shaw. He released Marjory. Told her to go. She went. She went fast.

He opened the gun. Alice gave him the bullets. He loaded it, closed it, took off the safety.

"HOWARD!" he roared.

Howard's head snapped towards him. Blood ran down his face from the wound on his temple. He snarled, blood dripping from his mouth.

Shaw raised the gun.

"Move away boys," he said.

Howard distracted, Robbie sidled along the wall. Clubs still raised and keeping a wary watch on Howard, Darren and Jamie backed up to Shaw.

Shaw looked down the sights at Howard's pulped and twisted face. The bandage had peeled away from his cheek, revealing the raw, angry wound beneath.

Growling like a scrap yard dog, Howard took a step towards him.

Shaw increasing the pressure on the trigger.

"Don't make me do it Howard," Shaw said, already knowing that he had no choice. Howard had been a dead man walking since Kate Walker bit him.

Howard lunged. Shaw squeezed the trigger. The bullet struck Howard square between the eyes. He was dead before he hit the floor.

Shaw turned to Darren.

"Where's Ben?" he asked.

The living room had been ransacked. Furniture turned over, cushions ripped, curtains pulled down. Buckets of snow, sat in front of the fire for melting, were upturned.

The room was dim. It took Shaw a moment to locate Ben amid the chaos.

He was lying on the sodden rug in front of the fireplace. The fire had been doused by a bucket of slush. The room already chill.

Shaw knelt down beside him. There was a mass of swelling down one side of the old man's face, the eye black, puffed up, sealed closed. Shaw felt his carotid artery. Ben's good eye fluttered and opened.

"He's alive - Ben's alive - get Marjory," Shaw yelled.

Commotion in the background. Yelling, running feet.

Ben's lips moved. Shaw put his ear to Ben's mouth. There was a raspy intake of breath, then silence.

"I'm here, I'm here." Marjory bustling through the

chaos.

Shaw looked up at her.

"You're too late."

He saw the way her face crumpled, but he didn't care. He wanted to hurt her. Wanted to lash out. Swear, hit someone, blame somebody for the mess they were in. Marjory just happened to be first in line.

The others were there behind her, staring silently at the lamentation before them. Shaw cradling Ben's head. Marjory, tears welling in her eyes standing before them. The anger in Shaw's face.

They huddled together - Alice, Darren, Robbie, Elizabeth, Lucy - thin, pale, pathetic creatures, watching him from the shadows. They had no chance of surviving. None. It was hysterical they were even trying.

"And then there were eight," he said.

Nobody joined in with his laughter. Not one of them cracked a smile. They were wretched, the lot of them. Himself included.

His laughter died a sudden death.

"Where's Toby?" he asked.

He hadn't seen the dog since he'd come back inside.

He stood up.

"TOBY!"

He whistled. No panting. No pattering of paws. Nothing. He looked around the group.

"I haven't seen her," Elizabeth said.

They all shook their heads. A sickening sensation in Shaw's stomach.

He strode out of the room, along the hall, whistling and calling for the dog. His imagination in overdrive, thinking about the damage Howard could have inflicted on her.

The kitchen was as chaotic as the living room. Chairs overturned, crockery smashed. Soup covered the walls in a vomit splatter. Lentils, rice, flour and sugar had been spilled and strewn across the floor. Jars of jam and peanut butter smashed and ground underfoot.

Shaw called for the dog again. A whimper from the store. Shaw yanked the door open. The dog leapt at him.

"Whoa, whoa, girl," he said.

He stroked her, feeling along her body for any tenderness, any signs of damage. She was trembling all over, but otherwise seemed fine. She was lucky Howard was satisfied with locking her in the cupboard.

She licked his hands, licked his face, was all over him.

He gathered her into his arms. The anger he'd felt, the feelings of fear and bereavement and of utter helplessness, melted away as he stroked her and breathed in her dog smell.

The others came through, treading cautiously. He saw the fear on their faces and felt ashamed that they were afraid of him.

"I'm sorry," he said, his voice hoarse.

He did not know how they would respond, but they came to him. Hugged him, hugged each other, and Shaw realised and accepted that he was one of them. He belonged.

His anomalous sense of well-being lasted around twenty-five seconds. Peace, love and harmony. Yeah, right. The impromptu love-in was all very well and he hated to be the one to break up the party, but the truth was, they were living in a world of pain and there was one question above all others that needed to be asked.

"Did Howard bite anyone?" He looked round them. "Alice?"

She shook her head. He didn't come near me or the girls, or Marjory."

"Jamie?"

"Nah, he whacked me a couple of times, but no bites."

"Same here," Darren said.

"He didn't bit me either. What about you, Robbie?"

All eyes on Robbie.

"No. No, he didn't bite me."

"You sure?"

"Positive."

"Great, then we're all clear." Shaw grinned at them. "All we have to contend with now is no food, no water and no fuel. It'll be a breeze."

It wasn't funny, but they laughed anyway. When it got as bad as this, there was little else to do.

46

The wound was on his inner arm, just above the wrist. Robbie hadn't lied. Howard didn't bite him. Not really. The skin was barely broken. It wasn't what anyone would describe as a bite. Not a proper bite. More of a puncture wound. Tiny, red at the edges. No point in mentioning it. He didn't want any fuss. It hurt like hell though. Was kind of itchy and throbby at the same time.

He surreptitiously scratched at it through his sleeve. There was instant relief immediately followed by an increased desire to rub at it some more. He resisted. Didn't want to draw attention to himself. But the itch was driving him mad. He wanted to push up his sleeve and have a real go at it. Had the feeling that if he did, he wouldn't be able to stop. He'd scratch and scratch until he'd scratched right through his arm. Hell, it itched.

"Robbie?"

He jumped like he'd been caught with his hand in the biscuit barrel. Shaw staring at him.

"Yeah?"

"Want to give us a hand here?"

They wrapped the bodies tightly in sheets, carried them outside and laid them in the snow. There was no time for ceremony and burial would have to wait.

Back indoors, Robbie found the hammer Howard had used to attack Ben. The sight of a few strands of Ben's fine, white hair caught in the congealed blood on its head made his gorge rise. He kicked it under a sideboard.

Furniture was righted. The blood-stained, sodden rug rolled up and put outside beside the bodies. Wet ashes and sodden logs were cleared from the fireplace, a new fire set and lit. The buckets were refilled with snow for melting. The mess on the kitchen floor was swept and cleared. The splattered soup cleaned from the wall. A food inventory taken.

The potatoes, carrots, turnip and onions were in the store Toby had been locked in and had likewise mercifully escaped Howard's attention. The tinned goods were intact and some of the packets and plastic bottles had survived, but otherwise, his rampage had cost them dearly.

"Ketchup, ketchup," Alice said, "there's plenty of ketchup, but not much to put it on."

She was so thin, so fragile, the scar on her face stark against her pale skin. Robbie wanted to put his arms around her, protect her. Hold her close to him.

"It's as if he was trying to destroy any chance we had," Darren said, muscling in, as usual. He put a hand on her shoulder. Robbie willed her to shake it off. She didn't.

Most nights he fell easily into sleep, exhausted by the relentless physical activity required to keep them warm, watered and fed. But not this night. This night he lay awake, tormented by the throbbing itch in his arm. Tormented by the thought of how close he was to Alice. Tormented more by the fact that Darren lay on the floor between them.

Darren, always in the way, always with the jokes, always with the touching. Darren with his hand on her shoulder. His hand on her back. His hand on her arm. And her never, ever pulling away from him. Smiling at his stupid jokes, letting her hand brush against his. He hated Darren.

Didn't much like Shaw either. Not any more. Was always watching him. Frowning when he caught Robbie scratching his arm. It was his arm - he was entitled to scratch it. Wanted to scratch it now. But he wouldn't. Wasn't going to give into it. No matter how bad it got, he wouldn't give in.

He gave in.

He awoke to Elizabeth yelling.

She was standing at the window - pointing above the snow line.

"Blue sky, I can see the sun!"

Around him, the others roused themselves, and, one by one, shuffled bleary-eyed to the window. The blood on his scratched arm had dried during the night, crusting his sleeve to the wound, but at least the itchy throb had subsided.

He joined the others at the window. It was true - above the snow drift smudging against the window, they could see the sun rising in clear, blue sky.

A ripple of excitement ran through the group. A rash of smiles broke out on their pale faces. Darren put his arm around Alice's shoulders. Lucy bumped against his wounded arm, setting off the cycle of itching and throbbing again.

"Careful!" he snapped at her.

She immediately apologised, a startled look on her face. He felt a pang of guilt. He was Mr Nice, Mr Happy-to-help-out. He never snapped at anyone. Now everyone was getting on his nerves. Even Alice. Why was she so blind? Why didn't she just tell Darren to get lost?

Elizabeth and Lucy ran upstairs. The others followed, Robbie trudging up behind them. They looked out of the landing window. For endless days there had been nothing beyond the glass but rushing, whirling shades of white. Now they could see the village. A chance at last to get outside, go on a foray for supplies.

Darren had to stay at the Lodge with Elizabeth, Lucy and Marjory. The logs they had brought inside before the big blizzard were disappearing fast. With the snow all iced up, the stack outside was more out of reach than ever. Apart from boiling snow melt and fetching in fresh buckets of the stuff, which they now had to hack out with a hatchet, they were to scour the Lodge for wooden furniture they could break up and burn.

Robbie, on the other hand, was chosen to go on the expedition with Shaw, Jamie and Alice. He snickered as they waved goodbye to Darren and the others. This was his chance to get close to her without him getting in the way.

Their feet crunched satisfyingly over the hard, icy snow. The surface was uneven, the going slow, but it was good to be outside after being cooped up for so long. Makeshift sledges, fashioned from fish boxes, slithered on the ice behind them.

They had two targets - the hotel and the shop at the filling station. Their previous raid had made a dent in the hotel's supplies, but Howard had been picky - there was still plenty there for the taking.

Raiding the filling station was Robbie's idea. They'd be able to load up on crisps, confectionery, cereal bars and soft drinks. The idea of chocolate had caused a frisson of excitement - Alice almost swooned at the thought of it, smiling at him when he suggested it.

He had visions of the two of them giggling like kids as they emptied the shelves. Maybe sharing a Bounty or a packet of Maltesers between them. Yeah, Maltesers - he bet she was a Maltesers girl. He could see them now, popping the chocolate into each other's mouths. Laughing, teasing each other. The two of them alone together. It would almost be like having a date.

"I'll go with Alice," he said, when they got to the filling

station.

"No, you come to the hotel with me." Shaw said, "Jamie can go with Alice."

He protested, but Shaw insisted. He argued against the decision. Shaw was adamant. Robbie had to raise his voice to be heard but he wasn't shouting, nothing like it, but Alice - the way she looked at him you'd think he'd just kicked the dog.

He conceded. It wasn't like he had any choice. Even if he did get to go with her, it wouldn't be any good. She'd be annoyed with him. The mood would be spoilt. So Alice went off with Jamie and he trudged after Shaw and Toby.

The dog bounded about in the snow, leaping at little bits of ice Shaw kicked up. Bloody dog. He did feel like kicking it now.

His body flooded with hot shame. He'd never deliberately hurt an animal in his life, let alone kicked a dog. It was frustration doing it to him.

They went in through the front of the hotel this time. Past the lounge and the reception, through the back into the kitchen.

No wonder he was frustrated. He was so near to her for so much of the time, but they were never alone. He couldn't touch her. Well, he could try. He could do what Darren did. Casually lay his hand on her shoulder or waist. Brush his hand against hers. Press his leg to hers when they were at the table. He could do it, but he was scared. Scared that she would jerk away from him, brush him off. Reject him. Why couldn't she see that he loved her?

"You okay?"

He looked up, startled out of his thoughts. Shaw staring at him again. What was with the guy?

"Do you fancy me or something?"

"What?"

Shaw looking like he couldn't believe what he was

hearing. Then again, Robbie could hardly believe he'd said it. It just kind of slipped out. He was tempted to repeat himself, but Shaw's expression made him think better.

"I'm fine."

"You sure?"

"Yeah."

He turned away from Shaw. Began picking stuff off the shelves. Not looking at what he was taking. Not caring. Chucking anything and everything into the bin bag. Hating himself for sounding like a petulant schoolboy. Hating Shaw for making him feel that way. Who did he think he was anyway? Always calling the shots. Telling everybody what to do and when.

His arm started playing up again, the itch buried beneath layers of clothing. He looked around the kitchen, found a wooden spoon, stuck the handle up his sleeve and rubbed. Instant gratification. Until he stopped and the wound started screaming. So he rubbed some more, rubbing and rubbing and rubbing and he opened his eyes and Shaw was standing in front of him. Watching him. Not even pretending to be doing something else.

"Robbie?"

"I've got an itch, okay." He pulled out the spoon, threw it across the kitchen. It clattered across a stove top.

Shaw still staring at him.

"What?"

"I think we've got enough. Let's go." His voice annoyingly, disturbingly calm.

They tied the bags up and carried them out to the fish boxes, then began to haul them down to the filling station.

Alice and Jamie came out to meet them, grins on their faces, boxes already filled and ready to go.

"Looks like you two are on a chocolate high." Shaw grinned back at them.

"Don't worry - there's plenty there for everyone. We had to dig a path to the door, but once we got in it was great. We've got loads of goodies, plus a heap of other stuff - WD-40, matches, torches, batteries. What about you guys?"

"I think we did okay, eh Robbie?"

Robbie grunted in reply.

He was sandwiched between Alice and Jamie ahead of him, laughing and joking during the trek back, and Shaw following behind. Watching him. Always watching him. His back itching where Shaw's stare bored into his back. Arm itching, back itching. It was a torment.

The harsh lines of a scowl settled into his face like they were there for the long haul.

47

The days grew ever shorter, the nights longer. They huddled by the fire, feeding it chair legs, hacked up shelving, skirting boards. Some nights they talked, but increasingly, as darkness fell, it brought with it a sombre hush. They would stare at the flames, watch paint blister, peel and burn on the furniture they had sawn and chopped, until one by one, they bedded down for the night. Huddling into sleeping bags and quilts. Yearning for sleep to come quickly.

Often, too often for Shaw, hours would pass between him first closing his eyes and the merciful onset of sleep. They were active during the day. Sleep should not cheat him the way it did yet he faced too many hours of wakefulness with nothing to do but think. Think about what was, what had been and what yet might be.

Strangely enough, his thoughts of what had been rarely strayed further back than the death of Barry Bell. His life in the old world had already taken on a dreamlike quality. Thinking about it was like reading about something that had happened to someone else.

If it was like that for him, he wondered what it must be like for Lucy. Her memories would fade faster than his. Perhaps she would forget her old life altogether. Her parents, her family home, nothing more than a fading dream. Maybe it was for the best that this new world was the only one she would really know. Her new future would be all the less painful for her. If she survived.

There wouldn't have been much chance of that happening if the blizzard had gone on any longer. What would they have done to survive? How far would they have gone when the last of their food supplies had been eaten?

What would hunger and desperation have driven them to do?

He hoped they would never have to find out. In the meantime, though there was no sign of a thaw, blizzard season was, it seemed, over and there was food to be had.

After their first post-blizzard expedition to the hotel and filling station, they trampled a path to the village and began systematically raiding the houses they could gain access to for food, fuel and toilet paper. The path soon became grey from use. Made grimy by trodden-in coal dust. The coal dug out from bunkers, dragged back to the Lodge on sleds. Fed to the range to keep it going.

There was no running water anywhere, but the cisterns in the houses were still full. As they came upon them, they took it in turns to experience the luxury of a flushing toilet without having to fill it with used water first.

It was the last gasp of the old civilisation. With no running water, personal hygiene was a luxury long gone. They were down to the essentials of basic hygiene. They wore hats most of the time - inside as well as out. The men had beards. They all wore layers of clothing. As there was no spare water for washing down, and therefore no reason to strip, Shaw's body had been permanently clothed for weeks. He assumed the others were in the same state. In all likelihood, they stank, but as they all stank together, nobody commented on it.

They hardly ate like kings, but with the village now open to them, neither were they starving. For now that was enough, but during the long nights, with dawn still several hours away, questions about the future churned over in his mind.

They hadn't had time to plant anything for the coming year before the snow came. Growing weary of a diet supplemented by carrots and turnips was not a luxury they would have the following autumn.

Most of the livestock was dead. A few of the highland cows had been spotted moving around. They had survived thus far, whether they made it to the spring was another matter.

A forlorn trip to the barn confirmed what he already knew. The sheep were dead, their emaciated bodies a desolate sight. A testament to their failure. He was glad it was not something Ben had to witness.

They were eating now but there was a finite amount of food they could scavenge from the village. Even if they managed to scrape through the year, they would not have any spare stores to set by for next winter. He had wanted to do it before, but now they had no choice. Come the thaw, they would have to take their chances and head south. In the meantime, they did what they had to do to survive.

There had been no screaming through the night since the death of Molly MacAulay and so they went about the village without fear of being attacked. They raided houses, giving no thought to whose home they were in. They had long since become inured to the sight of corpses. A slippered foot sticking out from the end of a sofa or a dead body slumped on the floor hardly warranted a second glance.

Even Lucy was unperturbed by the dead, though in one house she did spend a few moments contemplating the sight of a cat lying dead beside an empty dish.

"Poor kitty," she muttered before going through the cupboards in search of food.

The cold, at once their enemy and friend, helped. The

houses were now effectively refrigeration units. The rank smell of purification no longer hung in the air as they went about their business.

The raiding parties teased each other about their hauls. Somewhere along the way, a game developed with points being awarded for items looted. Tinned prunes were at the bottom of the heap, garnering one point. Processed peas were worth two. A Fray Bentos steak pie, coming in its own pie dish and providing the group with freshly baked pastry, not to mention tasty gravy and meaty goodness, scored ten. It was the closest thing they got to fresh food out of a tin.

Bonus points were awarded for Pot Noodles and anything out of the norm, like chicken fillets or an all day breakfast in a tin.

Using the calendar on Darren's digital watch as a starting point, Elizabeth had been marking the days on a wall calendar in the kitchen. When she flipped the page over to December, she asked if they would be celebrating Christmas.

The idea took hold. In the midst of the dark winter, they had something to look forward to. Preparations began slowly, picking up as the month progressed.

Ten point food was put aside for Christmas Dinner. Boxes of decorations were scavenged from lofts. On Christmas Eve, they gathered around the fire to listen as Alice read Dickens' *A Christmas Carol* by candlelight. On the day itself, there was great excitement. Snow still had to be gathered, water boiled, the fire tended, but otherwise it was a day of fun and celebration.

They began with a game of Monopoly, playing with real money taken from tills at the shop, filling station and hotel, but the focus of the day was on the feast to come. For once, they would eat until they were sated.

They had a toast, glasses filled to the brim with wine or Coca cola according to preference.

"This was your idea, Elizabeth," Shaw said. "You should make the toast."

"Okay," she said, a wide smile on her face. She raised her glass of cola. "Here's to a Merry Christmas!"

"Merry Christmas!" they echoed.

Shaw took a long taste of wine. Today, he would let go a little.

Then it was onto the food. Soup to start with. Three tins of Granny's between them - two of Potato and Leek mixed with one of Scotch Broth - served with oatcakes.

This was followed by a buffet consisting two Fray Bentos Steak Pies, three tins of Grant's Minced Beef and Peas, one large tin of Ye Olde Oak Ham, two cans of hot dog sausages, Smash instant potatoes, tinned corn, tinned carrots, tinned peas and a jug of instant gravy.

After eating a bit of everything, Jamie sat back in his chair, holding his stomach. "I'm bursting," he groaned.

"You'll not be wanting any pudding then?" Marjory asked.

"Too right I will," he replied, to much laughter.

"Why don't we open the presents before pudding?" Alice suggested.

"Presents? We get presents too?" Jamie asked.

He wasn't the only one who looked surprised.

"Elizabeth, Lucy and I have a confession to make," Alice said. "We've been keeping some of our finds from you all - but it was done with the best motives."

Taking that as their cue, Elizabeth and Lucy left the kitchen, returning several minutes later with a bundle of gifts.

"Sorry about the wrapping paper," Elizabeth said, "it was all we could get at the shop."

She passed around parcels wrapped in brightly coloured paper proclaiming birthdays, engagements, weddings and the arrival of new babies.

The packages contained bars of chocolate and packets of fancy biscuits.

"We can have a midnight feast," Lucy said.

Shaw laughed along with everyone else, including Robbie, who had finally emerged from a persistent sulk. No doubt his good spirits were enhanced by the fact that he'd managed to get himself seated in between Alice and Darren, who had excused himself from the table.

He returned to the kitchen, a grin on his face. "I've got something for everyone as well. I thought we might try our luck with these," he said, throwing a pile of scratch cards into the middle of the table.

Everyone whooped and grabbed a card. It wasn't long before echoes of nothing here, ran around the table. Scraped cards were tossed aside, the pile on the table grew smaller.

"What a rip-off," Jamie said.

"No, wait a minute," Robbie said, "Yessssss." He punched the air. "I've got a winner. Ten thousand pounds."

Darren led the cheers.

"What are you going to do with it?" Jamie asked.

"Buy a car," Robbie grinned.

Pudding consisted of jelly and tinned fruit. Afterwards, there was hot chocolate and coffee. Shaw produced a bottle of Cointreau and a box of chocolates as his surprise contribution.

Despite everyone declaring how full they were, they sat at the table for a long time afterwards, drinking, nibbling at treats, chatting and laughing.

As he looked around the table, Shaw thought they looked genuinely happy. He felt happy himself. Yes, him, Shaw - happy! What a thought. Ha, sentimental fool that he was. Must be the drink getting to him. Well, let it get to him. It was a good feeling, getting slowly squiffed after such a long period of abstinence.

With the exception of Lucy and Elizabeth, they were all either tipsy or getting there. Jamie had screwed his face up at the wine, but was getting merry on a couple of tins of lager. Bless him.

Shaw raised his glass.

"To us and to getting plastered."

They laughed. It was a good sound. The best sound. He chinked his glass with Robbie's. "Good man," he said, grinning broadly at him.

Robbie grinned back. They were all happy. All one big happy family. Darren and Robbie like brothers. Darren leaned into Robbie. Told a joke, mucked it up, laughing before he got to the punch line.

Robbie stood up.

"Where you going?" Shaw asked him.

"Toilet."

"A man's gotta do what a man's gotta do." Shaw laughed, took a gulp of Cointreau then eyed the glass suspiciously. "This stuff's too sweet," he declared. He picked up his wine glass, drained it, banged it on the table. "More wine," he demanded. "Let's keep the red wine flowing."

Darren handed him a bottle, then moved into the empty seat beside Alice.

Shaw filled his glass.

"Keep the wine flowing," he laughed to himself. He looked across the table at Darren and Alice and raised his glass again.

"To young love."

"I'll drink to that." Marjory squealed as Darren kissed Alice lightly on the lips. "To young..."

"Whassup Marj?" Shaw asked, as her words tailed off.

He followed the direction of her gaze.

Robbie, standing in the doorway, a murderous look on his face.

48

She'd been beside him all through the meal. Their arms brushing against each other. Hands accidentally touching. The brief sensation of her skin on his. Filling each other's glasses. He knew she had feelings for him. It was there, in the way she looked at him. The way she smiled at him. Darren was nothing more than a distraction.

Darren, with his stupid jokes. Pretending to be such a nice guy. Everybody's friend. Well Robbie had the measure of him. Knew what he was really like. Sneaky. That's what Darren was, sneaky and sly. Worming his way round them all. Slithering around Alice. Knowing exactly what he was doing. Just the same as he'd known what he was doing when he grabbed Robbie's arm.

He'd done it deliberately. Setting off the itch and the *throb throb throbbing*. Just when he'd had it under control. Just when it had become a background pain, an irritation he could live with, Darren had to go digging his fingers into it. Bringing it to the foreground. *THROB THROB THROB.*

The room suddenly claustrophobic. Elizabeth's giggles stabbing his head. Marjory's drunken laughter setting his teeth on edge. Jamie shouting. Everyone talking at once. Being so loud, so happy. Darren sniggering and laughing.

Mocking his pain. Making Robbie want to punch him. Hit him hard. Hurt him.

He stood up. Said he was going to the toilet. But all he wanted to do was get away from them. Get away from them all. Except Alice. Not Alice. He loved Alice. Wanted her. Needed her.

He stood outside, in the cool hall. The party continuing without him. As if he'd never been there. Breathing in. Exhaling. Deep breaths. Nice and slow. Gritting his teeth against the urge to scratch. Knowing from bitter experience that the short term relief would only lead to an increasing spiral of pain and misery. He pulled his sleeve up. Letting the cold get to the wound. Thinking it would maybe settle down the itch. Thinking about going outside, plunging his arm into a bank of snow.

Hearing them in there. The cheers louder. Opening the door. Seeing *him* kissing *her*. Feeling the rage inside.

He ran at Darren, hit him in the face, knocking him from the chair. From the chair *Robbie* had been sitting in. Alice screamed. He didn't care. It was time this thing got sorted.

Darren on the floor, looking stupid, hand over his nose and mouth. He hadn't seen that one coming. None of them saw it coming. Not even Shaw. Pissed as a fart. Took his eye off the ball. Clueless. The lot of them.

He kicked Darren, caught him in the gut. Heard the *oof* of air being expelled. Darren doubling up. Robbie yelling.

"You're not laughing now!"

Alice still screaming. Why was she screaming? All of them screaming and yelling. The noise swirling around his head. Biting at him like a plague of midges. Darren was going to get it now. Robbie kicked. Kicked again.

It was dark when he woke up. He was on a bed. His head throbbed and his mouth was dry, his tongue thick and furry. He'd never been much of a drinker. Never had a hangover. He guessed he had one now. Maybe not just a hangover.

The back of his head was tender. Someone had hit him. They'd actually hit him. What the hell... It started to come back to him.

He'd lost it. Was kicking Darren. Everyone screaming and yelling. He groaned. Felt sick. They hated him. They all hated him. Alice hated him. He curled into a foetal position and wept.

He awoke to grey light. The sky had clouded over but there was no sign of snow. He was in the room he'd been sleeping in before they all moved back downstairs. He sat on the edge of the bed, the quilt wrapped around him, rubbing at the wound on his arm.

He'd tried the door - it wasn't locked. He could leave anytime he wanted. He opened it a crack. Heard the murmur of voices downstairs. Closed it again and sat on the bed, imprisoned by his own shame.

He couldn't face them. Couldn't stand the thought of facing them.

He could smell coffee.

They'd all be down there, drinking, eating, laughing and joking with each other, not caring about him. Glad that he wasn't with them, casting a pall over their happy time.

He'd ruined Christmas. Ruined it for little Lucy. Ruined it for all of them. Alice - how could he face her again?

"How's your wrist, Robbie?"

He jumped. Looked up. Alice, standing by the open door. He pulled the quilt over his arm.

"I didn't hear you come in."

Gabbling the words, his face burning up.

"Sorry," she said. "I didn't mean to startle you. I just wondered how you were and how your wrist is."

"What do you mean? There's nothing wrong with my

wrist."

"I've seen it, Robbie. We've all seen it."

He hung his head, unable to meet her gaze.

"Let me take a look."

He could hear her crossing the room towards him, old floorboards creaking beneath her feet. Her hand appeared, reaching out to him. He uncovered his wounded arm, still unable to look her in the face.

She held his arm, her touch gentle. Tears pricked at his eyes.

"Come to the light."

He stood up, letting her lead him to the window. He watched her as she peered at the wound. A few stray hairs wisped out from beneath her beanie. He longed to caress her face.

She looked up, catching him staring. His fading blush immediately reignited.

"It's a bite, isn't it?"

He pulled his arm away.

"Robbie, Howard bit you, didn't he?"

"It's hardly a bite," his voice defensive, "more of a scrape."

"Marjory will have to look at it."

"She didn't do Howard much good, did she?" Blurting the words, anger rising.

She turned away from him. She was going to leave him there, alone. He put his hand on her arm to stop her.

"Please - don't go."

She looked at his hand on her arm. Looked into his face, pity in her eyes. *Pity!* He didn't want pity. There was only one thing he wanted from her.

He tightened his grip and pushed her back against the wall. He leaned into her body, aroused and hungry for her.

"I love you Alice."

He kissed her hard on the mouth. Her lips were soft, his dry, rasping against hers. Ignoring her struggling against him, he pushed his free hand under her top, reaching up for her breast. He felt her nipple hard beneath the smooth fabric of her bra. He yanked the material down and tweaked her nipple between his fingers. His mouth was still clasped on hers as he came in his pants.

He gave a low moan and loosened his grasp on her arm. She immediately squirmed away from him, a look of horror on her face.

"What are you doing?"

Screaming in his face. Angry. Disgusted.

A babble of apology rose to his lips, but before he could get it out, she was gone. Fleeing downstairs. Back to them. Back to *him*.

He slumped onto the bed, head in hands. He was finished.

He thought they'd come. Stampeding up the stairs. Angry with him. Angry because he'd lied. Angry because he'd hit Darren and ruined Christmas. Angry because of what he'd done - tried to do - to Alice.

But they didn't come. No-one came. They had abandoned him.

He sat for a long time, not moving - not even to pull the quilt around his shoulders. He grew cold, his fingers numb, his mind numb.

Numb. No pain. No hurt. No humiliation. To be forever numb. Bliss.

It wasn't cold enough in the room. He would have to stir himself. Go downstairs. Walk out of the front door into the snow covered world beyond. Walk through the cold, white numbness until he could not walk any further. Until he fell and lay still in the snow.

He'd heard that hypothermia wasn't such a bad way to go. There was the initial cold, shivery stage, but beyond that there was warmth as you slipped into unconsciousness.

Making the decision gave him strength. He stood up, catching sight of himself in the bedroom mirror. He'd lost his hat. His hair hadn't been cut in months. It hung around his face, lank, lifeless. His face pale and spotty beneath it, eyes red-rimmed, pink from crying. No wonder Alice had spurned him.

He looked away and, treading lightly, walked to the door. It stood ajar, the way Alice had left it. He stepped into hall and listened.

Voices, coming from the kitchen. Everybody busy. No-one thinking about him.

Quiet as snow falling on snow, he walked down the stairs. He crossed the hall to the front door, not stopping to collect anything on the way. He hardly even existed. There was nothing he needed. Not now.

"Going somewhere?"

He jumped. Heart pounding, he turned.

Shaw. Standing there, watching him.

49

"Felt like taking a walk."

"It's pretty chilly out there."

Robbie shrugged his thin shoulders. "No matter."

He opened the door.

Shaw closed the gap between them, spoke quietly, his lips close to Robbie's ear.

"I can't let you do this."

Robbie tried to push Shaw away, but Shaw stayed close and tight. Put his hand on the door, closed it.

Robbie turned to Shaw, a scowl on his face, but there were tears in his eyes. He looked so young, so pathetic. Shaw put a hand on his shoulder, half expecting him to pull away. Instead he let out a sob, leaned into Shaw and cried like a baby. When the worst of it was over, Shaw led him through to the kitchen. Marjory was boiling snow melt on the range, decanting the boiled water into jugs. Elizabeth was cleaning. Lucy sitting at the table, drawing. Sometimes a kid had to be a kid.

Shaw told Robbie to sit down. He sat. An obedient puppy. Who knew how long that would last? Shaw had watched Robbie tugging at his sleeve, rubbing at his arm, had long suspected he had been bit. Now he knew for sure, but what to do about it was another matter.

Lucy slid a sheet of paper across the table to Robbie.

"This is for you," she said, "because you're the best at

playing games."

Robbie looked at the drawing, mustered a smile. "Thank you."

"Shaw said you weren't well, and that's why you hit Darren. Do you feel better now?"

"A bit," Robbie replied.

"Good," Lucy said. "We don't want you to end up like Howard."

Shaw stared at her. *Out of the mouths of babes.*

Unaware of the thick silence that had taken a sudden stranglehold on the room, the girl had already turned her attention to another drawing.

"What can we do?" Shaw asked.

Marjory looked at him. Even in the dim light of the hall he could see how puffy her eyes were, how slack the skin on her face.

"Sedate him?" she suggested.

"Are you kidding me?"

"No, not really. If he's got what Howard had, then I don't know what else there is to be done. I don't have a magic cure I'm keeping from you. There's only so much I can do. I'm a retired nurse, not a miracle worker."

Her voice increasingly querulous through the tirade.

"Marjory, have you been drinking?"

She glared at him.

"Don't you take that tone with me."

He felt like grabbing her and giving her a shake. Instead, he stared her down. She caved in, looked away from him, muttering.

"Just a couple to take the edge off."

"Bloody hell Marjory, you've got to keep it together."

She turned on him. "You were drinking yesterday! We were all drinking yesterday."

"Yes, and look what happened."

"That wasn't my fault."

"Maybe not, but you're sure as hell not helping now."

Their voices rising in anger.

"I can't give you what you want - can't you see that?" Marjory yelling at Shaw. "You keep asking me to fix everything, but I can't do it. The boy is already dead - you know it, I know it. Let's face it, we're all as good as dead - and you wonder why I drink?"

"STOP SCREAMING AT EACH OTHER!"

Elizabeth, standing in the kitchen doorway, shouting at them, crying. Lucy clinging to her. Robbie behind them, eyes lost in the dark hollows of his face.

"You should have let me go," he said.

Shaw shook his head. "No, not like that."

"How then?"

Shaw didn't have an answer.

The porch door opened. Toby appeared, panting, wagging her tail. Alice, Darren and Jamie piling in behind her. Their laughter brought to a sharp halt when they saw the scene before them.

"What's going on?" Alice, looking between them.

"I've got the disease," Robbie said. "Everyone knows it. According to Marjory, I'm as good as dead already."

"She's been drinking," Shaw said. "Don't listen to her."

"In *vino veritas*," Marjory said.

Shaw told her to shut up. She ignored him.

"In wine there is truth," she said. "Though in my case, it was the dregs from the Cointreau bottle."

"Will you shut up!" Shaw, exasperated.

"Is he safe to be around?" Darren asked.

"Safer than you, you sneaky shit!" Robbie spat at him.

"I'm not the one behaving like a lunatic," Darren snarled.

"That's enough," Shaw barking over them. "Darren, go to the kitchen."

"But-"

"Just do it. Robbie, come with me. The rest of you - I don't know - do what you like."

Shaw hustled Robbie into the living room, closed the door behind them. He threw a few chopped-up chair legs on the fire, warmed himself in front of it. He could hear the muted tones of the others in the kitchen.

"I hate him!" Robbie blurted.

"Calm down," Shaw said.

"I am calm. But I still hate him."

Shaw watched as Robbie gave one of the sofas a half-hearted kick. He felt sorry for the kid. All diseased up and broken-hearted to boot.

"She doesn't think of you that way," he said, his voice gentle as he could make it.

Robbie slumped. Bravado gone.

"I know," staring at the carpet. "I'm like a brother to her. That's what she said." He looked up at Shaw. "What are you going to do with me?"

"During the day, we'll watch you. Keep an eye on you, take care of you."

"And at night?"

"Make sure you're warm and comfortable..."

"And?"

"Lock you in your room. I'm sorry."

"It's okay. If Marjory had her way she'd put me down."

"Don't pay any attention to her - she's... not coping."

"Lost the plot, more like."

Robbie gave him a watery smile. Shaw did his best to return it. Truth was, he didn't feel much like smiling.

"Well," he said, "if she hasn't lost it already, she's well on her way."

"Aren't we all?"

"Maybe."

They stood in silence for a few moments. Shaw still by the fire, Robbie scuffing his toes against the sofa.

"Shaw?"

"Yeah?"

"Why are we even trying?"

"I don't know," Shaw replied truthfully. "Maybe it's

because there's nothing else we can do."

They gave him a hot water bottle and an extra quilt for warmth, a piss bucket, a jug half-filled with water and a glass, a hurricane lamp and a box of matches.

"You be okay?" Shaw asked.

"I'll be fine," Robbie replied.

"You know we've got to do this, right?"

"I know."

"See you in the morning."

"See you."

Shaw closed the door on Robbie and locked it.

"You okay?" Darren asked him when he walked into the living room.

"About as good as can be expected," he replied.

"It doesn't seem right," Alice said. "Locking him up like that."

"There's nothing else we can do - if we let him sleep in here and he turns in the night, we'd be dead before we woke up," Shaw said.

"I know that. I understand - but it still doesn't feel right."

"Have you got any better ideas? What do you want me to do - go up and shoot him right now?"

Alice's face crumpled.

"Steady on, Shaw," Darren said.

Shaw held his palms up. "I know - I'm sorry - Alice, really I am."

"It's okay," she said. "It's been a long day."

The mood in the room was subdued as they settled down for the night. The excitement of the build-up to Christmas no more than a disintegrating memory.

Sleep came quickly to Shaw that night. He gave himself willingly to it. He woke once, during the night. There was a brief moment - a split second before he opened his eyes

- when he was back before it all happened. Lying in his own bed, on the other side of the world, the people he loved close by him. Then it was gone. He wasn't there - he was here, in his new reality. Lying on the floor, in the Lodge. At least Marjory wasn't snoring. The God of Small Mercies must be smiling on them. He rolled over and went back to sleep.

"Where's Marjory?"
    Lucy, looking down at him.
    Shaw rubbed the sleep from his face.
    "I don't know. Have you checked the kitchen?"
    "She's not there."
    "Maybe she's in the bathroom," sitting up, coming to.
    "She's not there either."
    He stood up. "Why don't you go and have another look."
    She ran off, taking the dog with her.
    Shaw was still rubbing the crick in his neck when Lucy returned.
    "Marjory's gone," she said.

50

Shaw rapped on the bedroom door.

"You okay, Robbie? I'm opening up now."

No reply. Probably still sleeping, rolled up in his double duvets, wrapped against the cold. Everyone else was scouring the Lodge for Marjory. Maybe she'd taken a fancy to sleeping in a proper bed herself. Who knew what was going on in her drink-addled head? Once he'd got Robbie roused, they'd join the search for her.

He turned the key. The copper tang of blood hit him as soon as he opened the door. He stared at the blood-soaked bed.

"Oh no," he said quietly. "Oh no, Robbie."

He wasn't wrapped up all cosy like. He was lying on his back, across the bed, arms splayed out. The sleeve on his wounded arm pushed up to the elbow. The wound wiped out by a deep gouge running from his wrist, half-way to his elbow. There were cuts on the fingers of his other hand from holding the broken glass he'd used to cut himself.

Knowing it was way too late, Shaw felt for a pulse in Robbie's neck. His skin was cold to the touch, the beat of his heart long gone, its last act to pump the blood out of his arm, over the bed.

He should have let the poor bastard walk out into the snow. He'd prefer to freeze to death himself than go like this. But he had taken that choice away from Robbie and now he was going to have to live with that knowledge. He rested the back of his hand against Robbie's cold cheek.

"I'm sorry," he said.

"Be careful."

He turned. Alice.

"Don't get any blood on you," she said. "If it gets into any cuts..."

Shaw took his hand away from Robbie's face. Unconsciously stepped back from the bed.

"Poor Robbie," she said.

"It's my fault."

"You didn't bite him, you didn't infect him."

"No, but I could have let him walk out yesterday."

"Really, could you have let him go like that, knowing he would die out there, alone?"

Shaw shook his head. "No, but he died alone anyway."

She sighed. "Maybe it's better this way."

He looked at her. The moment stretched between them.

"Maybe it is," he finally said. Then, "Any sign of Marjory?"

"She's not here and her coat and boots have gone."

Shaw closed the door behind him. The dead didn't get up and walk around. Robbie wasn't going anywhere. They could take care of the body later. Right now, they were more concerned with the living. What was left of them.

He went downstairs with Alice and called everyone to the kitchen.

"Robbie's dead."

The words hung in the air awhile, fat, heavy, ripe.

"How?" Elizabeth finally asked.

"He cut his wrist," Shaw said. "Bled to death."

He saw no reason to be other than truthful. They were

all just going to have to suck it up. Himself included.

"Which wrist did he cut?" Lucy asked. Shaw stared at her. "Was it the one with the bite on it?"

"Yes, it was," Shaw replied. "Why do you ask?"

"Maybe he didn't mean to kill himself. Maybe he was trying to get rid of the itch. He was always scratching it."

"Maybe he was," Shaw said.

"So he didn't mean to kill himself then," Alice said. "It was an accident. A tragic accident."

She squeezed Shaw's arm. It was a good try. He appreciated the sentiment, but didn't take much comfort from it.

"Accident or not, Robbie is dead, but we're still here, and right now we've got a problem to deal with."

"Marjory," Darren said.

"Marjory," Shaw agreed.

"What we gonna do," Jamie asked, "send search parties round the village?"

"I don't think there's any need for that," Shaw replied, "I've got a good idea of where she might be."

"Yeah, me too." Darren said. "She's in the bar, isn't she?"

Shaw took Alice and Darren with him. They walked in silence. He didn't know what Alice and Darren were thinking about, but his mind was on Robbie. He couldn't help but think he'd let the boy down.

They entered the bar cautiously. First, it was the old pub smells. A little more dusty, a little fainter, but hanging on in there.

Then it was the new smell. The fresh smell. Foul and unmistakable.

Brandy bottle on its side on the bar, contents pooling around a half-filled glass. Marjory, on the floor, beside an overturned barstool. Her head broken. Cracked against the brass foot rail. See the smudge on the dull metal? A smear of blood, a scrap of skin, a few hairs. No shit Sherlock.

Her glassy eyes staring at the bottom of the bar. At the foot scuffs, the dust bunnies, the little mounds of sticky grime that gathered where bar met floor.

Shaw laughed.

Alice stared at him, appalled.

Darren screwed his face up against the smell.

"Her bowels opened when she died." Shaw informed them. "Her bladder too. Happens all the time. Perfectly natural. She died lying in her own pish. What a way to go. Good old Marjory."

"Stop it," Alice told him.

"Why?" Shaw asked. "It's what she would have wanted."

"You're being horrible."

"Am I?"

"You know you are. It's not like you."

"How would you know that? Maybe this is exactly like me." Needling her. not caring.

"Shaw, take it easy, man."

"Why don't you kiddiewinks toddle on back to the Lodge?"

"What are you going to do?" Darren asked.

"I'm going to stay here with the dead people and the ghosts and raise a glass to good old pissy-pants Marjory."

"Please, Shaw." Alice, pleading.

"Come on, Alice." Darren with his hand on her arm. "Leave him."

"Good lad," Shaw said. "Just do one thing for me."

"What?"

"Look after the dog."

Darren nodded, pulled Alice to the door. She opened her mouth to speak. Shaw raised a finger to his lips.

"Hush now," he said.

He turned to face the gantry, the sick smile on his face reflected on dusty mirrors, as the door banged behind them. Yeah, he was just going to have to suck it up. Robbie with his gouged arm, and all the rest of it. Suck it up, Shaw.

He took a bottle of Highland Park from the top shelf. Poured himself a large one. Swallowed it, relishing the warm trail it blazed down his throat.

He looked down at Marjory, decided he didn't fancy her company after all. Nor that of Kate Walker, lying in her heap by the pool table.

He picked up the bottle and took it through to the residents lounge.

"This'll do," he said aloud.

He selected a few bottles from the bar. Lined them up on a table by a comfy chair and settled himself down for a bender.

Days and nights blended. He drank in the dark. Drank in the murky light. Passed out. Dozed off. Woke up. Drank. The fire fairy came and lit a fire in the hearth. Left a pile of sticks beside it. The heat was good. He tossed a few sticks on. Forgot about it. Woke up in the cold, but the fire fairy came again. Life was a peach.

The food fairy dropped by. Left him a flask of stew. Might have been hot once. He ate it cold, dripping it down his front, mashing it into his mouth. Bored with the effort of chewing after a few mouthfuls.

He put time, energy and effort into breaking the cigarette machine open. Lit a cigarette. His first for five years. Sucked in the smoke. Coughed once, twice, got the nicotine buzz, sucked again. No better time to take up an old habit. Blowing smoke rings at the ceiling. Ash spilling down his front.

Time oozed on by. Opened his eyes once to see two Alices in front of him. He said hello to both of them, passed out again.

Sometimes he ate the food the food fairy left. Mostly he

didn't. Felt peckish one time and had himself a feast of salted peanuts and pork scratchings. Gave him a hellish thirst. Took a couple of tins of lager to slake it. Fell asleep in a nest of rustling packets and crumbs of fried pork fat but when he woke up they were all gone.

The cleaning fairy had been.

The fairies never spoke to him. Until one day -

"Shaw! Wake up!"

Same words over and over again. Shaking his shoulder. Pulling and tugging at him. *Wakeup-wakeup-wakeup-wakeup-wakeup-wakeup-wakeup-wakeup-wakeup-wakeup-wakeup-wakeup-* Until, bleary eyed, he woke up.

They were standing in a semi-circle. All of them staring at him. Toby licked his hand. He scratched her ear.

"Good girl."

A grin hatching unnaturally on his face.

"Shaw?"

He looked up. Had forgot they were there.

Darren speaking to him.

"The snow. It's melting."

51

The thaw announced its arrival by seeping beneath the front door. Snow melt puddled across the tiled floor of the porch, soaking into the hall carpet beyond. The frozen world, though harsh, had at least given the impression of being clean and crisp. Now it became a quagmire.

Melting snow bloated the ground, turning it to bog. What had lain hidden for so long was now revealed. The shed roof had caved in under the weight of the snow, the radio destroyed in the wreckage. Frozen sheep carcasses were exposed, rotting as they thawed. The bodies of Ben, Howard and Robbie, were released from their icy preserves and now lay in mucky slush.

Beneath a top layer of water-logged mud, the earth was still iron hard. Burial would have to wait. Meantime the bodies decayed within their stained shrouds.

Miraculously, though they were down to the bones of their haunches, several highland cows had survived the snows. Even more astonishing, someway, somehow, a few scraggy sheep had also hung onto life. As soon as it was possible to do so, gates were opened to allow the animals freedom to roam in search of food.

Houses previously cut off by deep drifts of snow, became accessible, but the bodies entombed there were now rapidly decaying, filling the homes with foul stenches.

Foraging for food and other supplies became a dirty job.

As the group battled to stay warm they had thought the snow their enemy. Now they floundered in a wet world, with a new set of hazards to be overcome.

Mould and mildew crept into the Lodge. The temperature had risen but perpetual dampness chilled them to the bone. Despite their best efforts, mud was trailed inside. It was impossible to keep it at bay.

Shaw opened out a map on the kitchen table.

"We head south," he said.

He had returned two days after the thaw began. When he went back, he went back clean and he went back sober.

His regeneration began with a pair of scissors he found in reception. After trimming his beard as close as possible to his face, he shed his filthy clothes. Using icy water from a toilet cistern in one of the guest bedrooms, he scrubbed himself down before dressing in clean clothes scavenged from the staff quarters. He was welcomed at the Lodge with teary smiles and open arms.

"Where to?" Darren asked.

"We need to find somewhere we can make a go of things - grow food, raise livestock. It's the only way ahead for us. We can't keep living on what was left behind. Sooner or later it's all going to turn bad or run out."

"We need a place with good resources," Alice said. "A clean water supply, fertile ground, somewhere to live." She traced a route on the map as she spoke.

"We need to get south of Drumochter Pass - into Perthshire. Plenty of fertile land down there and a better climate."

"Okay," Shaw said. "We can check things out as we go. You never know - there might be a group we can join forces with."

"Maybe in Ullapool," Darren said.

"Possibly," Shaw replied. "Or, for all we know, they've got things organised in Inverness. We've been cut off up here - could be the rest of the world is getting back on its feet. If we don't find anything feasible on the way, we'll push on to Perthshire."

Excited by the prospect of leaving the death and misery of the village behind, the group prepared for their exodus. They filled their fuel tanks with red diesel taken from barns. Every day, Shaw drove out of the village in Howard's Range Rover. Every day going a little further, testing the road. Checking out the high ground.

Then one day, with a thin, watery sun struggling valiantly above him, he returned to the Lodge with a smile on his face.

"We go tomorrow," he announced.

It was sometime near the start of February.

52

They travelled in two vehicles. Elizabeth, Lucy and the dog rode in the Range Rover with Shaw. Alice, Darren and Jamie following in a pick-up.

Neither of the girls showed any sign of being upset at leaving. They seemed just as eager as Shaw to get away. He pressed his foot on the accelerator as they passed the last house. He had no idea what was ahead of them, but he was glad to be leaving the village and its ghosts behind.

His mood lifted as he drove. It felt good to be moving. Patches of ice lurked in shadowed spots. Pot holes had erupted, road edges crumbled, but the going was better than he had dared to hope. They passed vehicles, parked haphazardly on the side of the road, catching glimpses of long-dead drivers slumped over steering wheels, but they were few and far between.

The chatter in the vehicle dried up, the mood dipping as they passed through a desolate hamlet. Two ponies lay dead in a muddy field, coats matted, ribs jutting. Crofts were littered with the carcasses of dead cows and sheep. Of human life, there was no sign.

"Maybe we're the last ones alive on the planet," Elizabeth said, in an unwitting echo of Shaw's own thoughts.

"Maybe there will be someone in Ullapool," Lucy said.

"Maybe," Shaw said, thinking surely someone there had survived. Maybe even a decent sized group of them.

Perched on the coast, Ardmair was another dead hamlet. They drove by a line of holiday homes, hollow sentinels looking over the pebble beach, empty save for a pair of oystercatchers.

The road twisted up and over the hilly landscape until finally they were on the last climb. At the top of this steep hill, they would see Ullapool, with its many resources, laid out before them. Soon, they would know whether anyone there had survived.

"What's that?"

Elizabeth, pointing at the bend near the top of the hill.

Shaw peered ahead, trying to make sense of what he was seeing.

"It's a barricade. A barricade!" He grinned.

"Why are you smiling?" she asked.

"A barricade can only mean one thing," he said, "Survivors. Not Screamers - real people. Uninfected people."

He drove to within a few metres of the obstruction before pulling over and getting out to examine it.

Right on the bend, just below the peak of the hill, it filled the width of the road, flanked on one side by a sheer drop to the valley below and on the other by a steep, gorse-covered bank. It was a serious bit of work - a deep wall of tangled metal and wood, made up of cars, farm machinery, shopping trolleys, bits of fencing, gates, doors, layered with strata of unidentifiable heavy objects. It would take a tank to plough through it.

The others gathered close by.

"Can we get through?" Jamie asked.

"We can give it a try," Shaw replied. "HELLO - IS ANYONE THERE?" he hollered at the blockade.

No response. He tried again. This time, he got an answer.

"Move away," a voice called. "Go back to your vehicles and leave."

The tone of the voice was as unwelcoming as the words, but Shaw was delighted to hear it.

"We're not alone," he said to the others.

"They don't sound too friendly," Darren said.

"They're suspicious, that's all." Shaw said.

"WE COME IN PEACE." Jamie yelled.

Darren punched him on the arm. "Idiot. Why didn't you ask to be taken to their leader?"

"Move away," the voice repeated. "Go back to your vehicles and leave."

"You're the first survivors we've come across," Shaw called.

"LEAVE NOW." A different voice.

"Maybe they think we're Screamers," Darren said.

"We're not infected," Shaw called. "We aren't crazy, we're not going to hurt anyone. We want to help."

"Get in your vehicles." The first voice again.

"We can work together," Shaw called.

He couldn't blame them for being suspicious - maybe they'd had a whole load of Screamer attacks - but once they realised that they were good guys, they'd surely welcome them in.

"*BLOODY HELL!*" Darren screamed as the first bullet whizzed over his head. The second whistled by Shaw's ear.

"*RUN!*" Shaw yelled. No-one had to be told twice.

He clambered into the Range Rover, ear ringing from the shot. One smart three-point-turn later, he was pelting down the hill, behind the pick-up. They drove back over the next hill, out of range, out of sight, before pulling over beside the pebble beach at Ardmair.

They got out of the vehicles, staring at each other, faces still registering shock.

"I guess Ullapool's off the agenda," Jamie said.

"Looks like it," Shaw replied.

A snort of laughter erupted from inside him. The others looked at him as though he was mad. Maybe it was shock, maybe he'd finally lost the plot. Whatever it was, once the laughter got a hold of him, it wasn't letting go. It shook him loose from the inside out.

Jamie cracked first. Started giggling, pointing at Shaw. Pretty soon the rest of them were infected. Standing, by the side of the road, hooting and howling like getting shot at was the funniest thing in the world.

53

With no other choice, they retraced their route back north until they came to Ledmore junction, from where they picked up the route going east across country.

The single track twisted and turned through dark forest. Several times they stopped to clear fallen branches from the road. It was time consuming work and the day was short. With the sun low in the sky, Shaw pulled into a picnic spot and suggested setting up camp for the night.

There were few houses in the area and none close by. The likelihood of Screamers stumbling upon them was remote. There were tables and benches, a barbecue pit and a stream nearby.

"Nice," Darren said, looking around. "All mod cons."

"I've just been in there," Alice pointed at the wooden building behind her, "There's a certificate on the wall - Loo of the Year Award! There's running water, soap, toilet paper and - the toilets flush!"

"Loo of the Year," Jamie grinned, "This place is pure luxury."

They foraged for dead wood and built a big fire for warmth and another in the barbecue pit for cooking. They dined on hot dog sausages and baked beans, made smoky by the fire, washing the food down with hot, sweet, black tea.

Lucy, being the only one small enough to do so comfortably, slept in a sleeping bag across the back seat of the car. The others unrolled bed mats around the fire and climbed into sleeping bags.

They woke with the cold light of dawn. The fire had long since burnt out. Shaw busied himself lighting a new one in the barbecue pit. No matter what lay in store for them, they could at least start the day with a hot breakfast.

A rummage in the back of the pick-up produced a tin of corned beef and a couple of cans of boiled potatoes. While the others roused themselves and began packing up camp, he sliced, fried, clashed the pan.

"I love corned beef hash," Jamie said, when they sat down at one of the picnic tables to eat.

"Food of the Gods," Darren agreed.

"What's the plan?" Alice asked, as they finished eating. "Are we going to check out Inverness?"

"After what happened at Ullapool?" Jamie said.

"We'll take a look," Shaw said. "We're going that way anyway. If we don't like what we see, we push on."

54

They viewed the city from the other side of the Kessock Bridge. The drive down had been uneventful. A few more fallen branches on the road. Nothing they couldn't handle. Wrecked cars. Burnt out cars. Nothing blocking the road. Bodies lying in the street in a few of the small villages they passed through, soft tissue rotted, bones exposed. Dead livestock in fields. Death, decay, dereliction. Same old, same old.

"Anything?" Darren asked.

Alice handed him the binoculars. "Looks like the whole city's been on fire," Alice said.

Shaw peered through the rifle sight at collapsed roofs, blackened buildings broken windows. Looked like there had been a riot.

"Nothing's moving," Darren said.

"The road looks clear enough," Shaw scanned what he could see of the dual carriageway on the other side of the bridge. "There's a few abandoned cars, but it looks like there's plenty of space to get around them."

"At least there aren't any barriers," Jamie said.

"Not that I can see," Shaw said.

"What do you think?" Alice asked. "Do we go into the city or head south?"

"Could be some good supplies there." Darren suggested.

"If they haven't all been burnt or looted already," Alice said.

"There might be Screamers," Elizabeth said. "Lots of them."

"Not to mention all the dead bodies," Alice said. "It will be pretty rank, don't you think?"

"What do you think, Shaw?" Jamie asked.

Shaw looked up from the rifle sight. "I don't like the look of it - I say we head south, but let's not take any chances. Jamie - you ride shotgun with me. Darren, you do the same for Alice. You girls," he said to Elizabeth and Lucy, "Stay low in the back."

They nodded. Shaw handed the gun to Jamie.

"Keep your eyes open," he told him.

"Yes, boss," he said, not quite managing to keep the grin from his face as he weighed the rifle in his hands.

They drove across the bridge. On the other side, there were vehicles crashed, parked in the middle of the roundabout and on the verges, but only a few on the road itself, and they were easy enough to get around.

The dual carriageway rose steadily away from the Beauly Firth, passing industrial estates, retail parks, housing schemes. A movement caught Shaw's eye. He turned his head. It was only a curtain blowing from a broken window.

"Look out!"

Jamie, yelling.

Ahead. Bridge spanning the road. Movement. Faces glimpsed. Shaw pulled hard on the wheel. The car veered to the left. A battery of breezeblocks hit the road to the right of them. The nearest missing them by millimetres.

Behind them, the pick-up swerved. Swung hard fast around the debris. Shaw, watching in the wing mirror. Thought she was going to make it. The back end fish-tailed. The truck skidded. Hit the crash barrier, turned on its side. Screeched along the road, sparks flying. Elizabeth screaming Alice's name.

Shaw hard on the brakes. Nippy gear change. Reversed down to them. Speedy, speedy. Shouting at Jamie as he's getting out of the car.

"Shoot to kill."

From the bridge. Voices shouting. Coarse laughter. Excitement. *Screamers. Did they work together? How many of them?*

He ran to the overturned pick-up. *Please let them be okay.* The door swung open, forced upwards. Alice's head appeared. Gash on her forehead.

"Get out of there," Shaw yelled. "Screamers."

Expecting them to stream over the road at any moment.

He grabbed Alice, hauled her out. Darren right behind her, clambering out, blood on his face. Still clutching the gun.

Yelling. Whooping and hollering. Shaw glanced over his shoulder. Screamers coming down the embankment. Running towards them, blood up.

"Move it!" he yelled. They ran to the Range Rover.

"Hurry! Get in!" Jamie at the wheel, gunning the engine.

Darren and Alice clambering into the back seat. Dog barking. Kids yelling *hurryhurry*. Shaw getting in front. Grabbing the rifle. Car already moving. Pulling the door shut. Something blocking it. A man, running alongside. Grabbing on to him. Dirty fingers encircling his arm. Digging in. Holding on. Eyes narrow slits in a twisted face.

Go Go. Go.

Alice and Darren yelling at Jamie from the back. Telling him to move.

The attacker hanging on. Gripping. Pulling Shaw out. *Winning.* Shaw sliding. No space to butt him with the rifle. Felt himself going. Being dragged out. Slipping on the seat. Arms from behind, holding onto to him. Jamie, pedal to the floor. The attacker being dragged along the road. Still hanging on. Shaw prising his fingers off. Darren's arm, at the side of the seat, punching at the man's face. Again and again and again until the grip loosened. Till he was gone, the door slamming shut on the vacated space.

Staring ahead.

No sound now but the engine.

55

In a lay-by south of Inverness, Shaw cut a patch of hair from Darren's head and glued the edges of the cut on his scalp together.

"Superglue?" Elizabeth, holding the first aid kit, closely watching the proceedings.

"That's what it was designed for," Shaw said. "For patching up wounds in Vietnam. That's why it works so well at sticking your fingers together"

He cleaned the wound on Alice's forehead with a Dettol-soaked cotton pad. "It's just a scrape," he told her. "A plaster will do the job."

"Just as well the first aid kit was in the car," Elizabeth said.

"Just as well," Shaw agreed.

More than half of their supplies had been lost along with the pick-up. Heading south, they took it in turns to sit cramped, four in a row, in the back of the vehicle. The dog in the foot-well, jammed between the legs of whoever had the luxury of sitting in the front passenger seat.

They stuck to the A9, by-passing the small towns and villages on the way.

Nobody was in any hurry for another encounter with unfriendly natives.

They passed wrecks and crashes and vehicles parked haphazardly at the side of the road, drivers still belted in, dead at the wheel. Corpses lay on the ground beside open doors, flesh and skin partially stripped, rotted, eaten by birds, insects, mammals. Skulls revealed, bared teeth grinning from shrunken gums.

Sometimes they had to drive slowly to get by, bumping over verges, scraping by barriers. They had plenty of time to look. Plenty of time to take in the sights. A wizened baby, strapped securely in a car seat, mother slumped at the wheel. A child, curled up on the grass, new trainers on his feet. A dog, lying dead in the back of an estate car. A woman, dressed in beige, skeletal hand still clutching her handbag. The charred bodies of people trapped in burnt-out vehicles. All of this they saw, and more, but long stretches of the road were clear.

"We need to find somewhere before it gets dark," Shaw said.

He could feel the weight of the mountains pressing down on them as they drove through the bleak landscape of the Drumochter Pass.

There were patches of snow on the tops and in the shadowed hollows of the hills, but mostly the scree covered slopes were grey and forbidding, the metal skeletons of dead pylons marching uselessly over them.

"There's a place over there," Alice said.

A solitary farmhouse, its white-painted walls stark against the dismal moor. A bed and breakfast sign hung from a post at the road end.

Shaw turned onto the single track road and drove up to the building. The house was solid, made of stone. He cut the engine. Everyone piled out, began stretching arms, rolling shoulders. Knocking out the kinks.

Shaw looked around. Apart from the eerie silence, everything seemed old-world normal. No rotting corpses. No broken glass or burnt-out cars, just an old Mondeo with three flat tyres sitting out front.

"Vacancies," Jamie read from a sign in the window.

Darren tried the door. It was unlocked. He opened it, called hallo. The house was still. He pushed the door open wide, stepped into the hall, called out again. His call was met with the same stillness. They went inside.

A grandfather clock stood silent in the hall. In a small study, a body on the floor, dressed in blue overalls. Upstairs, a bed with a candlewick bedspread. In the bed, a woman with tightly permed hair and flaking, parchment skin. Head resting against a floral-patterned pillow. A tea tray on the bedside table.

Life went on until it stopped. Shaw closed the door. Checked out the rest of the bedrooms. All empty. *Vacancies.* He went downstairs. The others were in the kitchen.

"Anything?"

Darren turned to him, grinning, flecks of dried blood clinging to the side of his face. "There's loads of food. Tins, cartons, packets. All good stuff."

"And this." Jamie lit a ring on the hob. "Calor gas."

"And this," Elizabeth, turning on the tap. "Running water."

"Look what I found!" Lucy, dragging a bag of dried dog food from the utility room.

"Looks like we've struck gold," Shaw said, eying the sack of Field & Trial.

He found the dog run at the back of the house, wire chewed where the animals had tried to bite through. There had been two of them. The remains of one amounted to little more than a pile of gnawed bones. The other, its companion long eaten, eventually starving to death.

They ate well that night.

Darren served up. "It's kind of a stew," he said. "It started off life as a couple of tins of lentil soup and I added a few things."

"What kind of things?" Lucy, eying him suspiciously.

"Good things," Darren winked at her. "Ham, corn, carrots. A little Field and Trial."

Lucy's eyes widened until she realised he was kidding her.

"Ha, ha - you fell for it," Jamie said.

Lucy punched him on the arm.

Jamie wired in as soon as his bowl was put down to him. "Oh man, this is good - even if it is dog food."

"We haven't been reduced to that - yet," Darren said.

"Maybe we could stay here a few days," Alice suggested. She glanced at Shaw. "It would be good to rest up."

"Feed up," Jamie chimed in.

"Clean up," Elizabeth added.

Shaw looked round the table at them. Pleading eyes in tired faces looked back at him.

"I guess it won't do any harm to take it easy for a couple of days." he replied.

"Yessssss!" Jamie punched the air.

They brought in peat from the stack at the back of the house, lit a fire in the living room. Heated water on the hob for washing. Warmed the beds with hot water bottles. Drank coffee, ate biscuits.

In the morning, Shaw stood outside, warming his hands on a cup of coffee, watching as the sun rose over the hills. After a while, Alice joined him. They stood in silence for a while.

"I've been thinking about what happened in Inverness," Shaw said.

"You mean the Screamers?"

"Yes - well, yes and no. What I mean is - I don't think they were Screamers."

"What else could they be?" Alice, frowning at him.

"People. Just people."

"But that man - the one who was holding on to you - it was crazy."

"I know, but did you get at look at his eyes? Barry, Kate, Howard, Molly MacAulay - they all had the same look in their eyes. You could see there was something going on, something not right. That man yesterday - what I saw in his eyes wasn't the same. Maybe he was crazy to do what he did, but he wasn't Screamer crazy. Didn't try to bite me, just wanted to get me out of the car, or, more likely, try to get the car as well as the truck. He was desperate and he was scared. Fear and desperation, not a good combo."

"In a way, that kind of makes it worse," Alice said. "If you're right then we have to be as wary of other survivors as we do Screamers."

"Just gets better and better." Shaw gazed over the glacial valley. "You know we can't stay here long," he said.

"I know," she answered. "Just give us a couple of days."

He nodded. "Two more nights, then we move."

The urge was in him to push on, to find somewhere they could live instead of scavenge, but he could see the sense in resting up. They were safe here and with running water on tap and plenty of food available, the burden of chores was lifted from them. They all bathed. Shaw and Darren shaved their beards. They ate. They rested, they relaxed. Then they packed up and left.

South of the Pass, they came off the dual carriageway and followed a twisting road through the countryside.

"We won't find what we're looking for on the A9," Shaw said.

"What are we looking for?" Jamie asked.

"I don't know," Shaw replied, "but we'll know it when we-"

He stopped the car in the middle of the road.

"What is it?" Alice asked.

"There," Darren had seen it too. "Smoke."

They looked at the wispy strand of smoke rising from the forest.

"Screamers?" Darren asked.

"I don't know," Shaw said. "Let's check it out."

"Reverse, reverse," Elizabeth shouted. "I think I saw something."

They were in the middle of the woods on what was beginning to feel like a futile pursuit.

Shaw reversed. Couldn't see anything.

"There," she said, "It's a track."

Shaw looked. "I think you're right," he said, looking at the leaf covered ground beside an overgrown hedge. "Well spotted."

He turned, drove slowly along the rough track. After a few metres it veered to the left, taking them deeper into the woods.

"There," Alice pointed ahead. "That's it!" she said.

The cottage sat in a clearing in the middle of the woods, smoke rising from the chimney. Drifts of snowdrops grew in clusters in the garden. The boarded up windows on the ground floor weren't such a pretty sight.

"Looks like someone's home," Shaw said.

"I don't think Screamers would bother boarding up windows," Darren said.

"No, you wouldn't think so," Shaw replied. "But let's take it easy."

He opened the door, got out, walked to the gate. There was no way anyone inside didn't already know they were there.

"Hello," he called. "Is there anyone there?"

His scalp prickled. He knew he was being watched. One of the upstairs windows was open. Thought he caught a glimpse of someone. Maybe a trick of light. A reflection on the glass. No - there was definitely someone there.

"There's six of us," he called out, "and a dog. We're not infected and we won't do you any harm."

He glanced back at the car. The others watched him intently.

"We've got food," he called. "We're looking for somewhere safe to stay."

He watched the window.

"My name is Shaw."

He stood quietly for a moment, waiting for an answer. When it came, the voice was cracked, the words difficult to understand.

"I'm sorry," he called, "I didn't understand."

A few beats of silence then it came again, still raspy, but louder, clearer.

"Tell the others to get out of the truck and stand where I can see them."

"Can we trust you?" Shaw called back.

"You're still standing."

He couldn't argue with that logic. He motioned to the others to get out. They came and stood by him. He pointed at them, one by one, and called out their names, "Alice, Darren, Jamie, Elizabeth, Lucy. The dog is called Toby."

The dog ran the length of the fence, sniffing and peeing.

"It's nice here," Elizabeth said, looking at the garden.

"Can we come in?" Shaw asked.

"Stay where you are. Don't move."

Shaw stared at the window. He couldn't see anything, but the sensation of being watched had gone.

Suddenly the dog jumped the fence and went bounding round the side of the cottage. Shaw called her back. He heard her barking. Called her again. She reappeared, tongue lolling, tail wagging. There was someone with her.

"It's a crazy woman," Jamie whispered.

Shaw hushed him, but the boy had a point.

The woman was dressed in jeans and heavy boots, her

top half layered in sweatshirts and an oversize combat jacket. Her hair was unkempt, sticking out at all angles, but the most notable thing about her was the rifle she was pointing at them.

Shaw raised his hands without prompting. The others followed suit. She had a wary look in her eye - like a wild animal. He thought of deer on the road, the way you had to go careful with them, never knowing which way they'd jump.

She took a few steps towards them, studying them one at a time. When her gaze dropped to Lucy, she stared, her eyes widening. A large tear rolled down her face as she lowered the gun.

PART THREE

56

Chrissie's generation - Generation X - grew up in the shadow of the mushroom cloud. Radiation sickness, death, destruction - instant apocalypse - and all it would take was the press of a button. Cockroaches would survive while the children of the Cold War perished.

They relied on MAD to save them. Mutually Assured Destruction. Reagan with his finger on one button, Gorbachev with his on the other. If he does it, I'll do it.

Protect and Survive. What a hoot. Take down the internal doors in your home and use them to build a shelter. Store water, hoard corned beef. Prepare an improvised toilet, using a bucket lined with a polythene bag. Remember to keep a stack of fresh bags handy, as well as toilet paper and strong disinfectant.
Lock your pets outside.

Good citizens could follow government issued guidelines to the letter but it wouldn't have made one little radioactive speck of difference. It was all smoke and mirrors. Something to keep the people occupied. Because when that bomb went off, they would all be dust.

Scorched on the road, gone in an instant, just like those people in Hiroshima and Nagasaki. Nothing left but shadows. That's if they were lucky. Better to be vaporised in a teeth-melting fast-blast than to suffer the horrors of radiation sickness. *Whoomph,* gone. Sayonara, my friend.

But suddenly, the Cold War was over and the Wall came down. The Berlin Wall that is. No longer separating East from West. The bomb was still there, lurky, lurk, lurk, but the insidious fear had gone. It wasn't the all-consuming threat it had been.

Nightmares about the symptoms of radiation sickness - bleeding from the eyes, leaching blood from the bowels - were last week's news. There were too many other things to worry about - rising oil prices, climate change, food shortages, HIV, AIDS, terrorists, anthrax, obesity and starvation, genetically modified food, Chlamydia, dirty bombs, biological warfare, paedophiles, MRSA, cancer, super bugs, bird flu... on and on it went.

There was so much to worry about that it was difficult to keep up. Immigration, unemployment, new food scares every week. The politics of fear pervaded every aspect of daily life. People were too fat, not exercising enough, drinking too much and everyone was living too long.

People carried on despite the fear. With terror of the bomb all but gone, there was nothing else to match it for immediate destruction on a grand scale. All the other stuff added together couldn't compete with that one big, all-consuming threat.

If they could survive the risk of nuclear holocaust for so long, they weren't going to sweat the small stuff. And so people continued to buy flat-packs from IKEA, book long-haul flights to sun-drenched holiday destinations and watch reality television. Everything just kept on keeping on.

Until it stopped.

There was no mushroom cloud. No bang. It wasn't big and it wasn't biblical. No darkening skies, no roiling sea. Armageddon slithered up unannounced. No horsemen, no angels with trumpets. Just Doctor Austin's film on YouTube.

He uploaded it just before the net went down and the screens turned black. Not many people saw it, but it scared those who did. Chrissie was one of them.

He said that Falling Down Flu wasn't a flu. It wasn't even a virus. It was a rogue prion. Voice off-screen asks, what does that mean?

Doctor Austin replies, What it means is that basically, we're finished.

57

She could have shot them, taken their food, kept the dog. A companion to help stave off loneliness. Or a food source, if she became desperate enough.

Chrissie had learned that people were bad and people were dangerous. They would hurt her if they got the chance. Even so, something stopped her squeezing the trigger.

It wouldn't have been the right thing to do. Something inside her told her she would regret it.

It wasn't just her conscience, or a moral hangover from the old days. There was something else, something about the one called Shaw. She liked the cut of his jib. He stood there, exposed, yet so still and calm.

He didn't have that crazy look in his eye - the one she'd seen up close. Calm was good. And when the rest of them came piling out, the only look they had going on was post-apocalyptic Brady Bunch.

There was nothing of the mob about them, but Lucy was the clincher. She reminded Chrissie of Phoebe. Crying was pointless. It achieved nothing. And yet her eyes welled. Embarrassed, angry at herself for showing weakness, she swept her tears away with the back of her hand.

The Brady Bunch called *them* Screamers. Chrissie got it straight off. It was a good name. *Screamers*. That's when they were most dangerous - when they were screaming and carrying on. That's when they were ruthless and out of control. They had no fear. Didn't care about anything. That's when they had most chance of getting you.

But it wasn't just the Screamers you had to watch out for. It was the other survivors.

The ones who weren't like the Brady Bunch.

58

In the beginning, Chrissie stayed away from the ghost town of Feldybridge. But there were good things to be found there, things too good - too useful - to be ignored - and so finally she succumbed.

By her third trip, the place was hardly freaking her at all. She got to know the locals, even fell into conversation with a couple of them. Her favourite was Mrs Bun. Mrs Bun lay in the street outside the baker's shop. Chrissie would wish her a good morning, and Mrs Bun would wish her one right back.

Every time Chrissie saw her, she looked a little more dried out. She told Mrs Bun that it wasn't doing her pale skin much good lying in the sun all day long like that, even if it was autumn, but the woman just laughed her off in that good-natured way she had.

It was only a game. Although she did speak out loud to them, Chrissie wasn't hearing voices. Dead people weren't talking to her. All the same, it got so that she looked forward to seeing them whenever she was there. Everybody likes to see a familiar face.

Although she thought it was likely that there was a survivor somewhere in Feldybridge, she never came across one. Never saw any sign of one either. Those little shops were all hers.

She kept her guard up. Aside from her conversations with the corpses, she didn't make any more noise than was necessary. She proceeded mainly with caution, but it was impossible to stay on red alert the whole time. All that resulted in was her jumping at her own reflection, which happened on several occasions.

She was picking up a few things from the hardware store when she heard the engines. *Cars.* Cars meant people. Yeah, she made jokes to herself about talking to stiffs, but the reality was that loneliness was killing her.

At this point in time she was aware that the corpse conversations could be the thin end of the wedge, but what kind of a state might she be in six months hence? Would she still be joking, or would she actually be hearing voices by then?

The thought of speaking to real live people was tantalising. The prospect excited her so much, she almost ran into the street to flag them down. She was at the shop door when her sense of self-preservation finally kicked in.

Instead of going into the street, she lost herself in cautious shadows. No need to rush things. No harm in taking a little time to suss the incomers out.

She huddled down as the vehicles drew near, watching through the window. Different sounds became audible over the engines. Yelling, whooping, smashing glass.

The convoy roared by the store. People hanging out of vehicles, throwing missiles. Chrissie ducked behind a row of shelves as the store window shattered.

When they'd gone by, she crawled through to the back on her hands and knees. She hid there until it was dark. It gave her plenty of time to think. She came to the conclusion that she wasn't in need of any new friends after all. She'd stick with the corpses, thanks.

She couldn't risk taking the car. They might hear it and follow her. Instead, she slunk through unlit streets to the outskirts of the village. It took her several hours of feeling her way in the dark before she managed to circle around to the woods. She had a couple of head torches she'd lifted from the store, but she couldn't risk using them until Feldybridge was well behind her.

In the woods, shadows jumped at her. She stumbled several times despite the torches, managing to swallow a scream when the tip of a branch tickled her cheek.

The sound of rustling in the undergrowth tensed her to the point of pinging apart. She started breathing again when the torchlight was reflected in the eyes of a roe deer.

At one point, she thought she was going round in circles. That she'd seen this log, or that boulder before. At the point of weeping in frustration, she came across a trail she'd used. It led to the river. She knew her way to the cottage from there.

Ten minutes later, she was inside, doors bolted, feeling lucky to be alive.

Now she was on permanent red alert. Jumping at shadows. Tensing at creaks. Despite the fact that it was coming on winter, she didn't dare light the range during the day in case the smoke attracted attention.

The invaders had no such concerns. Black smoke belched into the sky, enough of it hanging over the woods to suggest they'd burnt the entire village down.

Curiosity getting the better of her, Chrissie slipped furtively from the locked-down safety of the cottage and crept up the hill. Lying on a ridge, she surveyed the village through binoculars. Incredibly, most of it seemed intact. All except the church. The building had stood for centuries, withstanding the reformation and Jacobean battles, only to succumb to FDF. The invaders had concentrated their efforts there, feeding the fire to keep it going.

Chrissie retreated to the cottage. She did not emerge again until there had been no smoke for several days.

When she did finally come out, it was only to keep watch from the hill. The ancient church was a charred ruin. A few bodies lay in the streets where none had been before. Otherwise, everything was still. It looked as though the invaders had either killed each other or cleared out.

The following day, she returned to the hill and scanned the town slowly, in grid pattern. Nothing had changed. The new bodies still lay in the same positions.

She wanted to get her car back. Wanted the security of knowing that she could get in it and take off at a moment's notice. Without it, she felt stranded. But, caution still riding high, she forced herself to leave it for another day.

When she couldn't be any surer that it was safe, she walked into the village. The car was where she'd left it, mercifully unscathed. The same could not be said of Chrissie.

There were no more chats with the locals. She fancied she caught a look of hurt in Mrs Bun's eyes, but she was all done with Feldybridge. It wasn't safe anymore. Besides which, the invaders had been efficient looters.

Chrissie took what she could gather quickly and got out. From now on, she would stick to the cottage and the woods. It was safe there. As safe as it could be anywhere.

But it wasn't safe enough.

59

She was collecting firewood when the Screamer attacked. He came from nowhere. Suddenly, he was there, in front of her. Eyes crazed, teeth bared. A silent beat as they stared at each other. She blinked. He howled. She dropped the bundle of wood. He lunged. Snarling. The sound deep. Coming from his throat. Hands scrabbling to get at her. Fingers long and strong. Grabby. Filthy nails swiping by her eyes. Missing by a micron.

She swerved. Hand instinctively going for the sheath on her thigh. Pulling out the knife. Not thinking. Doing. Swiftly raising it. Drawing it across his throat. The blade razor-edged. Slicing through skin, muscle, cartilage. Arteries.

Blood spewed from the wound. A strong, wide arc of red. Spraying her. Droplets on her face. In her hair. Plasma raining on the forest floor. Gore splattering her boots. His eyes popping. Surprise. Shock. Rage.

He lunged again. But he was already weakened. Blood spurting forth with every beat of his heart.

Shocked by what she'd done, Chrissie stepped backwards. Out of reach. Stumbled over a fallen branch. Fell into a snapping tangle of dried twigs. He staggered towards her. One step. She tried to get up. Two steps.

Her sleeve caught in the branches. Dead shoots snagging her hair. Three steps. Almost upon her, he collapsed onto his knees. The gushing flow easing as he bled out.

He reached a hand out to her. At her. Fingers curling. Still trying to claw at her. Dirty nails visible through a red, bloody coating.

He gurgled. Blood bubbles foaming at his mouth before he collapsed backwards. He died staring at the canopy, the slash on his throat a raw, wide grin.

Chrissie untangled herself and stood up. She stared down at her assailant. At the wound she'd drawn across his throat. Breathed in the coppery tang of blood already coagulating, turned and threw up.

One quick puke and it was over.

Still holding the knife, Chrissie held her hands out before her. Look ma, no shakes. She wiped the blade on a handful of ferns and slipped it back in its sheath.

She'd acted on instinct and she had no regrets. If she'd taken even a second to think about it, she'd be dead and he'd be... He'd be what? Eating her? Tearing her apart? Violating her body? Or would her death at his hands have been enough to satisfy him in itself? Would he simply have left her lying there and gone on his way?

She gazed down at him, accustomed now to the slash in his throat. He was quite the country gent in his Barbour jacket and Hunter wellies. She went through his pockets. Found a penknife. It wasn't much of a blade. She had better. There was a leather wallet containing a driving license, two credit cards, one debit card, and a few notes. Fat lot of good they were. His name was Gordon Lees.

Chrissie had no inclination to bury Gordon Lees. Leaving him for the creatures of the forest to feast upon, she gathered up her bundle of firewood and headed back to the cottage.

On the way, she listened for unexpected sounds. Twigs cracking, leaves crunching underfoot, but all she heard was the normal soundtrack of the woods. Small birds twittering. The raw cry of crows. The burble of water from the river. The rattle and sigh of rust-coloured leaves in the light breeze. Even so, she picked up her pace as she went.

Gordon Lees had snuck up on her. Others could easily do the same.

By the time she got back her scalp was prickling, her body sweating, nerves jangling. Her hands, no longer steady, shook as she bolted the door.

She sighed, leant against it, felt peace for a moment. Until the thought went through her mind, that perhaps she had locked one of them in there with her.

Knife in hand, she checked the cottage. Every nook and cranny of it. Including places in which no-one could possibly hide. Drawers, small cupboards, behind cushions. Everywhere.

When she'd done, she made sure the door was still bolted, the windows locked, and checked the cottage all over again.

She drew the curtains before dark. She knew - part of her knew - that she was turning in on herself, but she couldn't stop.

She tried singing, stomping about. Filling the cottage with noise instead of letting the shadows creep up on her. But now that it had arrived, she could not push back the fear.

Sounds she had grown accustomed to developed new, threatening resonances. She jumped at every creak, every sigh, every click of the old cottage and woke in the morning, unrefreshed from her sleep.

The thought of one of them sneaking in haunted her. When she couldn't take it any longer, she boarded up the downstairs windows. Winter closed in soon after.

Snow fell day after day after day. Now all she cared about was staying warm. She was forced to light the fire, no matter whose eye the smoke caught. But no-one came. The world had been smothered beneath a freezing, white blanket. There was no more anything except isolation.

The long dark nights were occasionally punctuated by days of such astounding, glistening beauty, she thought she must be hallucinating. On one of those days, she lay on her back in the garden. Gazing up at the clear blue sky, she made a snow angel. Standing up to inspect it, she saw one angel, one set of footprints.

There was her. Only her. Everyone else was dead. She was the last human on earth.

Weeks, then months went by. Finally, the snow melted. The days were grey, but growing longer. Snowdrops blossomed in the garden. And they came.

60

The sound of the engine alerted her. She understood straight away that it was the smoke from the chimney that had brought them to her. She should have stopped lighting the fire during the day as soon as the snow cleared. She'd grown careless. Too used to being warm.

There was more to it yet - the snow may have gone, but the days were damp, the air chill. Light the fire and risk attracting attention. Leave it unlit and invite pneumonia in. She'd made her choice. Now it was time to pay the price.

She watched and waited by the bedroom window, wondering if after all she'd been through that this was finally going to be the end. Wondering if she would care if it was. Thinking maybe she was ready to give in now. To submit. But when the four wheel drive pulled up in front of the cottage and her heart hammered in her chest, she knew that she would not give up without a fight. She wasn't ready to die.

This much was clear - they were different. Unlike any other survivors she had encountered. No noise. No whooping and hollering. No smashing of glass or obvious murderous intent. The girl was the clincher. Lucy didn't look anything like Phoebe, but she was a little girl and that was enough.

Chrissie had dreamt about her daughter all winter long. The pain of her loss increasing over time. She wondered how that could be so. Wondered how she could stand the pain and still go on. When she saw Lucy, she gave up. Caved in. There was no more fight in her. If she'd got it wrong and they were going to tear her apart, so be it. She lowered the gun.

Alice went to her. Hugged her. Chrissie stiffened then relaxed. It felt strange to be held. To have someone so close to her she could feel the warmth of their breath on her cheek. She wasn't sure if she liked it or not, but still she let them in. She opened her door and welcomed them to her world. The moment she did so, her world ceased to exist.

She was no longer the last human on earth.

61

It wasn't easy being the last person on earth. Any sane person would think she'd be glad of the company. But she was used to being alone. To having only her own thoughts, her own sounds, for company. It wasn't long before she began to resent the newcomers.

The interlopers moved into her space, filled her world with their noise. They talked constantly. They laughed and joked and asked questions, endless questions, until she thought her head would burst.

Where had she come from? Where had she been? Had she met anyone else along the way?

Chrissie clammed up. Didn't tell them a thing.

They touched her stuff. They all touched her stuff. Every one of them. They moved things, used things, filled her space with their own things.

They cooked in her kitchen, then expected her to eat with them. They ate her food. Gave her their food. Acted like they all belonged together. Chrissie simmered with resentment.

Lucy drew pictures for her. Drawings of Chrissie and the cottage. Sometimes with Lucy or one of the others drawn alongside.

Chrissie didn't ask for the drawings. She didn't want

them, but Lucy gave them to her anyway. Not knowing what else to do, Chrissie accepted them. Said thank you. Stuck them on the wall to make the kid happy.

She don't know why she was supposed to make her happy. She wasn't Phoebe. She wasn't anything to Chrissie. None of them were.

She'd made a mistake letting them in. She wanted things back the way they were. She wanted to be alone again.

She'd grown accustomed to being the last person on earth. Now she didn't want to share her world. Not with them. There was only one other person she wanted to be with, but she was dead. They couldn't just bring another kid into her world and think she'd be just as good. That she'd fill the gap.

She didn't want Lucy. She wanted Phoebe. And if she couldn't have her, she didn't want anyone.

Chrissie was already teetering on the edge. When they took the boards off the windows, she went right over.

They said that if bandits or Screamers happened upon them, a few boarded up windows weren't going to make much difference to their chances. They said they didn't like living in the permanent twilight of the downstairs world.

That dim world was Chrissie's safety zone. When they ripped the boards off the windows, they exposed her. Frightened, she fought back.

Bright spring light flooded into the kitchen and she freaked.

Later, much later, Shaw told her that as breakdowns went, hers was quite spectacular.

62

Chrissie screamed and yelled and swore. Words she didn't know she knew came hurtling and spitting from her lips. Her emotions, unchecked by manners, politeness, social etiquette, civilisation, ran naked and wild. There was no civilisation.

At first they gave her free rein. They stood back while emotions toyed with their faces. Oh look, that one is shocked. This one perturbed. Scared, worried, anxious, uneasy, distressed. Chrissie laughed at them all. Taunting, goading.

They tried talking to her. Gentle voices. Asking her to calm down. Telling her to take it easy. No-one was going to hurt her. Telling her she was going to hurt herself. Telling her what to do in her own home. The home they had invaded, taken as their own. Who the hell did they think they were?

She upped the ante. Grabbed a plate, smashed it against the wall. The sound was good, the effect on their faces better. She snatched up a glass. Aimed it at the window they'd exposed.

They snatched her. Grabbed her while she wasn't looking. Hands all over her. Pinning her down. Shaw's voice. Telling her they weren't going to hurt her. It was for her own good.

They manhandled her up the stairs. The last person who had done that was her mother.

She didn't make it easy. Fought against them every step of the way, hanging onto the banister while they shoved and pushed and dragged her. Yelling instructions at each other. The dog barking in the hall below.

They tied her to the bedstead. Saying it was for her own good. Saying it over and over while she thrashed and fought against them. When they'd finished tying her down, they locked the door behind them. Left her alone. Like her mother had done to her. Like she'd done to Phoebe.

Nobody kissed her on the forehead. Not this time. Didn't matter, she'd only dreamt it before. Hadn't she?

She wasn't sure now. Wasn't sure about anything. Neither were they. They thought she might have turned Screamer. She heard them say so. She didn't blame them for that. Was thinking the same thing herself.

She slept. She slept a lot. Long and deep, like hibernation. Except that every so often, she'd wake up and when she did, Shaw was there. Sitting on a chair by the window, reading while he babysat.

At first she screamed at him. Yelling at him to untie her. Cursing him inside out and upside down. She didn't much fancy the cut of his jib now. In fact, she hated, loathed, despised him. He was the reason she was tied up, a prisoner in her own home. It enraged her further when he barely glanced at her, face impassive, before going back to his book.

Funny thing was, even though his presence infuriated her, she soon got used to him being there. After a while she stopped yelling at him. It made her throat hurt and took up too much energy. Besides, she couldn't remember what it was she was angry about.

She was just so very tired.

Days passed. They fed her. Let her go to the bathroom. They made her use it with the door open, Alice standing outside, but she was beyond caring about those sorts of niceties.

When she'd been calm for a while, they stopped tying her up.

She spied on Shaw. Watching him through her eyelashes whilst she pretended to sleep. His face was lined and creased, and fell easily into a frown. But when he smiled, he looked alive - really alive. She imagined that though life with him might not be easy, it would never be dull.

The cut of his jib was starting to appeal again.

63

One day she woke up and Shaw wasn't there. Chrissie's chest tightened. She didn't want to be on her own. Not any more. A sick feeling swelled inside her. She threw the covers back. What if they'd listened to the vile things she'd said? What if they'd believed her? Thought she really did want to be alone. Forever and always on her own.

The door was unlocked. Her skin prickled. They had abandoned her. Left her free to roam and fend for herself. Thinking she'd done it before so she could do it again. But she couldn't. Not now. You couldn't give something to a person - companionship, support - then snatch it away and expect them to be the same as they were before. It wasn't right. Wasn't fair.

She snorted, mocking herself. Fair? What exactly did that mean? Life hadn't been fair in the old world and life wasn't fair now. All that had happened was that the veneer had been stripped off. It was every woman, man and child for their own self.

The thoughts swirled angrily, bitterly, through her head as she opened the door. She peered into the dim hall. A creak on the stairs made her hackles rise. Her worst fear had been realised. A Screamer, here in the cottage.

271

Sniffing her out. Hunting her down.

She glanced into the room. They'd taken her weapons away. Left her with nothing with which to defend herself. The key. Still in the door. She slipped it out of the lock. It was old, heavy. She held its bow tight in her fist, the shank protruding between her fingers. The end was chunky, blunt. She'd have to pack a good punch to drive it into the Screamer's eye. She'd have to be up close. Snapping teeth, stinking breath, body heat, kind of up close. It was risky, but it was all she had.

Footsteps, reaching the top of the stairs. Sweat prickling at her hairline. Fist clenching ever tighter around the key.

Shaw stepped onto the landing. Raised an eyebrow. Bid her a good morning. Chrissie leant back against the door frame. Closed her eyes, let out a long sigh.

She wasn't alone.

"Are you okay?"

She opened her eyes. Shaw, standing in front of her. Body heat close. She smiled. "Yeah, I'm okay."

He put his arms around her, his embrace tentative at first. Tightening as she leant into him. She buried her face in the thick fleece of his checked shirt, breathed in the smell of him. He'd been outside. She could smell it on him, on his shirt, on his skin. Leaves, damp earth, ozone. Familiar scents clinging to an unfamiliar body.

"I'm not alone," she whispered.

The hubbub of conversation faded as Chrissie walked into the warm kitchen. She had dressed in clean clothes. Lost the mad-woman-in-the-attic hairstyle. There was a pause as they stared at her, and she stared back at them. They were sitting round the table, yet they seemed to fill the room with their heartbeats, their breath, their life. They seemed to belong.

"Tell us about Phoebe," Lucy said.

Chrissie frowned, wondering how they knew about her.

Wondering what else they knew.

"You've been talking in your sleep," Elizabeth said.

"You were delirious," Jamie added.

"Come on, sit down." Darren pushed out a chair for her.

She glanced at Shaw, feeling nervous, and maybe a little embarrassed about the moment they'd shared upstairs. Wondering if a moment was all it would ever be.

She hadn't realised how much she'd missed the contact, the warmth, the comfort of other people. She was a herd animal, not a lone wolf. She didn't want to be on her own. She wanted to be part of something.

She smiled. It felt weird on her face as she stretched dormant muscles. It must have looked okay though, because they smiled back.

She sat in the chair Darren had pushed out for her, pulled it into the table. Was absorbed into the group.

She told them about Phoebe, the dogs, the mob at the supermarket and about everything else she'd been through. They told her about the people they'd lost and about what they'd been through. It took a while.

They drank black coffee and ate soup as they talked. There were moments of light among the tales of loss. Laughter erupting often enough so that when Chrissie smiled, it no longer felt unnatural. And through it all, the eating, the talking, the sharing, small looks passed between her and Shaw. Each recognising something in the other.

They'd only met, were little more than strangers, but Chrissie already felt as though she had known him a long time.

64

Somewhere during the days and weeks that followed, they stopped existing and started living again. The clearing and planting Chrissie had done the previous autumn was rewarded by fresh spring greens, carrots, beans and early new potatoes. These few simple vegetables tasted like manna from heaven to palates jaded by long months of preserved food.

They became farmers. Turning the soil, planting, planning a year of fresh fruit and vegetables. They were helped by a gentle spring. Everyone worked, each contributing in their own way.

Although they didn't have the manpower to keep someone on permanent look-out, they were always aware of the possibility of a Screamer happening upon them. They kept the guns oiled and the knives sharp, but none came. Perhaps the harsh winter had killed them off.

They became adept at hunting, gathering, scavenging. One day Darren and Jamie returned from a foray, grins plastered across their faces.

"Wait till you see what we've got." Jamie pulled a crate from the back of the Range Rover. Inside there were hens. Live hens.

"Where did they come from?" Chrissie asked. After

the harsh winter, she was amazed that there was any livestock still alive.

"They were in a barn. Most of them were dead, but not these beauties. But wait - you haven't seen the best yet." The group crowded round while Jamie proudly brought out his treasure. An undernourished, dull-feathered cockerel.

"He doesn't look like much now, but we'll soon get him up to scratch."

"But how did they survive?" Shaw asked.

"Sacks of grain and a leaky tap. We got there just in time - most of the grain was gone."

"But we found more - tons more - in a store," Jamie said.

The garden was sectioned for planting, so they built the chicken run on the woods side of the wall. A few weeks later, plumped-up and cared for, the hens started laying.

In the hope that the rooster had been nourished adequately enough to do some roostering, they left a clutch of eggs baking under a broody hen. With any luck, they'd soon have a few chicks bolstering the flock.

With seven of them living there, plus the dog, the cottage was filled to the rafters. Elizabeth and Lucy slept in the Parlour, Chrissie in one bedroom, Alice and Darren in the other. Jamie cleared the box room and kitted it out with a camp bed and a few home comforts he'd scavenged. Shaw slept in the kitchen with Toby.

Chrissie often lay in bed, staring at the ceiling, picturing Shaw lying in the room below. Wondering if he was thinking about her. If he felt the same ache, the same desire.

She told herself not to be stupid. In the old world, their paths would never have crossed. But this was the new world, and their paths had more than crossed. They had intertwined, throwing them into almost constant close proximity. Close, yet never alone. The group was small, but there was always someone else around.

She hugged herself under the duvet, wishing it was his arms she was in instead of her own. Longing to breath in the smell of him once more.

The idea that she would ever be close, be intimate, with anyone again, was so remote that she had never given it any head-space. Now that there was at least the possibility, her desire was killing her. She felt like Tantalus, the sweet fruit within sight, but agonisingly out of reach. It was torture.

Exquisite, bitter-sweet, torture.

65

In the evening, when work was over, the group gathered in the kitchen to eat and talk. They discussed what had been achieved, or not, that day, chewed over problems and decided who would do what in the days to come.

When the dishes had been cleared they would play cards, sing, or read by the light of the paraffin lamps. Sometimes they'd forget the lyric of the song they were singing. They'd hum until someone managed to pick it up again, or else it would dwindle away, perhaps never to be sung again. Old songs fading, no-one writing anything new.

The main entertainment was reading. They took it in turns to read out loud to each other. Even though they eked the books out, it didn't take them long to work their way through the small collection in the cottage. When they started reading the same stories over, Shaw suggested going on a foray to collect some more. He asked Chrissie to go with him.

She hesitated. Since arriving at Birch Cottage, she'd never been further abroad than Feldybridge. She hadn't even been that far since the mob had burned down the church. Her chest constricted at the thought of venturing out into the world, pulse racing at the possibility of

277

encountering a blood-thirsty mob. Mouth drying at the prospect of getting up close and personal with a grabby, bitey Screamer.

But she also realised that her world had become small. Perhaps too small. If she didn't do something about it, the danger was that it would continue to shrink, and her with it.

Good. She was pleased that she had rationalised her response. She didn't hesitate for long. She said yes.

The fact that she would be spending several hours alone with Shaw was merely an added bonus. Nothing to do with her leaping at the chance.

Nothing at all.

66

Shaw drove. Chrissie sat in the passenger seat, excited at the prospect of a day out with him. Her worries about encountering mobs or Screamers had all but gone since they'd made the decision to head to Pitlochry, some fifteen miles north of Feldybridge.

Several forays had been made there during the previous months, each without incident. Like Feldybridge, it seemed that everyone in the town had either died or abandoned the place.

The small Victorian town had catered largely for the tourist trade. Though the gift shops and cafes contained little of use to them, the outdoor shops had been a tremendous source, amongst other things, yielding decent boots and waterproof gear. They had been concerned with the practical aspects of survival. Until now, it had not occurred to anyone to visit the library.

Chrissie and Shaw exchanged some conversation at the start of the journey, but now that they were finally alone, there was an unexpected awkwardness between them. There had been so many things she wanted to say to him, ask him, but now that she had the opportunity, her mind was uncooperative and had gone blank.

The harder she tried to think of something to say, the harder it became. She'd come up with an idea then dismiss it as trivial or try-too-hard. She snuck a couple of glances at Shaw, but he was staring intently at the road ahead. He wasn't giving anything away.

The silence between them thickened, solidifying with every passing mile.

Finally, they made the turn for Pitlochry. Chrissie stared out of the window as they approached the outskirts of the town. Potholes, caused by frost upheaval, pitted the road. Weeds growing in the cracks.

Victorian villas lined the street. Gardens, once picture-postcard neat were now overgrown. Grass knee-high. Bushes leggy. Guest-house signs, paint peeling, colours fading after the harsh winter, stood forlornly outside properties where every room was vacant. Corpses excepted.

Nothing shone on the abandoned buildings. Windows were grubby or broken, metal tarnished. The old world was fading.

"It's a ghost town." The words dry in her mouth.

They passed restaurants, estate agents, a church. Each building as desolate as the last.

"Yeah," Shaw said, "It is."

"Funny how there are no bodies anywhere though," she said. "You'd think there would be a few."

"I was thinking the same thing myself."

She glanced at him. He was frowning.

"What is it?" she asked, the earlier awkwardness dwindling.

"I could have sworn there were bodies in the street the last time I was here."

"Maybe they were further up - nearer the centre of town."

"Maybe," he said, but he didn't sound convinced. "I don't like to say it, but this place is giving me the creeps."

"Me too. Was it like this before?"

"No, it was fine. Don't know what it is today." He shrugged and took the empty sacks they'd brought from the back of the Land Rover. "Come on, let's get this done."

He had parked right at the library steps. There were three cars parked in the marked bays, but here were no other people. Alive or dead.

All was peaceful. Birds twittered. The sun shone, though it's warmth was not enough to stop a shiver running through Chrissie. She had the skin-crawling feeling they were being watched.

Shaw was already pushing open the library door.

The previous night, she'd indulged in fantasies about their jaunt. The laughs they would share choosing books together. How they would gently mock each other's choices. Creating new memories, forgetting, for a time, the harsh realities of their new lives. But there was no forgetting. Inside, he went one way, she the other.

There was no indulgent picking and choosing. Without either of them saying so, their seemingly gentle mission, now had a sense of urgency about it. Neither of them wanted to spend any longer in the library than they had to.

Chrissie was in the fiction department. She gave the horror section a swerve. They had plenty enough of that in real life. Otherwise, she randomly picked books from the shelves, throwing them into the sacks.

A water stain in one corner of the ceiling explained the damp, musty smell permeating the room. Come next winter, the entire book collection would be mouldering.

There was a stand at the end of one of the shelves. She spun it around. Classics. Twain, Austen, Hardy. She took enough of them to finish filling the sacks. For better or worse, her arbitrary selection would have to do.

"I'm done," she called to Shaw.

"Me too," he called back.

The sacks were too heavy for her to lift. She dragged the first one to the door, leaving it there for Shaw to carry out to the Land Rover. She went back for the second, wondering if it was just her, or was the smell getting worse? Maybe a sewage pipe had burst somewhere. They would have toilets in the building, so it was possible.

She was most of the way to the door with the second sack when she stopped to rub an ache in her back. The smell was definitely getting worse.

"Shaw, can you smell that?"

No answer. He must be outside loading up.

She bent down to grab the sack again. Heard a sound. She straightened up. Turned around.

"Shaw?"

A woman appeared from behind a shelf.

A second passed as they eyed each other.

Her hair was frizzing free from tight plaits. Name badge dangling from a black cardigan. Blouse stained, hanging over a loose skirt. Tights laddered. Dribbled excrement drying on her legs. Mouth twisted. A crazed look in her eye. Librarian turned Screamer.

The librarian opened her mouth. A dry screech rasped from the back of her throat. She ran at Chrissie. Full pelt. Was on her in a heartbeat. They fell. Chrissie landed on her back. Her hands against the librarian's shoulders, trying to push her off. The librarian bearing down, teeth gnashing. Foul breath flowing from between her cracked lips.

Chrissie's arms weakening under the weight of her attacker. She couldn't get to the knife strapped to her thigh. She was hemmed in. Full sack on one side. Solid book shelf on the other. The librarian squeezing her lungs empty.

She thrust her head at Chrissie. Chrissie twisted her face away. Teeth scraped against her cheek. The librarian reared for another bite. Chrissie squeezed her eyes tight.

No thought in her head but that a whole new world of pain was coming her way.

67

She heard the snap of the librarian's jaws. No pain followed. No bite. The librarian slithering down her body. Bumping against her. Grabbing at her. Howling. Nothing making sense.

Chrissie opened her eyes.

Shaw, gripping the librarian's ankles. Dragging her off. The librarian writhing and snarling. Shaw had a tiger by the tail.

Chrissie scrambled to her feet. The librarian twisting around, trying to get at Shaw. Chrissie grabbed a book from the shelf. Brought it down on the librarian's head. Thumping the hard cover down again, and again, and again. The corner driving into her temple, her eye. The librarian squealing. Chrissie thumping her over and over.

When she stopped squealing and started moaning, Chrissie tossed the book aside and pulled out her knife. She drove the blade under the librarian's ribcage, into her heart. The librarian gasped. Chrissie withdrew the blade. Blood blossomed across the librarian's blouse as her body went into a spasm.

Though she did not look at him, Chrissie was aware of Shaw standing beside her, both of them watching as life ebbed from the librarian's body.

When the twitching was done and the last breath had been drawn, Chrissie knelt beside the dead body and wiped her blade clean on the librarian's cardigan. The edge scraped across her name badge.

Blade clean, Chrissie stood up and slid the knife back in its sheath.

"Gracie Dawn, dead and gone," Shaw said.

Chrissie stared at the corpse. Tried to crank up some sympathy for Gracie Dawn, but the smell of bowels recently evacuated made her gorge rise.

"Do you want to hang around and sing the twenty-third psalm, or are we going to get out of here?"

Shaw looked at her, a wry smile on his lips. "Yea, though I walk through the valley of the shadow of death. Let's get out of here."

"It's okay - she didn't break the skin." Shaw, standing in front of Chrissie, cleaning her face with antiseptic wipes.

When he'd finished, she took in deep breaths of fresh air and exhaled slowly.

"You okay?" he asked, one hand resting lightly on her arm.

"Fine." She held out her hands. "Look, barely a tremble. And I didn't throw up. I'm getting better at this. Or worse. Depending on your point of view."

"Chrissie, look at me."

She looked up at his face. Into his eyes.

"What you did in there - you had no choice. If you didn't kill her, I would have. It's us or them. Either the Screamers win or we do. You understand?"

She nodded. He was standing close. So close.

"The book work was a little bizarre, I'll give you that."

He grinned. She smiled back. He bent his head. Gently kissed her. He hadn't shaved in two days. She kissed him back, hard. He pulled her tight. She wrapped her arms around him, tasting him, breathing him in. Wanting him. It felt so good as they melted together. But then he abruptly pulled away.

She looked at him. *What the... ?* He shook his head.

"Not here. It's not safe."

She glanced around. He was right. They were outside. Exposed. She could just picture a Screamer coming across them while they were making the beast with two backs. But she wasn't going to lose her chance. Not now. She'd seen the look in his eye, felt the way his body responded to hers. He wanted her every bit as much as she wanted him.

"Move into the bedroom with me," she said.

His eyes crinkled as he smiled. "I thought you'd never ask."

The four sacks of books they'd lifted from the library hardly made a dent in the space in the back of the Land Rover. Shaw suggested they make the most of the trip and pick up a few more supplies while they were in town.

"Nice choice of book, by the way."

"I just grabbed the nearest one to hand - didn't notice the title. What was it?"

"Self Defence for Dummies."

When she'd stopped laughing, she said, "I forgot to tell you thanks."

"What for?"

"For getting her off me."

"No problem. Any..."

"What's up?"

Shaw pulled up outside a supermarket in the centre of the town.

"Look at that," he said, nodding at the shop windows.

Chrissie looked. She saw a shop with lots of empty shelves.

"Looks like someone got here before us."

"Whenever we've been up here we've stopped off at this shop and plugged up any spaces with supplies. Last time we were here there was still plenty on the shelves."

"So, like I say - someone got here before us."

"And emptied the entire store?"

"Why not?"

"You'd need to be driving some serious wheels to wipe out the whole place - and look at it - there's no mess, nothing broken or trashed. That shop has been systematically emptied."

They slowly drove further up the street.

"There are no bodies anywhere," Shaw said.

"The outdoor shop has been cleared."

"So have the bodies. Somebody has moved them."

"Stop - back up," Chrissie said.

Shaw reversed down the street to a junction.

"Look there." Chrissie pointed up a side road.

Shaw looked. A barricade had been constructed about two hundred metres up the road.

"That's new," Shaw said. "Looks like someone has staked a claim."

"Maybe the natives are friendly. Do you think we should try to make contact?"

"Last time I tried that, I got shot at."

"Look there - did you see that?"

"Sunlight catching on binoculars."

"I had a feeling we were being watched when we got here. I put it down to the Screamer..."

Chrissie looked at the buildings surrounding them. At the first and second floor windows they couldn't see through. At the darkened interiors on street level.

"There could be a lot of eyes on us right now."

"I was just thinking it must have taken a few of them to get the streets cleaned up so well."

"Maybe they are from here and claiming it back."

"Inch by inch."

"What do you think?" Chrissie asked.

"I think we should get out of here while we can still get."

68

They had basic first aid knowledge and a couple of medical reference books, but nobody wanted to be relying on anyone else looking up the right chapter if they got ill, so they did their best to stay healthy. They took regular doses of vitamin pills and none of them was going to die from lack of exercise.

White goods had become white elephants. It was good-bye automatic washing machine, hello washboard and mangle. Almost everything they did demanded physical activity. Often lots of it. Digging, planting, hoeing, hunting, gathering, chopping, cleaning. And all this physical output demanded calorific input.

Every week, Darren and Jamie spent a couple of early mornings at the river. They weren't always successful, but more often than not, they returned with a fry of sweet, brown trout. After spotting a few freshwater crayfish, they were on a mission to trap them. Trial and error finally resulted in success - and a new source of food.

Shaw went on hunting trips. Sometimes, alone, sometimes with Chrissie or one of the others. If they were lucky, they'd be eating venison, but no-one turned their nose up at rabbit stew.

They learned how to stretch their food. Dried beans

and lentils and were used to eke out stews. Two eggs didn't go far in feeding seven people, but two eggs in a batter using dried milk, made a stack of pancakes. Similarly, a few handfuls of wholemeal flour kneaded into a dough with a little water, then rolled out thin and cooked on a skillet, made a whole heap of chapattis.

They worked hard, they had shelter and they had food in their bellies. They rarely talked about the world they had known before. There was little point. It was gone.

Incredible though it seemed, after all they had been through, after everything they had lost, life could still be good, new relationships formed.

The morning after the Pitlochry trip, there were a few nudges and jokes around the table as everyone realised Shaw had moved upstairs with Chrissie, but the only surprise to anyone was that it had taken so long.

Hard work though it was, the new world they had created for themselves wasn't all bad, but the fear that everything could go drastically wrong at any moment constantly narked at the back their minds.

Shaw, in particular, thought about all the tomorrows to come.

"What happens to them if anything happens to us?" he asked Chrissie.

"Then we die and they live," she replied. "Life goes on. Besides, anything could happen to any one of us at any time. There are no guarantees."

"Yeah, and don't we know it, but hear me out. No matter how or when we die - even if we get our three score and ten - at some point, there will only be one of us left. For argument's sake, let's say it's Lucy. Imagine her on her own. Going through the kind of winter you had. Having to live, and die, on her own."

He sat back against a tree trunk, and let his point sink in. They were in the forest gathering wood and had stopped for a break.

"So what do you suggest?" Chrissie asked. She had an

idea of where the conversation was going and she didn't like it.

"The group - it's too small. We've achieved a lot, learned a lot, but we're vulnerable. If anything happens to any one of us, it's going to have a big impact on the rest. I think we need more people."

"More people?" The idea horrified her. She raised an eyebrow at him. "Would that be the bitey kind of people or the shooty kind?"

"I knew you'd be like this."

"Like what?"

"Defensive. Shut down."

"If I am, it's because I've got good reason to be."

Shaw stood up. Started pacing. "There's a whole world out there, Chrissie."

"Yeah, and it's in one hell of a mess."

"Can't you see - new people would bring new skills and knowledge, and a better chance for survival."

"New people mean danger. More chance of death."

He stopped pacing, turned to face her. Looked her in the eye.   "We were new people once."

"Yes, but you were different. You didn't try to bite me or kill me."

"We can't be the only ones. There must be others out there like us."

"Are you sure about that?"

"No. But we have to try."

They stared at each other for a moment, neither willing to concede. Each convinced they were in the right.

They finished that day's work speaking only when necessary. Silence once again thickening between them.

It was their first row and they couldn't let it go. The subject consumed them in the following days. Tension simmered between them, radiating through the group as everyone decided which side they were on. In the evening, books were laid aside as they argued the pros and cons all the way around the woods and back.

Chrissie could see the logic of what Shaw was saying, but it only worked if the mythical new people weren't the killing and raiding and destructing kind.

He argued that there was strength in numbers. She said they risked destroying everything they'd worked so hard to achieve.

Darren was firmly with Shaw. The others wavered, recognising the truth on both sides. They had made a good life. They were vulnerable. Other people were dangerous. More people would help them grow stronger. Would give them more hands to help. And more mouths to feed.

"The ones in Pitlochry didn't shoot us," Shaw said.

It was their third night of arguing.

"Only because we never gave them a chance," Chrissie retorted.

"They could have shot us down at any time, but they let us leave. I've been thinking about it. They're like the ones up in Ullapool. They're only defending themselves. I think we should make contact with them."

"Are you crazy?"

"Chrissie - they cleared the bodies from the streets. They've gathered in supplies - they've probably got every resource in Pitlochry locked down by now. If they can spare the time to clear away bodies, there's got to be at least a dozen of them up there. They are like us. They are organised. They are working at it - trying to make things better. And if they're a little jumpy, well who can blame them?"

"I'll go with you," Darren said.

"No," Chrissie said. "I'll go."

The group fell silent. Everyone looked at her.

"It makes sense. They've seen me before and they know we didn't cause any trouble last time - maybe a couple of familiar faces will help. If anyone has to go, it should be Shaw and me."

69

Since the argument, they'd been sleeping back-to-back. She thought about reaching out to him. Putting her hand on his shoulder, or running a finger down his back. An invitation. But she was scared that he'd shrug her off. Ignore her. Reject her.

That was part of it.

Another part was that she was angry with him. She thought he was wrong. He had an idea and he was willing to compromise the safety of the group to test it. Did he not value what they had? Did he not see how good it was? And she was hurt. He had already rejected her. He had found her, but it wasn't enough. He wanted something more, something else.

Alice had told her how restless he'd been before. Always wanting to leave the village, to push south. He'd been right then. Perhaps he was right now?

No. Chrissie pushed the thought away. He was reckless. Seeking adventure for adventure's sake. Moving for the sake of moving.

On the eve of their last trip to Pitlochry, she'd been excited at the prospect of spending time alone with him. This time she was scared. If Shaw was wrong, there was a good chance they wouldn't be coming back. She closed her eyes and willed sleep to come.

"I hope I've got it wrong," Chrissie said.

Shaw glanced at her. They were in the same positions in the same vehicle. Visual triggers for the people in Pitlochry.

"Me too," he replied.

Fat raindrops splatted against the windscreen.

"Rotten day for it," she said.

"Not even the end of the world as we know it can change summer in Scotland."

He grinned. She smiled back. They had reached some kind of a truce. Whilst conversation hadn't exactly flowed between them, they were at least talking.

"That's new," Chrissie said as they passed a trashed BMW. The windscreen was smashed, passenger door hanging open. Boot and bonnet yawning wide. "I wonder where the driver is."

"Dead in the ditch," Shaw said.

The rain eased off as they approached Pitlochry. They straightened up in their seats as they came to the outskirts of the town. Though there was nothing discernibly different from their last visit, the scene was more desolate under grey skies. Windows darker. Gardens more dishevelled after a battering from heavy rain.

Already driving slowly, Shaw lowered his speed.

"They might have built a barricade further down," he said. "We don't want to surprise them."

Chrissie stiffened.

"What is it?"

She pointed through the windscreen. "There - up ahead, broken windows. It wasn't like that before."

She looked at Shaw. His mouth was set in a grim line.

The devastation became clearer as they moved further towards the centre of town. Windows had been smashed, shops trashed. Several buildings burnt out.

"We should turn round," Chrissie said.

"Not yet. Whatever happened here, it's over."

All the same, Chrissie took one of the rifles from the back of the Land Rover.

Shaw drove around debris lying in the street. Pieces of masonry. Burnt out furniture. A dog, stiff and dead, yellow fur matted. A maroon stain had formed around the knife stuck into its ribcage.

They turned onto the side road where the barricade had been erected. It looked as though a tank had driven through it, the wreckage spilling down the hill.

A woman's body lay among twisted metal. Naked, bloodied. Battered to a pulp.

There were more bodies. Presumably belonging to the people who had erected the barrier. Some had been battered. Others burned. Alive or dead when set alight, they couldn't tell. One man had been hung from a first floor window. Electric cable biting into his neck. Tongue, black and swollen, bulging from his mouth.

They called out, but there was no-one left alive to answer. Even the birds were silent that day.

70

When they got back to the cottage, Elizabeth and Jamie rushed out to meet them. Cries of welcome dried on their lips as they caught sight of Shaw's grim face, Chrissie's hollow eyes.

They delivered the news from Pitlochry in flat tones.

"What now?" Alice asked. "What if whoever did that to them finds us?"

"We won't stand a chance," Jamie said.

That night, when Chrissie put a hand on his back, Shaw turned to her. They made love. Slowly. Intensely.

When it was over, she asked him a question.

"You're leaving, aren't you?"

His answer came in the dark. "Yes."

After what they'd seen in Pitlochry, Shaw was absolutely convinced they needed to find more people. Strengthen their numbers.

"Maybe if we'd hooked up with the Pitlochry ones earlier, they would have survived," he said.

"And maybe we'd all be dead," Chrissie replied.

"Maybe - but how long do you think our luck is going to hold out? Jamie's right - if a mob like that finds us, we won't stand a chance."

He was right. But she was right too. Didn't make it any easier.

The next morning, Shaw and Darren packed for the journey. They would head south, towards the central belt. Towards everything they had thus far avoided.

Running across the waist of Scotland, from Glasgow in the west, to Edinburgh in the east, the central belt contained the highest density of population in the country. More people, more danger. More people, more chance of finding survivors.

They were taking the motorbikes they'd picked up in Feldybridge. They'd be better for getting around road blockages, faster for getting out of sticky situations. They loaded the panniers with food, water, bivvy bags, camping gear and ammunition.

Toby ran around Shaw's ankles, excited, knowing that something was up, not yet realising that she was with the stay-at-home crowd.

It hardly took any time before they were ready to leave. Chrissie felt sick inside as she handed them loaded rifles to sling across their backs. But she plastered a smile on her face and waved them off good-style. Backing them all the way because now that it had come to this, there was nothing else to be done.

For better or worse, what they'd had this few months past was going to change. She was scared of who or what they might find out there. Whatever they found, she hoped that nothing would prevent them coming back.

She kept her fears to herself. The others had enough of their own to deal with. Besides, giving them a voice would only strengthen them.

She glanced at Alice. A sheen of tears had glassed her eyes, but they didn't spill. None of them cried.

When Shaw and Darren had disappeared from sight and the sound of the engines faded to nothing, they turned back to the cottage. Back to the daily business of staying alive.

Lucy ran off to tend the hens. Elizabeth and Jamie went fishing. Chrissie had wood to chop. Alice was going to work in the vegetable garden. Something about the way she moved - the way she held herself - made Chrissie give her a double-take.

When the others had gone, Chrissie sought her out.

"What's wrong?" she asked.

Alice glanced at her briefly, then looked away, brow knotted. The scar on her cheek stood out stark despite her summer tan.

"Nothing," she said, "It's just Darren going, you know..."

Her voice trailed away as she gazed at the ground.

"Yeah, a man's gotta do what a man's gotta do." The bitterness of her own words caught Chrissie by surprise. "Yes, I know, it's hard," she said, toning it down. "I'm hardly getting out the bunting myself."

Alice gave her a diluted smile.

"Now tell me what's really up," Chrissie said.

Alice took a breath.

"I'm pregnant."

71

Chrissie reeled from a sudden rush of emotion, none of it joyful. It all came from the dark end of the spectrum. Fear was the biggest part of it. There was no elation at the thought of new life coming into the world.

There was no light in Alice's face either. All Chrissie could see was her own dread mirrored back at her. Alice was terrified.

Chrissie pulled her close, hugged her tight. The act both giving comfort and allowing her to hide the shock and trepidation playing havoc with her features.

"It'll be all right," she said, "Women have been having babies for thousands of years. Hundreds of thousands of years. It'll be alright."

She kept on telling her it would be alright, saying it over and over again, as much to convince herself as Alice.

Initial shock over, and with her face under control, she released the younger woman from her embrace.

"Let's have a cup of tea."

"But the garden -"

"The garden can wait."

They sat at the kitchen table, the way they had sat many times before, but never with such heavy hearts.

"How far on are you?" Chrissie asked.

"Maybe two months - give or take."

"How sure are you?"

"Two blue lines sure."

Chrissie raised an eyebrow.

"I picked up a testing kit last time we were in town," she said in answer to the implied question.

"That makes it definite then," Chrissie said. "Those kits are pretty accurate."

"It's definite alright."

"You had morning sickness?"

"No."

"Well that's something to be grateful for. Does Darren know?"

Alice shook her head. "He wouldn't have gone if I'd told him."

"But you didn't want him to go," Chrissie said.

"I know. But I didn't want to stop him either." Alice laughed. It wasn't much of a laugh, but it was something. "Crazy, isn't it?"

"That's one word for it." Chrissie said, "Don't worry. It'll be fine."

She'd recovered her composure and was giving sounding convincing her best shot. Truth was, she wasn't at all sure that it would be fine.

Sure, women had been having babies for centuries, but evolution had done nothing to reduce the pain and danger associated with childbirth. It was, as it had ever been, a bloody and brutal practice. Even with expert medical care, women died giving birth, and here they were in the new dark ages and Chrissie was no midwife.

They decided to keep the news from Jamie, Elizabeth and Lucy in case anything went wrong. It was still early days. There was a chance Alice would lose the developing foetus. It would be upsetting and it wouldn't be pleasant, but there were times when Chrissie thought a miscarriage might be for the best.

If Alice went full term, she would be bringing a child into the world who may never meet anyone of their own age. Shaw had been right. Even if they, as a group, managed to live and die in peace, in the end one of them would be left alone. It was a sobering thought.

As it happened, Alice didn't miscarry, she didn't get morning sickness, and her ankles didn't swell. But she was often brought to her knees by overwhelming tiredness. There was little she could do during these periods other than lie down and sleep.

It soon became obvious that something was up, and so the news of the forthcoming child was shared with the others.

They took the news better than Alice and Chrissie had. Finally, there was joy and excitement for the new life she was carrying. As far as Jamie, Elizabeth and Lucy were concerned, this wasn't something to be feared. The new baby represented hope for the future. A promise of something better ahead.

They worked with renewed vigour during the rest of the summer. Determined to cover for the times when Alice couldn't work. Eager to make sure everything was as good as it could be for when the new baby arrived.

They tended the vegetable plots. Salted and smoked the fish they caught and the meat they hunted. They methodically searched through Feldybridge for food, equipment, fuel, clothes, baby items. For anything that was or may become useful. Jamie taught Elizabeth and Lucy how to drive. Life went on.

Days then weeks passed with no sign of Darren or Shaw. Leaves turned gold and red. They blazed, glorious in the autumn sunshine before fading and dropping, becoming brown and brittle underfoot. Hours of light became fewer as the nights drew in, and there was a distinct chill in the air.

Alice passed through her tired phase and worked as hard as the others, though they wouldn't allow her do any heavy tasks.

Pregnancy suited her. Her face filled out. She developed a glow. Her lean figure softened.

She joked to Chrissie that she felt like one of those ancient fertility symbols. All boobs, bum and belly. Chrissie told her she looked beautiful.

She meant it too, but when she caught sight of Alice when she thought no-one was looking, she could see sadness in her eyes. She was missing Darren.

They didn't speak much about Darren or Shaw. Occasionally Lucy would ask if they would be home soon, and Chrissie would tell her yes, she hoped so. But as time went on and Alice's belly swelled, there was no sign of them.

72

They had discussed, planned and rehearsed what they would do if the cottage was attacked. But all the rehearsals in the world couldn't prepare them for how they actually felt when they heard the sound of vehicles approaching.

Hearts raced. Stomachs lurched. Adrenalin coursed through their bodies as they locked down and armed up.

The intruders pulled up in front of the cottage. Climbed out of their vehicles, arms raised, hands empty. Hailed them with the words, *Shaw sent us*.

Fear had them by the throat when the first lot arrived. It was a wonder no-one was shot. When panic subsided, they realised what the arrival signalled. Darren and Shaw were alive. They were achieving what they set out to do. They were out there finding survivors. The right kind of survivors.

They arrived in dribs and drabs, in ones, twos or threes, occasionally in a slightly larger group. Shambolic, post-plague families with no common blood. Related to each other by what they'd been through. Just like themselves.

The first lot caught them by surprise, but as more survivors came their way, a routine was established. They

301

served them a hot meal - soup or a stew - and listened to their stories.

Tales of scavenging for food, of trying to find somewhere safe to sleep were repeated over and over. The cities and towns offered rich pickings shelter and food-wise, but danger came in many forms.

Packs of feral dogs stalked streets across the country. In Edinburgh, wild animals, set free from the zoo, roamed the lanes and avenues. A woman from Corstorphine told them of how both her husband and herself had miraculously survived the disease, only for Frank to be killed by a bear in his front garden. She escaped as his head was torn from his body.

It wasn't only large animals wreaking havoc. One survivor's hideout was overrun by rats. In warm weather the air vibrated with the hum of bluebottles. Every corpse - human and animal - writhing with maggots.

Each person who arrived at the cottage had encountered at least one Screamer. They had different names for them - Crazies, Psychos, Sickos, Mentallers. Even Zombies. Sometimes they managed to evade them. More often, they had killed to survive.

A picture built up as new people arrived with stories to tell.

More recent encounters with hostiles involved mobs, similar to the one Chrissie had seen in Feldybridge. It seemed there were gangs of them roaming the country. Moving from one town to the next, devouring and destroying, like plagues of locusts.

It was a lawless world, far removed from the tranquillity they had created for themselves. Even as Chrissie welcomed the survivors, she wondered what Shaw had brought to their doorstep.

Anyone arriving late in the day was invited to camp beside the cottage for the night. Some of them had vehicles they were already living in. Motor homes or trucks. Others had been camping or sleeping rough. One more night wouldn't kill them.

Most of them seemed pleased to find the cottage and reacted with gratitude. Some Chrissie wasn't so sure about. More than once, she cursed Shaw under her breath.

No matter how grateful, how friendly, the new arrivals seemed, she made sure the doors were bolted at night.

In the morning, following a simple breakfast of porridge, one of the group would take them to Feldybridge and help them find somewhere to live.

New homes were cleared of old occupants, the bodies wrapped in sheets and taken out to the street. They were loaded onto a truck, taken to the burnt-out church and stacked in funeral pyres. When the stack was big enough to warrant the use of fuel, it was doused in petrol or paraffin and burned at night so that the smoke would not be seen from a distance.

In this way, corpses were slowly cleared from the village.

Shaw's predictions were uncannily accurate. As the survivors trickled in, they brought new skills with them. Some, like carpentry, were as useful for the new life as they had been in the old world. Some, like the candle-maker, were more vital now than they had been before, although these days no-one cared too much about pretty colours or fancily-named scents.

Other skills were non-transferable. The new world had no need for call centre managers. Even so, everyone had something to offer. Anyone who had survived thus far had already proved themselves.

From the moment they first came, Chrissie hoped for someone with medical training. Any kind of medical training. Didn't need to be a mid-wife. They would have been glad of a dentist, or a vet, or even a nit nurse. The closest they got was a woman from Cumbernauld who worked at the make-up counter in Boots.

Despite the lack of anyone with medical skills, Chrissie was astounded by the way people mucked in. Fishing parties were organised and the catch shared out. As more people arrived, a barter system developed.

A market was set up, making it easier for people to exchange goods and services. A carpentry job for a haunch of venison. Eggs for candles. There was a will to work together. Chrissie berated herself for being so cynical. Shaw had been right. They were stronger now. Yes, there were more mouths to feed, but there were also more people able to provide food. People were helping each other. Looking out for one another. At last, she could allow herself to feel hope for Alice's baby. All they needed now was for its father to come home.

As winter progressed, the unsteady flow of newcomers faltered then stopped altogether, but still Darren and Shaw did not return.

73

Five months after Darren and Shaw left, a letter was delivered to the cottage. It contained an invitation to a mid-winter celebration in Feldybridge. Chrissie read it several times over. To receive post - any kind of post - was strange in itself. To receive an invitation to a party was stranger still.

The piece of paper she held in her hand signified just how much their situation had changed in such a short period of time. With no involvement on their part, a social gathering had been organised. They were no longer central to the new community. They were on the outside.

Her immediate response was trepidation. What else had been going on down there that they didn't know about?

Overwhelmed by so many people concentrated in one place, she had kept herself apart from the village. Shaw would think that a mistake. It was possible he was right, but Chrissie had reacted on gut feeling. Some of the incomers made her feel uncomfortable. Despite the good things she saw going on like the clearing of the dead and the market, her instinct was to keep her distance. The invitation only increased her feelings of unease.

"But why don't you want to go?" Jamie asked.

"It doesn't feel right."

She could see the frustration in his face at her woolly response, but how could she articulate her feelings when she did not fully understand them herself?

"You have to go," he insisted. "We all have to go - it will look really odd if you don't."

"Why does it matter so much?" Chrissie asked. "We can have our own celebration here."

"Jamie's right," Elizabeth said. "We have to go."

Chrissie could see in their faces that this wasn't about a couple of teenagers wanting to go to a party. There was something more behind it. Something sinister. And that was exactly why she didn't want to go. Why she didn't want any of them to go.

Although she had stayed away from the village, Jamie and Elizabeth had spent a lot of time there. They knew more about what was going on than Chrissie did and she trusted them. If it wasn't important, they would not persist like this.

Relief was evident on their faces when Chrissie finally relented and agreed to go. So much so, that her trepidation deepened.

The celebration was to take place on the following day.

74

The gathering took place in the village hall. It had been decked with boughs of holly, candles and paraffin lamps. The price of entry was a contribution of food for the buffet.

An admission table had been set up in the vestibule. Contributions were, it seemed, compulsory. They handed over a couple of sides of smoked trout, a stack of pancakes and a bucket of freshly cooked crayfish. Behind the handing-over table, Chrissie could see that most of the other contributions had been scavenged from the old world. Tins of meat, cans of fruit, biscuits, chocolate.

Chrissie's thoughts of how wrong it was, of how they couldn't keep living on the past, that one day it would all run out, were stifled as they entered the hall proper.

There were many faces she did not recognise. She had known that some new arrivals had by-passed the cottage, going directly to the village instead, but had not realised how many of them there had been.

She couldn't take a proper breath. The room seemed too small, the faces too many, the sound of chatter and laughter too loud. Her stomach tightened.

"Are you alright?" Alice whispered.

"There are more people than I thought," she said.

Alice nodded her agreement. She didn't look any more comfortable than Chrissie felt. Jamie, Elizabeth and Lucy disappeared, swallowed by the crowd.

In the far corner, a man began playing a fiddle. The hubbub died down as people turned to listen. A woman Chrissie recognised, accompanied him on the mouth organ. Her name was Mo. She'd turned up at the cottage in a campervan. Someone they couldn't see over the crowd clanked on a set of spoons. People began dancing. Chrissie and Alice found a couple of seats on the periphery of the party.

"Where are the others?" Chrissie asked.

She peered through the throng.

"Jamie saw someone he knew," Alice replied.

Bottles appeared. Wine, spirits, beer. A tall man with a bald head and jug ears appeared in front of them, offering a choice of rum or vodka. They politely declined.

"You sure, ladies?" He leered down at them.

"We're sure," Chrissie smiled. Keeping it friendly.

"All the more for me." He shrugged and grinned before moving away.

Chrissie picked out faces in the crowd. The candle-maker, the make-up woman from Cumbernauld. Jamie, talking to a tall girl with close cropped hair. She looked about sixteen.

"Who is that with Jamie?" she asked.

"Her name is Iona," Alice replied.

"I assume she's the reason he's been spending so much time down here?"

Alice smiled and nodded.

Chrissie had been so caught up in watching Alice and keeping everything ticking over at the cottage that she'd lost sight of what else was going on.

Alcohol flowed around them. People drinking like there were no tomorrows. The volume increased. Chrissie cringed at an outbreak of raucous laughter. It sounded forced and try-too-hard.

"Do you think we've stayed long enough?" she asked.

"Don't you want anything to eat?"

"Not hungry," Chrissie replied, raising her voice to be heard. "Besides, this lot seem more interested in liquid refreshment."

"Yeah, let's go. The noise is killing me."

"You stay here," Chrissie said, "I'll round up the others."

She walked round the hall, looking for them. It wasn't a large room. It wouldn't take too many people to fill it, but it felt as though it was holding a multitude. It was more people than Chrissie had seen in a long time. And way more than she was comfortable with.

She glanced into a side room where the food had been laid out on tables. Two women and a man stood in a huddle in the middle of the room, speaking in low voices. On noticing Chrissie, one of the women nudged the other. The other turned and fixed Chrissie with pale, basilisk eyes.

"Buffet's not open." The words snapping from her lips.

Chrissie glanced at the tables behind her. The pancakes were stacked beside a bowl of salted crackers. Of the smoked trout and boiled crayfish, there was no sign.

Clocking her glance, the man, short, but thick-set, squared his shoulders. His nose sprawled meatily across his face. Looked like it had been broken several times over.

It was hardly party-wear, but out of habit Chrissie's knife was strapped to her thigh. No matter what went down, she knew that she'd use it if she had to.

As if reading her thoughts, the man's finger's curled. Thick fingers. Hairy knuckles. The trio undoubtedly had allies in the hall. Friends or people who were intimidated by them and who would do their bidding out of fear. Either way, they'd have back-up. Seasonal though it was, Chrissie didn't want their group turned to mincemeat.

She pulled a dumb-old-me grin up from her boots, plastered it across her face and told them she was looking for someone.

"Well they're not in here," the basilisk smirked.

Resisting the almost overwhelming urge to cut a new smirk in her throat, Chrissie made her excuses and left.

She told herself she was being paranoid, but scouting around the hall, she picked up on pockets of bad vibes. The noise level had risen in parallel with the amount of alcohol being consumed. There were no mixers. People were downing straight shots of spirits. Laughter was rising to the rafters, but there were rumbling undercurrents of violence.

It felt like something could kick off at any moment, and Chrissie didn't fancy some of the narrow-eyed looks coming her way.

75

They sat in silence on the drive back to the cottage. Inside, with the doors bolted and the curtains closed, Chrissie shared her impressions of the party.

She hoped they would laugh at her. Tell her she was being paranoid. That she was blowing the whole thing out of proportion. It was only a bunch of people letting off steam. No harm was meant. Trouble was, no-one laughed. They agreed with her.

She looked at their pale, worried faces and cursed herself for blithely ignoring the developing situation in Feldybridge. For thinking hiding out in the woods would be enough to keep them safe. She couldn't have been more naïve if she'd tried.

When she was done cursing herself, she cursed Shaw for bringing trouble to them. She'd had the thought plenty of times before, but had kept it to herself. Saying it out loud was like committing blasphemy.

The others stared at her, hollow-eyed in the lamp light.

It was Jamie who broke the silence.

"There's a girl," he said. "Iona."

He glanced at Chrissie. She nodded. He continued. "She's only here because of Shaw, and I'm glad of that, but some of the others..."

"What about them, Jamie?"

"She told me - there have been fights. Mostly over food. It's not so easy to come by now. There's a woman no-one has seen for a while. She arrived on her own. After she disappeared, a man started trading meat at the market. Iona saw it. She thinks..."

The words faltered on Jamie's lips.

"Iona thinks the man killed and butchered her?" Chrissie finished the sentence for him.

Jamie nodded. Lucy screwed her face up. Chrissie stroked her hair but, young though she was, saw little value in keeping the knowledge from her. They all had to survive in this world. To do so, they had to know what they were up against. Chrissie included. It was time she pulled her head out of the hole it had been in.

"I'm worried about Iona," Jamie continued. "Do you think she could come here?"

"To live with us you mean?"

The boy nodded. Chrissie studied him. She hadn't looked at him properly in a long time. His face had grown leaner these last few months, his body harder. He was shaving regularly. He was on the brink of manhood. And he was in love.

She felt a sudden burst of affection for him. If he had found someone, she wasn't going to stand in the way.

"Could she?" he asked.

"What about her group?"

"She doesn't have one. She met the people she came in with on the road here. Mostly she's been on her own." Chrissie looked at the others. "What do you think?"

"If Jamie says she's okay, then she's okay," Elizabeth said.

"Lucy?"

"She seems nice."

"Alice?"

"I agree with Elizabeth."

"You know," Chrissie said to Jamie, "there's no

guarantee she'll be any safer up here with us."

"I know," he replied.

"Okay then," Chrissie said. "She can join us."

The next morning, just as dawn broke, Jamie set off for the village. He went by bicycle. Engines attracted too much attention.

Chrissie stood by the blue gate and watched him go. He was young and in love. What trials and tribulations he had ahead of him, she did not know, but at least he had found someone to share them with. In this world, no-one could dare hope for more.

She suddenly turned her head. Stared into the woods. The warm feeling gone. Ice frosting her spine. Hairs on the back of her neck standing up.

The forest consisted of one shadow merging into another. Stippled bark of silver birch. Mossy hummocks. Brown, tangled briars. Colours muted. The only thing standing out were bare tree branches, stark against the grey dawn sky.

She couldn't see anything, but it didn't matter. She'd known it in Pitlochry and she knew it now. Someone was watching her

76

Iona returned with Jamie. He hadn't been gone long. She couldn't have taken any persuasion to join him. More likely, they'd already planned the move. Apart from the bike she rode, all she had with her was a small rucksack.

"It's all I need," she said. "Anything else just gets in the way."

Chrissie noted the knife sheath strapped to her lean thigh. Iona was going to fit right in.

She mucked in with the rest of them. Seemed happy enough to do whatever was required. Chopping wood, skinning rabbits, cleaning out the hen house. She didn't say much during the day, but sitting by the warm glow of the stove that night, she thanked them for taking her in.

We're glad you're here," Alice said.

"I didn't like it in the village." Iona plaited Lucy's hair as she spoke. "It was good to begin with, people helping each other, pulling together, trying to make it work, but there were others... A man called Carnegie - he was the worst. Him and the women he hung around with."

"Short, stocky guy with a broken nose?" Chrissie asked.

"That's him," Iona nodded. "He's really mean. He forces people to give him stuff."

"Why don't they stand up to him?" Alice asked.

"He's got followers. Anyone who doesn't do what they are told gets beaten up. Or worse. People are scared. Some are talking about leaving, others want to stay. They say no matter how bad Carnegie and his lot are, they are better off in Feldybridge than anywhere else they've been. They'd rather pay him off than take their chances elsewhere."

"What do you think?" Chrissie asked.

"I don't like the way it's going down there, and it's getting worse. If you hadn't taken me in, I'd have taken my chances on the road."

"How did you hear about Feldybridge - did you meet Shaw?" Chrissie's heart thumped as she asked the question.

Iona shook her head. "I heard the name, but never met him. I mostly stayed away from other people, but I met this group. They seemed okay. They'd met people who told them about Shaw. The way they told it made Feldybridge sound like paradise. I had nothing better to do so I hooked up with them. Decided to see for myself what it was like. To be honest, I wasn't even sure that Shaw was a real person."

"He's real," Chrissie said. "He lived here, with us. Him, and Darren too."

Iona looked up from Lucy's hair. "Darren? He's the dad, right?" she asked Alice.

Alice nodded, absent-mindedly stroking her swollen belly.

"Where are they now?" Iona asked.

"I wish I knew." Chrissie gave Alice's arm a squeeze as she replied.

It had been a long time since anyone had turned up with the words, *Shaw sent us.*

For a while, they had been a beacon of light in the dark, but thanks to Carnegie and his sidekicks, that light had been extinguished.

Chrissie thought that Iona might be missed, but in the

following days nobody came looking for her. Inasmuch as she didn't want anyone sniffing around the cottage, it was a relief. But it was also sad that a young woman could disappear overnight without causing so much as a ripple.

If they thought about her at all, they probably assumed she'd run off. Or maybe they were waiting for some fresh meat to turn up at the market. In any case, it was better if she stayed away from the village. There was no argument from Iona. She'd had her fill of the place. Jamie was another matter.

Chrissie thought they should all stay away from Feldybridge. If they'd wanted to influence what was going on there, they should have been involved from the start. Maybe keeping out of it had been a mistake, but the opportunity was long gone. Their best plan now was to stay out of sight.

If they weren't a threat to anyone, if no one saw them around, maybe they'd be left alone.

Jamie disagreed. Said she was being naive. That it was more important to get information. That they had to know what was going on. Besides, nobody paid him any attention. In their eyes, he was just a kid. This rendered him practically invisible.

Right or wrong, foolish or wise, he was adamant. He had the burning conviction of youth on his side. Chrissie envied his simple clarity of vision. She over-thought things so much, she didn't know if she was seeing anything straight anymore. It didn't help that she'd been spooked in the woods a couple of times now. Couldn't shake the feeling she was being watched.

Not sure now whether the feelings were real or imagined, she kept them to herself. They were in a watchful enough state as it was. No point in winding people up any tighter.

There was no dissuading Jamie from his mission. A couple of days later, he sloped off with a fry of trout to trade. He returned with a handful of candles, half a loaf of hard bread, and a whole barrel of news.

77

Unable to resist the lure of superstores and all the easy pickings they had to offer, Carnegie organised raiding parties. They swooped around the peripheries of conurbations, plundering out-of-town stores and siphoning fuel.

As might be expected, many stores had already been ransacked or burned out. But some were strangely untouched. Aisle after brazen aisle of dizzying, consumer choice and all free for the taking. They came back from those trips laden down with booze, cigarettes, chocolate and tinned meat. Returning in the following days to clear the shelves.

On one such raid, they came face-to-face with a rival gang. There was no parley. Carnegie's crew immediately and gleefully threw themselves into bloodthirsty battle. They won the skirmish, showing no mercy in victory.

There were whispered tales of women from the other mob being gang-raped then tied to trucks. They were dragged up the A9, screaming themselves hoarse, until the clothes and skin had been flayed from their bodies. Their raw, red corpses left as carrion on the road.

Surviving men had their testicles cut off and stuffed in their mouths, left to choke or bleed to death as they were hung from lampposts.

The gore-fest fired Carnegie's crew up. Problem was, rival gangs were few and far between, so they came up with a new blood sport. Collecting supplies became a side show to the main event of hunting down Screamers.

The lucky ones were shot. The less fortunate were hanged, and stripped, their stomachs slashed. Viscera tumbled warm and steaming from their torsos. A feast for rats and birds and feral dogs.

There was a rumour going round that Carnegie cut the ears from his victims and threaded them onto a necklace he wore next to his skin.

Back at the cottage, Jamie repeated the stories. When she heard about the necklace of ears, Chrissie said it sounded like Carnegie had read one Vietnam War memoir too many. She doubted he'd ever been a nice guy, but now he had the opportunity to give free rein to his fantasies and it sounded as though he was making the most of it.

There was a difference between killing a Screamer in self-defence and deliberately hunting down what were essentially sick people, and killing them for fun.

Jamie couldn't say how much of what he had heard was true and how much was propaganda, spread by Carnegie's goons to keep the people in check. But even if only a fraction of it had really happened, the picture was grim enough.

What he could tell them was that the people in Feldybridge believed the stories. They were sucking them up, every last word. When they'd chewed them over and digested all they'd heard, they mostly signed up to Carnegie's crew. Better to be on the winning side, than become a victim.

Anyone who voiced objections was summarily silenced. You were either with them or you were against them. There was no middle ground.

When Jamie finished talking, they sat in silence. Digesting all they'd heard.

Iona and Jamie gripped each others' hands under the table. Alice hugged herself, wrapping her arms protectively around her heavy belly. Sitting on either side of Chrissie, Lucy and Elizabeth instinctively leaned into her. She put her arms around their thin shoulders. It wasn't enough. She had to do more to protect them. All of them.

A low growl from Toby broke the silence. They exchanged startled glances as the dog stalked across the room, hackles raised. They got to their feet, overturning chairs, as her growls turned into a volley of barks.

Somebody was banging on the front door.

78

"Who goes there?" Chrissie demanded.

She stood against the wall at the side of the door, rifle loaded, safety off. Her stomach was in a tight knot but her hands were steady and there was no tremble in her voice.

"A friend," came the reply.

"Identify yourself."

"It's Nigel, the candle-maker. I spoke to Jamie today. He traded three brown trout for candles and some bread. I need to speak to you. Please."

Chrissie looked down the hall at Jamie. He gave a nod. She leaned over and unlocked the door.

"Open it," she called, "but do it slowly and keep your hands where I can see them."

When he'd opened the door, the candle-maker raised his hands above his head. Chrissie glanced over his shoulder.

"You alone?"

"The others are waiting at the end of the track."

She nodded him in, locking the door behind him and ushered him through to the kitchen. He'd been one of the early arrivals. Had eaten with them.

Elizabeth and Iona kept watch from the windows

upstairs while the others gathered to listen to what he had to say.

"Did Jamie tell you what I told him today?"

Chrissie nodded. The candle-maker wore spectacles. There was a crack in one of the lenses. His face was gaunt.

"Talking to him like that - telling him what I did - it was dangerous. Carnegie has eyes and ears all over the place. But you were so kind when we first arrived - I wanted to warn you before we go."

"You leaving?" Chrissie asked.

He nodded.

"They've gone on a night raid. They're not just looking for Screamers now. They're killing anybody they come across. They're killing for fun. We're getting out while they're away. While we still can."

"Where are you heading?" Jamie asked.

"To the coast," he replied. "We're going to get a boat, try for the islands. I'd advise you to do the same. You're not safe here anymore."

79

"Are we going?" Jamie asked.

The sound of the door closing behind the candle-maker was still ringing in the air.

Chrissie nodded. "Yes."

"When?"

"Now. We pack and leave now."

Her mind already churning over what they should take. The pick-up and Range Rover were fuelled up. They'd pack what they could in them and leave the car behind.

They'd made a home at Birch Cottage. Had planted, planned for the future. Now they would have to get out with what they could.

It was down to essentials. Food, water, sleeping bags, torches, first aid kit, matches, rifles, a few clothes.

"They're worse than Screamers," Alice said. She had packed a bag of baby kit they'd accumulated. Clothes, nappies, blankets.

"Much worse," Chrissie agreed. "Screamers have a disease. Carnegie and his mob don't have any excuse. There's no reason for what they do."

"They're just bad people." Lucy, behind them, listening in.

"Yes, they are bad people," Chrissie went to her and

323

gave her a hug, "but we're not."

"Can I take these?"

She showed Chrissie a box of Crayola crayons.

"Of course you can," Chrissie said, "They definitely count as essential."

When they'd finished packing everything else, they crammed as much extra food as they could into the back of the truck. Filling every space with cans from the old time and bags filled with strips of smoked fish and meat.

It was Alice who asked the question they'd all been avoiding.

"What about Darren and Shaw?"

"I don't know," Chrissie said. She'd been thinking about them ever since it had become clear that they had to get out. "I don't know how we can leave them a message without risking Carnegie's lot finding it.

"It doesn't matter," Jamie kicked at a stone, keeping his gaze away from theirs as he spoke. "They're probably dead."

"No, they're not dead," Elizabeth said. "I know it."

"I hope you're right, Elizabeth," Chrissie said, "but either way, we've got to get out of here. Did you let the hens out?"

"Yes, we shooed them out to the woods and scattered a sack of feed around. And we locked up the run, so they can't get back in."

Chrissie nodded. Better the birds took their chances in the woods, than risk mass slaughter by Carnegie.

She surveyed the moonlit scene. Her car was parked by the cottage gate. A sign that someone was at home. The cottage doors were locked, the curtains closed, but they'd left chinks so that the light from the lamps inside glinted through. Anyone checking on them would think they were inside, cosied down for the night instead of making good their escape.

Thinking about hens. Thinking about the cottage.

Thinking about anything other than Darren and Shaw.

She closed the tail-gate.

"Right, that's it - let's get out of-"

She stopped, mid-sentence. Her scalp prickling as she got that being-watched feeling again.

Beside her, Toby stared into the woods. The dog quivered as she emitted a low whine.

"Maybe it's the hens she hears, " Elizabeth whispered.

"Maybe," Chrissie said, keeping her voice low in return. Thinking the dog was used to being around hens. Knowing that the candle-maker and his group were long gone. Thinking they'd maybe left their own departure too late. That they shouldn't have taken the time to pack. They should have driven away there and then. Not given Carnegie's mob time to quietly surround them.

No, that was crazy thinking. Those guys whooped and hollered. They didn't do anything quietly. Except maybe this once.

"Let's go," she said. Maybe if they just got into their vehicles and left, they'd be let alone.

"C'mon girl," she said to Toby.

The dog took off, darting into the woods. Lost in the shadows in seconds. Jamie started after her. Chrissie grabbed his arm.

"No - we'll have to go without her," she said.

He looked at Chrissie as though she'd suggested abandoning Lucy.

"We have to go," Chrissie repeated. "Toby's got a good chance of surviving out there, but if we stay, we die."

He shrugged her off.

"It's not right," he said, but he stayed where he was.

"No, it's not - but we can't risk all our lives for a dog. For all we know, Carnegie's mob are out there right now."

He glanced at Iona.

"Let's go," he said, turning away from Chrissie. Knowing she was right and hating her for it.

A sudden commotion in the undergrowth stopped him

325

in his tracks. Twigs snapping. Leaves crunching. Branches creaking and cracking. Something coming towards them.

Toby came belting out of the trees. A figure loping behind her. Tall, determined. Coming straight at them. A Screamer. Chrissie pulled out her knife.

"Get the guns," she hissed at Jamie.

He ran to get them.

Chrissie raised her knife. Elizabeth gasped as the figure approached. Chrissie faltered. The moonlight playing tricks on her eyes. Yes. No, it couldn't be.

Then he said her name and she knew it was him.

Shaw.

80

Darren came out of the bushes behind him.

They stood at the tree-line, staring at the group. The group staring right back. It was no illusion - they really were standing there, but they looked different.

Neither man had carried any excess weight before they'd gone, but now they were leaner, harder looking. Shaw's face looked as if it had been scrambled up and put back together in a rush. A scar slashed across his face from his cheekbone, over his lips to his jaw-line. There was a scar on Darren's temple and a squint in his nose where none had been before. They had machetes in their hands, rifles across their shoulders.

Darren was first to break the tableau. He went to Alice, put a hand on her belly. He didn't seem surprised that she was pregnant.

"When is it due?" he asked.

"Save the baby talk till later," Chrissie said. Her words were addressed to Darren, but it was Shaw she was looking at. "Right now we need to get out of here."

Shaw nodded like it was nothing more than the welcome home speech he'd been expecting.

In the distance, there was the sound of an explosion. Everyone moved at once, piling into the vehicles. Jamie,

Iona, Alice and Darren in the pick-up. Elizabeth, Lucy, Shaw, Chrissie and Toby in the Range Rover. They drove with the lights off. No need to advertise the fact that they were on the move.

"It was you, in the woods, wasn't it?" Chrissie asked.

"Yeah, it was us."

"I knew someone was watching me. You freaked me out, you know that?"

"Sorry about that."

"That's why Darren didn't looked surprised when he saw Alice - he already knew she was pregnant."

"Yeah, but it was a shock when he first saw her."

"Why didn't you come to the cottage - why were you hiding?"

"Couldn't risk it. If Carnegie or one of his lot spotted us, they'd have come after you straight away. We needed to suss out how things were first. And, the truth is, we needed some time to rest up."

She glanced at him. "You okay? You look like you've been through the wars."

Shaw looked back at her. "I'm okay. Now."

He mustered a smile. Her stomach did a little flip. She had an urge to touch him. Trace her fingers over his beat-up face. Instead, she concentrated on the track they were following.

"How come you know about Carnegie?" she asked.

Shaw rubbed the scar where it ended on his jaw. "Ran into him down near Stirling. Let's just say we didn't hit it off. Who was the guy with the glasses?"

"Candle-maker. You sent him to Feldybridge. He came to warn us to get out."

Shaw nodded. "I thought he looked familiar. Funny, we were on our way to tell you the same thing when he turned up."

"Why now - expecting trouble?" Chrissie asked.

"Always."

She looked at him sideways. Caught his grin in the light

328

of the dashboard. Despite the many grievances she still held against him, she grinned right back.

They drove to the bottom of the hill that overlooked the village. The others stayed by the vehicles, Darren and Alice billing and cooing over each other, while Shaw and Chrissie clambered to the top for a look-see.

They were having quite the party in Feldybridge. The kind of party people ended up dead. Motorbikes screeched up and down streets lit by burning oil drums. Cars raced, careening round bends, tyres screeching. Occasional screams pierced through the cold night air.

"It's like this all over," Shaw said. "People have gone crazy."

"We're not all like that," Chrissie said.

"No, but there are more of them than there are of us."

"But why are they doing it - they're using up all the resources left from before. It won't last forever - what will they do when it's all gone?"

"That's just it," he said. "They don't care. They think we're all finished anyway, so what does it matter."

"So what do we do?" Chrissie asked, "What's the plan?"

"Plan? I thought you had one."

"My only plan was to get the hell out before they came for us."

"Sounds good to me," he said.

"That's it? That's all you've got?" Chrissie could hear her voice rising, but wasn't in any mood to tone it down. "You disappear for all those months, send a load of psychos our way and when you do turn up you don't even bring a plan?"

"I didn't send the psychos - I sent the candle-maker. And even if I didn't send anyone, they'd have come anyway. They're always on the move. Looking for easy pickings. And I didn't think I needed a plan - I thought you'd have one."

"My plan was to make a life at the cottage. What we're

doing now isn't a plan. It's called running away."

They left that one hanging. Tension throbbing between them as they lay side by side on their stomachs, propped up on elbows, looking down at the village.

Finally Chrissie turned her head, started to speak. Before she could get the words out, Shaw turned his head and kissed her on the mouth.

It was just a kiss, but it was enough. Enough warmth, enough feeling, enough connection, to remind them of who they were.

The resentment she felt ebbed away. She couldn't blame him because he didn't have any more answers than anyone else. He wasn't a hero or a saviour. He was just a man trying his best to survive in a world that had been turned inside out.

They stayed on the hill awhile, watching as the party in the village became louder, more unruly. There was an explosion. More screaming. A woman running. Three men chasing her. They caught her. Dragged her fighting and kicking into a building.

"Check out the front of the church," Shaw said.

Chrissie checked it out. Vehicles gathering. Motorbikes, a couple of trucks, cars, driving around, circling, then breaking away from the circle. Moving out, along the high street. Onto the road that led to the cottage.

"They're coming to get us," she said.

"That's what it looks like."

They lost sight of the convoy as it disappeared beneath the bluff of the hill. A short while later, petrol-fed flames whooshed into the night sky. They came from the direction of Birch Cottage.

Darren appeared beside them.

"The cottage is gone," Chrissie told him.

"What if they start looking for us?" he asked.

"Look," Shaw nudged Chrissie. The convoy was

returning to the village.

"They think they've burned us alive," she said.

They stayed on the hill, watching, waiting until the revellers passed out and the party waned. When all was quiet, they got into their vehicles and fled into the night.

81

They kept mainly to the back roads veining the country. The landscape had changed drastically since Chrissie's journey to Birch Cottage. Though many of them had been shunted into ditches, there were still plenty of abandoned vehicles around. But now there were also mudslides, fallen trees and ruptures in the roads to contend with.

Nature had been reclaiming her territory. Verges were overgrown, grasses creeping over barely-used tarmac. Every summer they grew, flowered, multiplied, inching across asphalt, recovering ground, until, gradually, roads became trails. In danger of becoming forever lost in chaotic undergrowth.

In the countryside cultivated edges blurred as hedgerows grew large and tangled. Wildflower meadows flourished. Cowslip, sorrel and ragged robin weaving through the ribcages of skeletal cattle, wending through the jaws of sheep long dead.

Cities, towns, villages, were in a state of decay. Wherever people had lived in any number, wherever they had built, making their mark upon the land, there was now dereliction. Peeling paint, dirty windows, broken glass, cracks in the pavements, potholes in the roads. Saplings sprouting from gutters.

Burst sewage pipes created cesspools in ruined streets. Weeds had taken hold in nooks and crannies, roots fastening to crumbling buildings, ripping at the pointing, eating into the brickwork. Tiny plants tearing down what homo sapiens had built up.

Despite their determination to keep a low profile, they were often forced onto main roads, where they felt exposed and open to attack. But no matter where they travelled, they were on the constant look-out for bandits and Screamers.

Here and there, they came across pockets of survivors. But there was fear and wariness on both sides. Guns were aimed, slow retreats made. The group forced back onto the road. Forced to keep moving, to keep searching for somewhere they could settle. Not just a cottage in the woods. They needed a place they could defend. Somewhere they couldn't be burned out of. And they needed someplace safe where Alice could give birth.

They spent several nights in a crumbling four star hotel on the outskirts of Aviemore. The ground floor had been trashed, mirrors broken, sofas and armchairs slashed. The bar had long-since been raided, but in the housekeeping store they found sachets of instant hot chocolate, along with tea, coffee and packs of out-of-date shortbread.

On the second floor they found a clutch of rooms, vacant, intact. They took up residence, boiled water on a camping stove and dunked soggy biscuits into hot chocolate, relishing the sweet taste.

They slept on king-size beds, wrapped in sheets mottled with mildew, their heads resting on damp pillows.

They knew from the start it was not a place they could settle. It could not be easily defended and it was falling apart. The roof was leaking, the building sliding to decay. They drank the hot chocolate, ate the biscuits and when they'd rested for a couple of days, they moved on.

82

Chrissie cursed as Shaw suddenly hit the brakes.

"What the-?"

She'd been dozing, trying to lose the lack-of-sleep buzz in her head. As soon as she saw his face, she shut up.

"Look - there."

She followed his gaze. Iona and Jamie leaned forward to see what was up. Darren pulled up behind them and then they all saw it.

Shaw looked at Chrissie, gauging her reaction.

They'd been travelling through Morayshire, camping out when they couldn't find shelter for the night. Chrissie hadn't had a decent sleep since the luxury of the damp bed near Aviemore. She felt tired and dirty. Everyone was grumpy. Tempers were fraying. Moods fractious. Their mission to find somewhere they could settle, seemed impossible.

Chrissie had the grinding feeling that they were going to live on the road, and die on the road. The appeal of laying down to sleep and never waking up was growing every day. But now this.

She nodded at Shaw, a knot of excitement in her stomach. The unfamiliar feeling of hope welling inside her.

It was a road sign. Brown, the kind once used to

denote tourist sites. It was partially covered by overhanging branches from above, unkempt shrubbery from below. Through the twiggy growth, the legend read, **Fort George**.

Chrissie tried not to get too excited as they followed the sign. Driving slowly, cautiously, along narrow lanes. The more hopeful she allowed herself to be, the more crushing the blow when it all went wrong. It was bound to be settled already. The inhabitants unwelcoming. The drawbridge up.

But no barricades blocked their progress. And nothing stirred as they drove through the small fishing village of Ardersier. The half dozen bodies lying on the pavements were skeletal. Their clothing weather-worn rags.

The village was a ghost town. Paint peeling, windows glazed with two winters' worth of mire, and gardens grew wild and tangled, but there had been no deliberate destruction. No glass smashed. No buildings burned. If gangs roamed these parts, they had by-passed Ardersier, leaving it to sink into natural decay.

When the Fort came into view, they stopped the vehicles, got out and treated themselves to a good, long look.

It sat on a promontory, thick, stone walls flanked on three sides by the sea. Nobody said a word. They didn't have to. They knew this was the place.

Fort George had been built to keep the highland clans in order after the Jacobite uprisings of the eighteenth century. Until the coming of the disease, the impregnable fortress had been an army garrison and tourist attraction.

As a fortress, it was a work of beauty, defended by deep ditches, a fearsome rampart and mighty bastions. The stone walls were designed to absorb artillery shot. Thousands of tons of earth had been put in place to absorb the impact of enemy cannonballs. Earth which could now be dug over to form vegetable beds.

The desiccated bodies of two Historic Scotland staff,

identifiable by their uniforms and name badges, lay in the shop. There were ten bodies in the small chapel, including a baby in a pram. Several more bodies lay throughout the Fort. Visitors. People still thinking it couldn't happen to them. These people had worked and toured and prayed until they dropped.

Of the soldiers, there was no sign. Perhaps they had been deployed to quell civil unrest. Or had fled to be with their families. Whatever their story, no-one would know it now.

Within the Fort, there were open fireplaces, gas cookers and two massive gas tanks. Enough to keep them going for quite some time.

They helped themselves to swords from the Regimental Museum. A few extra guns, ammunition, and maybe a grenade or two would have been handy, but the armoury had been emptied, presumably when the garrison departed.

They had running water, space to grow food and access to the sea for fishing. They even had room enough to keep livestock. If they could find any to rear.

The Fort had been designed to hold two thousand men so there was space aplenty for them. Most importantly of all, they would be able to defend themselves from any bandits or Screamers who came their way.

They started over again with the digging and planting. Got busy with the hunting, fishing and trapping. They skinned rabbits, gutted fish, plucked wood pigeons. Skin, gut, pluck, cook, eat. *Shrink-wrapped-pre-prepared-pre-sliced-pre-washed-ready-to-eat-microwave-in-five-minutes*. Old world terms. Historical fancy. Things Alice's baby would grow up knowing nothing of. Nothing was convenient now.

They worked hard. Clearing ground. Clearing the bodies from the Fort. They broke their backs setting up home. But they were energised. Invigorated by the fact that this time, they knew they could do it.

336

Finally, they had accepted the fact that the world really had changed. Nobody was in charge. Nobody was going to come along and save them. There would be no plane overhead, dipping its wings to let them know they'd been seen. There would be no dropped supplies. There would be no rescue.

There was no government, no law, no order, bar the one they created for themselves. It was a new age, a new time. They were adapting, and they were surviving.

But nothing lasted for ever.

83

They maintained a low profile. Cooking on gas, lighting fires for warmth only after dark. No smoke billowed from chimneys during daylight hours. But it wasn't enough.

Iona called the alert. A motorbike gang on the Old Military Road. Heading straight to the Fort.

They had drilled for such an occasion. The big doors at the sally port were closed and bolted. Then, armed with rifles, they took up their positions out of sight of the intruders.

The bikers rumbled along the approach road. A motley, hard-bitten crew of eight. Looked like they'd been on the road a long time. Maybe from the start. Maybe before that.

Chrissie chewed on her bottom lip as they roared up and down the length of the walls. Hoping that everyone held their nerve. No shots were to be fired unless absolutely necessary. There was to be no sound, no movement from within the walls. No clue given that there was anyone alive inside.

They circled the bikes, roaring up and down, up and down. But the Fort was locked tight. There was no easy access, at least not without heavy artillery and these guys weren't packing rocket launchers.

She willed them to move on. Instead they parked up their bikes and set up camp. When they'd lit a fire and it was clear they weren't moving on any time soon, Shaw signalled for everyone to move inside.

"Are we just going to leave them out there?" Jamie asked.

"Well unless you want to invite them inside, I don't see what else we can do," Shaw said.

"We could cut their throats while they're sleeping," Chrissie said, adding, "Joke," when she saw how the others were looking at her.

Later, in the privacy of their own room, Shaw asked Chrissie if she had been joking, or if she meant what she said.

"Maybe," she replied. "I don't know."

"Do you want to go out and do it now?"

She looked at him in the light of the solitary candle lighting the room. The scar stood out clear on his face. A gift from Carnegie when Shaw tried to stop him selling a girl into slavery. She'd been Elizabeth's age, maybe younger, with glowing blonde hair and a pretty face. A face too pretty for this world. If she'd been ugly, she might have lived.

Shaw managed to cause some damage before Carnegie's goons stepped in. He broke Carnegie's nose. In return, he'd almost had his face sliced off. He and Darren received a good kicking and were lucky to escape with their lives. The girl wasn't so lucky. Straight after he sliced Shaw's face, Carnegie cut her throat. He did it just to see the look on Shaw's face.

When he told the story to Chrissie, he said at least she'd died quick. Maybe she was lucky.

"Gee Shaw, how romantic - a moonlit stroll. Just you, me and the machetes," Chrissie said.

"If you didn't mean it, you shouldn't have said it."

They eyed each other across the room.

"Shaw, what's happened to us?" she asked.

He held her look for a moment before sitting on the edge of the bed and pulling his boots off.

That night, they slept with a valley of cold mattress between them.

In the morning, when Chrissie snuck outside for a look, all she saw was a blackened circle in the grass where the campfire had been. The bikers had gone.

84

Alice's waters broke one night in early spring. They'd read the books, prepared as best they could. Shaw had birthed lambs, which made him chief midwife. Having given birth herself, Chrissie was second in command. Darren mopped Alice's brow and gave her a hand to grip onto. The others boiled water, provided towels and waited for news.

It was a textbook labour. Alice got up and walked around. She changed position. She shouted at Darren for rubbing her back when she didn't want it rubbed. And when the contractions intensified, she went into herself and pushed when it counted.

Chrissie thought she knew what to expect, but she wasn't prepared for the overwhelming emotion she felt as the baby's head crowned. *It's coming. I can see it coming. One more push, Alice.*

She supported the baby as it came out. New life in her hands. Her eyes welled as she watched Darren's face on seeing his baby daughter for the first time. Tears rolled down his cheeks. She could have sworn she saw Shaw swipe one away when he thought no-one was looking.

She gently laid the baby on Alice's stomach. Alice smiled, before closing her eyes, exhausted.

341

Chrissie washed her hands in a bowl of water and went off to tell the others the news. They had a baby sister.

She returned to the birth room with a tray of biscuits and sweet, black tea. Jamie, Elizabeth and Lucy trailed behind her in a bubble of contagious excitement.

Chrissie was brimming with happiness, full of smiles. All the worry, the strain, the fear, of the past few months wiped out. There was life. There was hope. No. It wouldn't be the life any of them had expected - not even in their worst nightmares - but they could make something of it. At the very least, the new baby was going to be loved. She would be cherished by all of them.

This delightful, skipping-through-the-meadow daisy-chain of thoughts came to an abrupt end as soon as Chrissie entered the room.

The atmosphere was foreboding, the air ripe with the mingling scents of blood, sweat and fear.

Alice lay on the bed, eyes closed, face slick with perspiration. Strands of hair coiled darkly on her cheeks and forehead. Darren sat on a chair beside her, holding the baby in a soft blanket nest. The umbilical cord still attached to the placenta which was in a bowl next to him.

His gaze met Chrissie's as she entered the room. Eyes pleading, filled with pain. All traces of his earlier joy gone.

Shaw stood at the end of the bed and replaced the red, sodden towel between Alice's legs with a fresh one. He dropped the soiled cloth onto the ones already heaped on the floor. He looked at Chrissie, his face fixed. Shook his head. The movement small, the meaning behind it enormous.

The others stood silently in the doorway. Bubble burst. They could not stop the bleeding. Were unable to stem the flow. They watched, helpless, as Alice bled to death.

They had been given a life and, in the same breath, had one taken from them.

85

Darren named the child Abigail. She thrived and survived, growing up as strong and fearless as her mother.

She was not, as they had feared she would be, a lone child. As years went by, they picked up a few waifs and strays along the way. Like Iona, many of them had been surviving alone. Some had been leading a solitary existence for so long that they could not adapt to community life. They moved on, but others stayed. Not many, but of enough them to allow the group to develop and flourish.

It wasn't all rainbows and rosebuds. Squabbles erupted, fights broke out, rows flared. Shaw and Chrissie were called in to arbitrate. Disagreements were swiftly resolved. The people who were there, were there because they wanted to be there. They knew what it was like on the outside. The dangers. The aching loneliness. How hard it was to survive. Inside the Fort they were part of something bigger than themselves. They had something worth holding on to. Something worth fighting for.

By and by relationships formed and babies were born. The mothers survived, mostly. Finally, they were doing more than watch each other slowly die. The group was viable. They had a future.

From the history books in the tourist shop, they figured out how to open up the old wood-fired brick ovens. They no longer had to rely on diminishing gas supplies for cooking. Using sheep captured from the hill, they established a flock. Grazing them on nearby fields. Fences were mended. Using hand clippers, they learned how to shear, and then how to spin and weave and felt.

Ammunition was low and hard to come by, so they learned how to make bows and arrows and how to hunt with them. To hone their skills, they held archery competitions.

Jamie developed a passion for catapults, using them to hunt rabbits. Occasionally astounding the others by knocking a wood pigeon out of the sky.

On bad years, when crops were poor, they foraged for food from the old world. Going through the houses in Ardersier one by one. Marking each door as they went. Then going further a field, to Inverness airport and Nairn. Or south, to Balloch on the fringe of Inverness.

They were far from the badlands of the central belt and rarely ran into trouble. New arrivals were rare beasts, Screamers rarer still, the threat of bandit raids almost forgotten.

They felt safe. Grew complacent. They casually lit fires during the day. Thin trails of smoke rising above them. Beacons in the sky.

The mob came in a convoy of trucks, motorbikes and cars. A cavalcade of terror. Their whooping and hollering carrying on the breeze. The sound of it freezing Chrissie's blood in her veins. Bringing back the old fears. The old terrors.

The alarm went up. Inside, there was panic. People running, yelling orders. The sally port doors were bolted. Arms taken up, stations manned.

Outside the walls, the gang tore up and down in their vehicles. Yelling, whooping it up. They drove a truck into the door, but it held fast. They tried to breach the walls. They did not get in, but they did not give up.

Within the walls, they held fire. Watching, waiting to see what the mob would do. It was too late to pretend there was no-one home. They had given themselves away. The mob knew they were there and whatever they had, the mob wanted it.

When their initial assault failed, they set up camp outside the walls and prepared to lay siege.

The group quickly recovered from the shock of the attack.

Everyone there was a fighter. Surviving hadn't been easy. Establishing a new way of life tougher still. They had toiled hard for what they had and they weren't going to give it up without a fight.

Chrissie, Shaw and Darren planned the retaliation.

86

That night, while the mob caroused around fires, drinking, singing, sloping into the dark for sex with the women in their midst, the group prepared their arsenal.

The snipers snuck into the watchtowers with their rifles. Archers and those armed with catapults, lined the walls. Babies and toddlers retreated into the Fort with a handful of minders. Everyone else, woman, man and child, was armed and in the towers or on the walls. If they didn't have a gun, or a bow, or a catapult, they had a petrol bomb.

In the chill, grey light of pre-dawn, while the mob still slumbered, Shaw gave the signal. The attack was unleashed.

Fire rained on the mob as petrol bombs were lobbed over the walls. They got to their feet, running around ablaze, banging into each other as they tried to knock out the flames. Some burned where they lay, writhing on the ground, screaming as they cooked.

Those untouched by the bombs, ran for their weapons, only to be shot in the head by snipers. Or stumble to the ground, an arrow through their heart, shoulder, leg. Stones and ball bearings, fired by catapult, crunched into temples, knocked out eyes. The bandits squealed and screamed when they were hit. Their cries drowning in the blood gurgling in their throats.

Those uninjured scrambled to flee the hell raining down on them. One managed to get on his bike. He was opening up the throttle when Chrissie shot him in the shoulder. She watched, satisfied with a good hit, as he skidded to his death.

They didn't get them all. Some survived. Burning rubber as they made good their escape.

The group remained in the grip of siege mentality during the following days. Locked down. Preparing and waiting for the surviving members of the mob to return. Seeking vengeance for their fallen comrades. Revenge for their humiliating defeat.

Finally, with no sign or sound of them, and growing weary with the wait, they unbolted the sally port and ventured out.

Scorched bodies lay contorted on the ground. The smell of charred meat lingering around them. Dead eyes stared glassily at the sky. Arrows protruded from necks, legs, arms.

They walked among the dead, faces solemn. They had not lost a single soul, but there was no joy in Chrissie's heart. No sense of victory. Just heavy, dread, remorse at the wicked waste of life.

Shaw laid a hand on her arm. "Are you okay?"

"It's just so senseless," she said. "I don't-"

A sharp crack in the air cut her words short. Gunfire. Her eyes widened in shock.

One crack. One gunshot. Only one. But the shooter's aim was true. Chrissie's knees crumpled. A sob escaped her lips as she reached out to Shaw. Gently, she stroked his face. The bullet had gone through his forehead. He'd been dead before he hit the ground. Probably never even knew he'd been shot.

"There! He's there!"

Darren, yelling, pointing at a grassy hummock near the car park.

Chrissie closed Shaw's eyes and got to her feet.

She strode towards the hummock, the tremble in her legs subsiding with every step. She didn't stop to think. Had no fear of being shot. She paid no heed to the voices yelling at her, telling her to come back. The only thought in her head was to kill the person who had murdered Shaw.

She pulled her knife from its sheath. Circled around the hummock. The gunman sat on the ground, his back against it. An arrow protruded from his thigh.

Her mouth fell open as he met her gaze.

Carnegie grinned and pointed the handgun at her chest.

Finger on the trigger. Point blank range.

"I thought I'd killed you already," he said.

He squeezed the trigger.

This is it, Chrissie thought.

A hollow click. An empty chamber. Realisation in Carnegie's eyes. Followed by panic. Then fear as Chrissie grabbed a handful of his greasy hair and yanked his head back.

"No, please-" he begged.

Her heart was stone.

"You've just drawn your last breath, Carnegie."

Chrissie swept the knife across his throat, cutting deep through skin, muscle, cartilage. She let go of his hair as pink bubbles foamed on his lips.

She watched, eyes hard, as the life ebbed out of him.

87

Carnegie's corpse was dragged out of sight and left to rot. The remaining bodies were piled on a funeral pyre. Shaw's body, wrapped tightly in white sheets, placed ceremoniously on top.

The assembled group watched quietly as Chrissie stepped forward with a flaming torch and set it alight.

No words were spoken. There was nothing to say.

She stepped back, watching as smoke towered high into the still, clear sky. Wondering if it would act as a beacon. Wondering who would follow it, who would come.

But no-one ever came again.

No Screamers, no bandits, no rescuers.

No-one.

Acknowledgements

For supporting me in writing Each New Morn, my sincere thanks to Phil Jones, Mary Kate Thomson, Caroline Thomson and Pete Urpeth at Emergents.

For advice on the practicalities of surviving the pandemic, I am grateful to Charlie Thomson and Alex Scott.

Special thanks to Dr. Austin at the Zombie Institute for Theoretical Studies for agreeing to appear in Each New Morn. Check out the Institute's excellent lectures if you get the chance - www.zombiescience.co.uk

I appreciate the efforts of everyone who has cajoled and inspired me during the writing of this book. There are too many people to mention individually, but for their enthusiasm and encouragement, my particular thanks go to Isabel Reid and Angela Ford.

About the Author

L.G. Thomson was born in Glasgow and grew up in the modernist New Town experiment of Cumbernauld. Since graduating from art school in Dundee, she has worked in a variety of places throughout Scotland, including museums, remote islands, a large police station, a small shed, and a medium-sized croft. She has won a national writing competition and was short-listed for the Dundee Book Prize. She took a break from writing to raise her daughters, home-educating them for several years. She now lives in Ullapool, on the north west coast of Scotland, where she writes Thrillers With Attitude.

Out now - BOYLE'S LAW

A page-turning crime thriller set in Scotland - but with a diamond heist as well as lust and murder to contend with, be prepared for a view of the Scottish Highlands you won't get on any glossy calendar.

Available now from Amazon's online Kindle Store. Coming soon on paperback.

Coming soon - EROSION

Ten people are stranded on a remote Scottish island. The seas are fierce, the cliffs high, the landscape rugged. From the start there are undercurrents of tension within the group. A woman suspects her husband of infidelity and plans her revenge. Elsewhere, jealousy, lust and anger raise the temperature within the claustrophobic confines of the living quarters. It's not long before ten become nine. The battle for survival has begun.

Thank you for reading Each New Morn. If you have enjoyed the book, please consider leaving a review on Amazon.

www.thrillerswithattitude.co.uk

33720624R00199

Made in the USA
Charleston, SC
23 September 2014